About the first two Warren Crow mysteries...

The Long Stair

"Warren Crow is a consultant living in a struggling neighborhood in Albany, New York. The problems the neighborhood faces... will be familiar to anyone who has ever looked beneath the surface of a disinvested neighborhood... But *The Long Stair* is first and last a murder mystery... And as such it is a gripping read."
– Miriam Axel-Lute, *Shelterforce: The Journal of Affordable Housing and Community Building*

"*The Long Stair* is a suspenseful page-turner.
In fact it is one of the best mysteries I have
read with an upstate setting."
– John Rowen, *Schenectady Sunday Gazette*

Wilder Ponds

"White captures the beauty and solitude of the Adirondacks, as well as human aspiration and greed, in this fast-paced novel. *Wilder Ponds* is a must read for those trying to under-stand the many perspectives on Adirondack development."

– Pete Sheehan, co-chair, Sierra Club Hudson-Mohawk Group

Edge of Albany

A WARREN CROW MYSTERY

Kirby White

Fox Creek Press   Albany, New York

ISBN 0-9773501-2-6

Copyright © Kirby White, 2012

Published by Fox Creek Press,
an underground nonprofit publisher.

Formatted and Printed by The Troy Book Makers.

Cover design by The Troy Book Makers
Cover photos by Kirby White

For

Albany Community Land Trust
on its 25th anniversary

Also for

The other members of the
Community Development Alliance:

Affordable Housing Partnership

Community Realty

Community Loan Fund

United Tenants of Albany

Fox Creek Press

Fox Creek Press, Inc., is a not-for-profit corporation organized to publish books and other materials relating to the fields of affordable housing, community development and environmental conservation and to dedicate all net proceeds derived from these publications to the support of nonprofit organizations working in these fields.

Fox Creek Press shares office space with other nonprofit organizations on Orange Street in Albany's Sheridan Hollow neighborhood. It is named in memory of the creek that once flowed as a natural stream through Sheridan Hollow but has now been forced underground.

All net proceeds from the sale of this book will be passed on to Albany Community Land Trust and other organizations supporting ACLT's efforts to provide permanently affordable housing in Albany's neighborhoods.

For information, contact:
Fox Creek Press
255 Orange Street, #103
Albany, NY 12210

Acknowledgements

I am grateful to my friends and coworkers Bob Radliff, Louise McNeilly, and Roger Markovics, and my wife Nola, for their reading of preliminary drafts, their helpful editorial suggestions, and their help in moving this work toward publication. Responsibility for whatever faults the work may have is of course my own. –K.W.

Tivoli Park

The events described in this novel are entirely fictional, but the setting for these events is real. An important part of this setting is Tivoli Park – or, as it's more formally known, Tivoli Lake Preserve or Tivoli Nature Preserve – the large, undeveloped, mostly wooded area lying immediately north of Albany's West Hill neighborhood and south of the I-90 corridor. The area has been owned by the city of Albany ever since 1851, when it was acquired to allow the creation of a small reservoir (the 4-acre pond known as Tivoli Lake) as part of the city's water supply system.

Use of the pond as a water source was discontinued early in the twentieth century. For many decades thereafter the land served only as a convenient, if illegal, dumping ground for urban debris – and as a place where neighborhood kids could roam, ride bikes, fish, and build their various huts and hideouts in the woods.

In 1998, when a neighborhood group's lawsuit resulted in the closing of the polluting trash-burning plant located in Sheridan Hollow, a part of the settlement funded the creation of the W. Haywood Burns Environmental Education Center, whose mission was to include stewardship of Tivoli Preserve. Since then, the Center has promoted the use of the area as a permanent urban nature preserve. However, it has no formal control over the future of the land.

Meanwhile, in the absence of human intervention, nature has taken its course. Cottonwoods and oaks have grown tall. Sumac, honeysuckle, wild grape, reeds and cattails have crowded into all available spaces. Deer, raccoons, possums, rabbits, geese, turkeys, and songbirds have lived and raised their young here.

For the present, the preserve remains the bucolic place pictured on the cover of this book. The long-term use of this land, however, is yet to be determined.

1

This all began when Jesse knocked on my door, which got my attention because he had never knocked before. For several years he'd more or less had the run of my house. When he came over from his house next door he would just walk in and yell up the stairs at me. But things were beginning to change. He was thirteen now – almost half a foot taller than he was last summer – and I no longer saw him every day the way I used to.

I was at my desk, reading a proposal for a redevelopment project in Sheridan Hollow, the perennially neglected neighborhood that lies immediately north of Albany's Capitol Hill – and just east of where I live on the upper end of Orange Street. I just barely heard the knock and wasn't eager to be disturbed, but when it was repeated I went downstairs and found Jesse standing on my front steps.

"How come you didn't just come in?" I asked.

He entered slowly, looking uncomfortable and saying nothing.

"What's up, Jesse?"

"Nothing," he said. "I mean I don't know – just stuff going on."

"There's always stuff going on," I said. "But come on in the kitchen. I'll get you a coke."

"No, I just got to tell you something." He was still standing just inside the door, still looking uncomfortable, not at all like himself. "But you can't tell nobody," he said. "I mean you can tell them this thing, but not who told you it."

"Okay, sure, you can trust me."

"I'm serious. You can't tell nobody at all."

"Sure," I said again.

"You go over by Tivoli Lake sometimes," he said. "I see you jogging around on them trails."

"Yeah, jogging or walking, or else I just go over there to sit on a log and listen to the birds. And sometimes I see you riding your bike on those trails. You and your buddies."

"Wasn't with nobody today. Just me seen this thing."

"What thing? What did you see?"

"You know that one trail goes down in behind those apartments – from the parking lot there..."

"Yes I know it. I usually go down the trail from the end of Judson, but I sometimes come back up to Livingston that way behind Park View Apartments."

"Yeah, well, I go down that way 'cause the way it drops down you get a real good takeoff with your bike."

"And you went down this morning?"

"And I almost run into this thing. It was..." He grimaced.

"What was it?"

"There's this guy on the ground there, right in the trail..." I waited.

"This dead guy."

"Woah. You sure he was dead?"

"I didn't do no autopsy," he said, with a little of his old feistiness. "Almost crashed my bike trying not to run over it, and I just turned around and got out of there. But I seen enough to know this guy wasn't going nowhere."

"You could see he was hurt bad?"

"Wasn't hurting anymore, cause he was dead, but it must of hurt when someone done it to him. He had blood on him. And someone had, like, cut his ears off."

"His ears? You think someone actually cut them off?"

"Someone had to've. They was gone, and ears don't just fall off people by their self."

"Okay," I said. "It sounds gruesome. I guess we need to tell the police."

"Not us," Jesse said. "You. You got to tell 'em you seen it yourself."

So I was making my way up Judson Street. It wasn't how I'd wanted to spend the rest of the morning, but if I was going to tell the police I had discovered the terrible thing Jesse described, then I definitely needed to see it myself. But I didn't want to. I didn't want to have to look at it, and I didn't want to have to be the one to tell the police about it.

And I was worried by Jesse's apparent fear of having anyone know that he had seen it. I'd already started to worry about him in recent months – especially when I'd see him hanging out with other teenagers on certain corners a few blocks down Orange Street. I had never worried about the younger Jesse roaming the neighborhood all hours of the day on his bike, but for a teenager… well this was not the easiest or safest place for an African American boy to be coming of age.

I turned left onto Livingston Avenue and walked the several blocks to Park View Apartments, a set of brick buildings ranged along the north side of the street. The narrow space between the street and the buildings was nicely landscaped, looking almost park-like. I followed a driveway around to the back, where a narrow parking area lay between the buildings and the actual Tivoli Park, which did not look at all park-like. I had sometimes wondered how they could advertise the property as "park view" apartments with a straight face.

The "entrance" to Tivoli Park from the parking area looked like just what it was – a narrow dirt path where kids rode their bikes into the woods. The path dropped down steeply from the edge of the pavement before leveling and bending out of sight.

I went down, feeling stiff and unready. I didn't see anything until I was around the bend. Then I could see there was a body lying on the path, and I felt even less ready.

It was an older black man, white-haired but not frail, wearing jeans and a sweatshirt. He was lying on his back. And, indeed, his ears had been severed. There was some blood on the front of the sweatshirt. Otherwise the body looked undamaged, but he was unquestionably dead.

I turned around and left – probably just as fast as Jesse had.

Back on the street I briefly considered going directly down Livingston to the police station on Henry Johnson Boulevard. But I decided it would be easier – at least it would feel easier – to go home and use the phone.

I called and asked for Detective Reilly, whom I'd got to know a couple of years earlier, when Jonah Lee was killed in the Neighborhood Housing Association's office on Second Street and I became involved in trying to find out what he was doing that got him killed.

I was told that Reilly was in the building but that it would "be a minute." I was put on hold and waited at least five minutes. Finally Reilly picked up and I explained who I was.

"Oh yeah, I remember," he said. "Warren Crow. Used to call me with all kinds of crap."

I reminded him that it had mostly been him calling me. "This time I'm calling you about something different, but just as unpleasant."

I told him what I had seen.

"What the hell were you doing down there anyway?"

"Just taking a walk."

"That's what sidewalks are for," he said. "They don't have sidewalks down there."

"I'm a country boy, I like to walk in the woods, Tivoli Park is the nearest woods."

"Okay, whatever. Best way to get to this place would be from where – from the apartments?"

"Yes."

"Meet me at the apartments in five minutes." He hung up.

I drove my pickup back to Livingston Avenue, arriving at the apartments just as Reilly was pulling into the parking area. We parked beside each other and got out of our vehicles. He was the same balding middle aged man I remembered from two years earlier.

"Okay, show me," he said, with the blend of brusqueness and weariness that I also remembered.

I led the way down the narrow trail, but stopped five yards from the body and let Reilly go ahead.

He walked slowly around the body, studying it, then crouched, placed a finger on the man's neck, and, leaning forward, stared at the wound where an ear had once been.

"How long ago were you here?" he asked.

"I don't know – half an hour maybe. I went straight home and called you."

"Were you sure he was dead at that time?"

"I didn't touch him. I didn't see how he could possibly be alive."

"You don't know who he is?"

"No, I don't."

"You sure? You take a good look at him?"

I was standing several yards away, and I realized I still had not looked fully into the man's face. I moved up behind Reilly and made myself look carefully.

"No, I don't recognize him – though I guess it's possible I've seen him on the street, or maybe walking down here in the woods."

Reilly was still hunched over the body, his back to me, muttering something. "Yeah, just behind the apartments."

It confused me until I realized he was speaking into a cell phone. "Tell them to meet me in the parking lot in back," he said.

He stood up, closing the phone. "Technical guys be here soon. Let's go up there and talk a little."

We went back to the parking lot and sat in his vehicle.

"You spend a lot of time down in that jungle?" he asked.

"Maybe three or four times a week I go there to jog or walk."

"Still don't know why you'd go down there to do that."

"As I said, I'm a country boy, and I don't like running on pavement. Anyway it's nearby and a nice quiet place to be outdoors, whether it's walking or jogging."

He shrugged. "Usually see other people down there?"

"Not always. Once in a while."

"People like the guy back there on the path?"

"More often kids, but some older people. I can't say if he was one of them, but it's possible."

"Older African American men?"

"Some, though the older people you see there are mostly white."

"You live at the end of Orange Street, almost to Robin, right?"

"Right."

"So when you come over to this area, you just go up Judson and cross Livingston and go straight down into the park where the Tivoli Park sign is?"

"Yes."

"That's what you did this morning?"

"Uh… Yeah."

"But you wound up way over here behind the apartments?"

"I sometimes do that loop and come back up to Livingston over here."

He turned in my direction and peered at me, frowning. I was afraid he'd guessed I wasn't telling the truth, and I wondered if there was any way to tell that I'd actually come from the other direction. The crime scene technicians would no doubt look for tracks. I couldn't remember what the trail had looked like at that point and whether any tracks would be identifiable.

"Anyway," he said finally, "you ran into that scene down there. Tell me what you make of it."

"I have no idea what to make of it."

"Anything about it mean anything to you?"

"No – except obviously what was done to him was more than just a way to kill someone. It had to be a way to send some kind of message or make some kind of statement."

"So – any thoughts on who it was a message to, what it was about?"

"The only thing I can think of is some kind of conflict between gangs, but that doesn't seem likely."

"The guy didn't exactly look like a gangbanger."

"No, he didn't."

"Doesn't fit anyway," Reilly said. "Gangs don't hang out in the woods. They shoot each other and stick knives in each other, but they don't generally cut each other's ears off. They seem to think shooting or stabbing a guy sends enough of a message."

It was a relief to have him agree that what we had seen wouldn't be related to gang violence, which meant there would be no reason to think it was related, even indirectly, to Jesse.

"So you're not aware of any motive anyone might have to send some kind of message like this one?"

"No."

He took a small notebook from his pocket, like the one he'd had when I first met him in the NHA office the day Jonah was killed. He took a card from the back of the notebook and gave it to me. "In case you think of anything," he said. "And give me your number. Might want to talk again when we know a little more."

2

Back at my house I sat at my desk and stared at the cover of the proposal I'd been reading when Jesse knocked. If the project could be funded and completed it would be the first really positive thing to happen in Sheridan Hollow in many years – many decades, in fact. And it might possibly provide a role for me. A couple of hours earlier I'd been looking forward to studying the thing, but I couldn't concentrate on it now. I needed to shake the image of a dead man with severed ears. I thought about driving up to Cohoes with my canoe and paddling up the Hudson into the islands. But that would be only a temporary escape. I decided, instead, to take a walk down into Sheridan Hollow and see if Raymond was home. He was one of the two people – the other being Ronnie – with whom I could talk in confidence about this morning's experience. I had promised Jesse not to tell anyone that he had told me about the dead man, but I could trust Raymond not to tell anyone, and I did need to talk to someone.

From my house I walked down Orange Street as far as Lark, then cut over one block and continued down the long slope of Sheridan Avenue, past the long stair and the Gander Bay Bar, to Raymond's house, the front of which looked almost as abandoned as the boarded-up houses on either side of it.

I went down the narrow walk-way to the back of the building, knocked on the back door and went into the large kitchen that was also Raymond's living room and study. I found him sitting at his big plywood table, gazing intently at the screen of his laptop.

By way of acknowledging that someone had come in, he said "aih," in the Canadian manner, and continued to stare at the laptop for another long moment. Finally he looked over his shoulder and said, "Warren."

"I wasn't sure if you'd be here or at Zera's," I said.

"Just came from there," he said. "Still work here."

By "work," in this case, he meant the research he does on the land claims of various Native American groups. He is an expert on the subject, but he does not charge native groups for the work he does for them. He himself is Cree and was born in the country off to the east of James Bay. His paying work is driving a fork lift at night for the New York State Office of General Services. When his shift ends at two in the morning he goes to Zera's apartment on Third Street. They've been seeing each other that way – from two till mid-morning – for more than a year now.

"How is Zera?" I asked.

"Just back from a week in Honduras – visiting relatives in the Garifuna community on the coast where her ancestors lived for centuries. Otherwise still doing day-care. House always full of babies when I wake up in the morning."

"Is she managing to keep on with her course work?"

"Coffee's on the stove," he said, pointing. "Oh she keeps on. No stopping her."

I got a cup of coffee and joined him at the big table, which consists of a large sheet of plywood roughly framed with two-by-fours and supported by saw horses. Most of its surface was covered with piles of books and papers, all neatly stacked. His cat Mabel was sleeping on one of the piles of papers. The room, as usual, smelled of the industrial-strength cleanser with which he mops the old wooden floor.

"It's been a bad morning," I said.

"Oh?"

I told him about Jesse's visit and what had followed.

"Jesus!" he said. He got up and filled his coffee cup and sat down again. "You got some kind of lunatic running around over there?"

"I have no idea. I'm worried about Jesse, though."

"But he couldn't possibly have anything to do with it."

"No, he couldn't – other than being the one to find it. I just can't figure why he seemed to be so frightened."

"Scary thing to see. Why wouldn't he be frightened?"

"But what he really seemed uptight about wasn't so much the thing he'd seen as the idea of having anyone know he was the one who saw it. Which is not like him. Jesse's not shy – he doesn't usually try to hide his role in things."

"I don't know," Raymond said. "*I'd* be freaked-out by it. Seems natural to just want to forget all about it as soon as possible."

"Yeah, I'm sure that's part of it, but I can't help feeling there's something he hasn't told me."

"You going to ask him more about it?"

"I intend to try," I said. "But I'm not sure how much he'll say. He doesn't seem to be quite the same kid who used to tell you whatever he thought about whatever came up, whether you asked or not."

"He's coming into being a teenager. So really he's *not* the same kid."

"And I guess that's what worries me – what it means to be a black kid, thirteen years old, hanging out in this neighborhood. Really different from being eleven or twelve wheeling around the neighborhood on his bike."

"You're worrying about him getting involved with a gang?"

"I don't know, but that possibility is part of the world he's living in now."

"Whatever that world actually is – which is maybe not what some people are saying it is. You hear the talk about the Orange Street Boys and the Jungle Junkies and Original Gangsta Killas, and now even Crips and Bloods are supposed to be here, but I don't know what it amounts to. Some nasty stuff goes on, but how many kids are really involved? Like Jonah used to say – teenagers are going to run in gangs, but it doesn't mean most of them are gangsters."

"I wish Jonah was still around for a kid like Jesse to talk to."

"He's still got you to talk to."

"I wish I was sure of that," I said.

As it happened, I ran into Jesse on my way home. He was with several other boys on the corner of Lark and Orange. I was going to pass within a few feet of him, but he was making a point of not looking at me.

I didn't stop but as I went by I said, "Hey Jesse, I got a job for you – stop by the house later."

He muttered "Okay," still not looking at me.

I went home, made a salami and lettuce sandwich and took it back up to my office, where I woke up my computer to check my email, and found a message from Ronnie.

Hey Crow…

Any chance you could take a long weekend – meet me at the cabin Friday evening and go to the ponds Saturday/Sunday. It's a poor substitute for what was supposed to be our Labrador trip, but my goddamned project is finally more or less wrapped up and I'm desperate for some woods and water, and to see you. And more than see you – I've been living like a nun for weeks and I want to do something about it. In fact I want to do a lot about it. So… I know we talked about going to the ponds Labor Day weekend. But that's still weeks away – and I don't want to wait. How about it?

Love
Ronnie

She had enrolled in a graduate program at Cornell in January and had undertaken a wetland ecology research project at the beginning of the summer, which she had hoped to finish by mid-July so we could do the Labrador canoe trip we'd been talking about almost since we first got together last summer. But the project had dragged on until we were forced to give up on the planned four-week trip. It had left me feeling at loose ends, stuck in hot summertime Albany, missing the northern country that I visited most summers – and missing Ronnie, whose research site was in the Montezuma marshes west of Syracuse – not a quick and easy drive to or from Albany.

Her email was sunlight breaking through the clouds. It was now Thursday. My impulse was to go get my gear ready, keep my appointment with Helen Hamilton in the afternoon, but reschedule my one Friday appointment, so I'd be ready to leave at noon for the cabin on Fisher Lake, where her family owned the large tract of land that included the remote Wilder Ponds – the ponds that were the reason for our getting together the summer before.

But even as I thought about the possibility, the sun slipped back behind the clouds. I couldn't do it. I couldn't just go off to the ponds and leave things as they were in Albany.

I called her cell phone, reaching her where she was at work on the edge of a marsh.

"Hey!" she said. "You caught me up to my ass in mud."

"Sounds like a lot more fun than sitting in front of a computer in a hot stuffy upstairs room on Orange Street."

"I won't argue with that," she said. "Did you get my email?"

"Yes and it's breaking my heart."

"You can't do it this weekend?"

I told her briefly what was going on – the dead man in Tivoli Park and my worries about Jesse. "I don't know what it is but there's something really bothering him."

"All right," she said, "the ponds can wait till Labor Day. It will be the little house in the city this weekend. Tell Jesse I'm coming especially to see him."

"You may be just what he needs," I said. "But I'm jealous."

"Oh, I might find a way to spend some time with you, too."

"In that case you'll be exactly what Jesse and I both need."

3

The sun was shining again in my private sky when I set out to walk the several blocks to the Neighborhood Housing Association office on Second Street. It was shining because Ronnie would be arriving the next evening. And because the prospect of meeting with Helen Hamilton brightened my day as well. Now NHA's executive director, Helen had been one of the first resident members of the Association, which was a kind of housing cooperative where members had 99-year leases for their homes. At the time when NHA founder Jonah Lee was killed she was already putting in many hours a week as an unpaid office manager. After Jonah's death, when no one was sure the organization could survive without him, the board asked her to take the executive director position. They had to talk her into it – she claimed she wasn't "the executive type" – but in fact she quickly became a more effective executive than Jonah had been. Jonah was the bold entrepreneurial founder, but it was Helen who solidified the organization. Her patient, even-handed style was keeping the association functioning smoothly, with a remarkable lack of internal tensions.

Recently, she had succeeded in getting NHA recognized by the city of Albany as a Community Housing Development Organization (or "CHDO") under the federal HOME program. This recognition gave the association an opportunity to receive funding from the fifteen percent of the city's HOME block grant that federal law reserves for such community-based organizations.

A grant of CHDO money could be used for the kinds of rental projects the organization was already doing, but it would burden those projects – and their residents – with federal requirements for annual certification of the residents' income-eligibility. Rather than accept this burden, Helen and the board had decided to launch a "community land trust" homeownership program that would allow them to acquire and rehabilitate single family homes that would then be sold for affordable prices to low-income families – with the Association retaining ownership of the underlying land, which would be leased to the homeowners for renewable 99-year terms. The leases would give NHA the ability to see that the homes would remain owner-occupied and that when they were eventually resold by the owners they would be sold to other low-income families for affordable prices. The CHDO funds could be used to subsidize these homes, and, once the homes were sold to income-eligible families, there would be no required annual recertification of those families' incomes.

NHA had applied for CHDO funds to subsidize three of these community land trust homes. They had just received approval from the city and had begun looking at properties that might be acquired. I was meeting with Helen today to look at some possible acquisitions and to talk about the unusual form of homebuyer mortgage financing that would be needed.

The NHA office had recently been painted, and the smell of fresh paint mingled with the usual aroma of coffee and lilac-scented air freshener. Helen was at her desk in front of a computer, looking as neat and composed as ever. On the screen in front of her was a photo of a small house.

"I'm checking the multiple listing service every day," she said. "Then we get Harriet Jones to show us everything on the north side that's even a remote possibility. We've looked at seven so far. This one just up the block here on Second is probably the best of them. It's tenanted now, which would rule it out for us, but it sounds like those people might be leaving soon."

She scooted her rolling desk chair off to the side and motioned to a second chair, which I pulled in front of the com-

puter. It was not a great photo but I did recognize the property
– a small two-story house with an addition in the rear that
had probably once been a porch and probably now contained
a kitchen. The web page reported 1100 square feet of floor
space, including three bedrooms as well as a living room, dining room and kitchen. The property was owned by the estate
of its previous owner. The asking price was $80,000.

"I'm guessing we might get it for something like $60,000,"
Helen said. "It needs some work but it doesn't look like anything major. I'm thinking it won't take more than $20,000
to put it in pretty good shape, though of course we would
need to get Fred in there to do a structural inspection. With
$20,000 in subsidy we should be able to sell it for $65,000,
which would make it quite affordable for households below
80% of area median income."

"Okay. Do you think it would be salable, in this neighborhood?"

"That's the question – would someone who could qualify
for a mortgage want to buy a house on this block? We were
hoping to find something on Livingston, or the other side of
Livingston on Beverly or one of those little streets. But there's
nothing." She looked at me and widened her eyes. "Not a
thing."

"Really? That's surprising."

"Someone's buying. Someone or some kind of company
with a Manhattan phone number. Harriet says the realtors
have started calling them as soon as they've got a listing in
that area so the property never even shows up on the MLS. No
one I've talked to seems to really know who they are."

"Do you know how they're financing all these purchases?"

"They say they're paying cash. At least that's all anyone
sees at this end. They bring a check to the table and close the
deal and that's that. None of the kinds of hassles we have to go
through to buy property."

"And no one knows what their angle is?"

"Not really. Lots of speculation. They seem to buy almost
sight-unseen, as though they're just working from a tax map
and don't really care what's on the lot or what it looks like. But
whatever their angle is, it's some absentee investor buying up
a piece of our community. And I do not like it."

"I don't either."

"I guess it's what Jonah was feeling," she said, "when he got into his Sheridan Hollow project."

"Yeah, the feeling that the community was being invaded and something had to be done, at whatever cost, to stop it."

"Yes. But I'm trying not to do what he did."

"Right. Too many housing organizations get into trouble by paying too much money for too much real estate because they think they're facing a now-or-never situation."

"I don't want to do that. In fact I don't really want to be buying up property over beyond Livingston anyway. What I would really like would be to just go on patiently buying property right here in this immediate neighborhood – and make it a better neighborhood – but if we're going to help people become homeowners right now, this year, then we've got to find homes that people will want to buy."

"That is the problem. That's the choice you have to make."

"I know. We can't do everything – not all at once. So on with *today's* business. We did look at some places over west of Quail, and a couple over the other direction on Ten Broeck. Blocks that don't have quite so many problems. But we'd be looking at more rehab for those particular houses."

We went over the MLS information for the west-of-Quail properties and agreed on two of them where it seemed worthwhile to ask the contractor that NHA worked with, Fred Swanson, to do structural inspections and prepare estimates of rehab costs.

"In the meantime," Helen said, "I've set up some appointments for us next week with a pair of banks. Does Tuesday morning still work for you?"

"Yes. Good."

"Both of them are banks where we have mortgages on rental properties. So they know us, and we're current with all our loans with them. But I'm afraid they have no idea of what a community land trust is or how CLT homeownership works."

"And it will take a while for them to get used to the idea. You may not get very far with them this year, but it's good to start now to educate them."

"But even if they get used to the idea, how is it going to go with the legal nitty-gritty? I can hear those attorneys saying, 'Homebuyer mortgages where the homebuyer doesn't own the land? Oh you can't do *that*.'"

"But you can do it, and the attorneys won't actually kill the deal if they don't have a vice president telling them to kill it. But even so, learning to do leasehold mortgages on resale-restricted property will take extra time from both the loan officers and the attorneys, so the banks will question whether it's worth their while to pay for that time when all they'll get out of it is just a handful of loans."

"But as you said, the folks at Albany Community Land Trust *have* been getting mortgage financing for CLT homes."

"For almost twenty-five years – by hook or by crook. It's easier for them now than when they started. And it will be easier for you because of them."

"Those folks also said we should talk to the Community Loan Fund, which is just across the hall from them over there on Orange Street, and of course the Loan Fund's already been a big help to us."

"Yes, talk with all those folks over on Orange Street – the people with the Loan Fund, the Affordable Housing Partnership and the Land Trust. They understand what you're trying to do, and they'll have time for you."

Helen sighed. "So much to think about, so much to learn."

"Good thing you're smart," I said.

"Nonsense." She stood up. I stood as well. She walked with me to the door and gave my shoulder a light pat as I went out.

It was after four when I got home. I didn't feel like going back up to my stuffy office so late in the day, so I got a beer from the refrigerator and went out to sit on my front steps. The street was empty, the red brick pavement baking in the late afternoon sun, the entire block quiet – no vehicles moving, no pedestrians. I was hoping Jesse would come by on his way home.

Eventually he did appear, wandering up the sidewalk from the direction of Henry Johnson Boulevard. When he noticed me he hesitated for a moment but then came on.

"Sit down a minute," I said. "I just want to fill you in."

He sat down on the step beside me and stared straight ahead into the street.

"I went and looked at it," I said. "And told the police and showed a detective where it was. When I left, a bunch of crime scene people were headed over there to do their technical stuff. By now they should have taken the body away. I told the detective I'd found it myself. I didn't mention you."

"'Preciate it," he said.

"So it's over with. It was an ugly thing to see, but you did the right thing telling me about it, and now there's nothing more you need to worry about."

He continued to stare silently into the empty street.

"I don't want to push you," I said, "but if there's anything else about this thing that's still a problem for you, I hope you'll let me try to help."

He gave me a quick look and shook his head. He was still very tense.

I backed off and asked, "How's your mom doing these days? I don't see her much."

"Me neither. She got a new job."

"You mean she's not working for Ellis any more?" For as long as I had known Mina Johnson, she had worked for a property management company cleaning apartments after they were vacated – a job requiring much more than a quick once-over with a vacuum.

"No, she still doing that, but now she got another job too, evenings, cleaning for College of Saint Rose."

"That adds up to an awful lot of time working on her feet every day. How's she holding up with it?"

"Real tired," Jesse said.

"I should think. Does she really need to do that much?"

"She saving up."

"To help with your college costs, I suppose."

"I tell her she don't need to – I don't even know if I *want* to go to college, but she don't want to hear that."

"Neither do I," I said. "Not everyone should go to college. But you've got a better head than most people, and you should go. You'll *like* college."

He didn't respond. After a while he said, "Well, guess I better be getting on home." But he continued to sit.

"And by the way, Ronnie's coming this weekend. She said to tell you she's coming specially to see you."

"Yeah, right," he said, "she coming to see *you*." But he smiled.

I took a long walk, out along Livingston to Quail, then down and around Washington Park and back along Lark Street. Back in my kitchen I poured some bourbon and stir-fried some beef and peppers and onions and broccoli, and listened to Terry Gross on WAMC. Later I poured another drink and took it out to the front steps, where the air was cooling. When it was fully dark I went inside and went to bed and dreamed of Ronnie.

4

Drinking my morning coffee at the kitchen table, I listened to WAMC's local news to see if there was any mention of a body found in Tivoli Park. But there was nothing. I assumed the police wanted to withhold the news as long as possible – or at least until they had more information – but it was just a matter of time before the media got wind of it one way or another.

After two cups of coffee, I walked up to the end of Judson, crossed Livingston, and then jogged down the trail into the park. It was nice to be able to loosen up with this easy downhill stretch. As I approached "Tivoli Lake" – a marshy pond covering only a few acres – the sun was just showing through the trees in the direction of Philip Livingston Middle School on my right.

Beyond the pond I turned west on the dirt road that parallels the railroad tracks. As usual there were bicycle tracks on the sandy surface of the road – but today there were also the tracks of at least one motor vehicle. Normally, locked gates prevent four-wheeled vehicles from reaching this road from the streets. My guess was that the police had been able to drive in here yesterday to explore the surroundings of the murder.

As I often did, I ran hard for several hundred yards on this level roadway, then slowed to a walk to catch my breath and listen to the quiet. On my right I could hear the stream where it flows back into the open from its extended captivity in a giant culvert. The railroad tracks were beyond the stream here, and beyond the tracks thick woods dampened the sound of traffic on I-90 to a faint whisper. No sound reached me from the streets to the south. In the marsh behind me redwing blackbirds were whistling. Up ahead a cardinal was announcing himself with his *birdy-birdy-birdy* call.

I walked to the point where the trail down from the apartments joined the road from the left. Part of me wanted to go up that way and have a look at the murder site, but the part of me that wanted nothing more to do with it prevailed. I continued up the dirt road. Five minutes later I was about to turn around and go back the way I had come when I spotted a familiar figure coming toward me.

I didn't know his name, but he was someone I met from time to time on these morning outings. He was a compact, tidy man, probably in his fifties. He was always dressed in neatly pressed shorts and a button-down shirt. He always carried a carved wooden walking stick. When we met we would usually exchange a few words about the weather – or about the fallibility of weather forecasters, or sometimes other examples of human fallibility, which he seemed to relish.

Today I said, "You know, we see each other often enough down here but we've never introduced ourselves. My name's Warren Crow."

"Robert Goodwin," he said. "That's *Robert* not *Robin*, and it's *Goodwin* not *Goodfellow*."

"So I guess you're just a regular human being," I said, "not the famous wood sprite."

"Not the famous wood sprite," he said with a chuckle, "but I'm not a very regular human being either, though I *pretend* to be quite regular."

"Do you live nearby?" I asked.

"You might say so."

"But you'd rather not say exactly where?"

"Forgive me, but I do take pleasure in not being *placed* that way, especially here in this place which is almost not a place at all."

"I'm not sure I follow you," I said. "Why doesn't this qualify as a place?"

"Places like this just don't exist in the middle of cities. Cities don't own places like this for a century and a half and not *do* anything with them and just let them go wild."

"Except in Albany."

"Albany's just another city in most ways, but then it's got this big gap – this big blank right here up against the West Hill neighborhood. Which means regular rules don't apply here. Anything can happen here."

I was thinking of the murder and trying to decide whether to tell him about it. In the meantime I played along with his peculiar way of talking about the place. "Of course you could say regular rules apply *only* here," I said, "but not in the rest of the city. Here the trees grow up and live until they die of natural causes, the mosquitoes breed, the birds eat the mosquitoes and build their nests, the deer browse... But I guess you're right that some *human* rules don't apply down here. In fact..."

I decided to tell him. Reilly had never told me *not* to tell anyone about the dead man, and I was curious about how the whimsical Robert Goodwin would react. I described the body to him as I had first described it to Reilly – as something that I myself had stumbled on. "So I guess it's true anything can happen here," I said.

He stared at me. "His ears cut off? My God, how bizarre! What can it possibly mean?"

"I certainly don't know."

"It can't possibly relate to this place. I mean I have sometimes thought that if my luck were to run out and my health were to fail I could come down here and just crawl into a thicket and die and the worms could consume me, and years later someone might or might not stumble on my bones. But what you're telling me... It doesn't belong here."

"Or anywhere."

"But especially not here."

"So I guess you haven't seen anything or anyone down here that might relate in any way to such a thing..."

"Definitely not – and I don't want to." He punched the ground forcefully with his walking stick. "This casts such a shadow. I have always so much enjoyed the little conversations with you and the few others I meet now and then down here – with all of us *nameless*, and, in being nameless, somehow *innocent*. Now when I meet people I'm going to have to work very hard to avoid wondering..."

"I apologize for spoiling the innocence..."

"No, it's not your fault. It's just something that you saw and told me about, like when you told me about the doe and fawn you had just seen, or the turkey brood – but oh so different!"

He looked thoroughly disconsolate, and I really did feel bad about having cast a shadow over the pleasure he took in the place.

We parted and I jogged back along the dirt road and up the hill and went home and took a shower.

When I sat down at my desk I found a phone message from Reilly asking me to call, which I did – hoping no evidence had been found to cast doubt on my claim that I'd simply stumbled on the body.

"I want to update you," Reilly said. "Because you're the only one I know who seems to spend time down there."

"There's a nonprofit group that oversees maintenance work on the trails – the Haywood Burns Environmental Education Center. You could call them."

"Called them. Guy I talked to said none of that's been done since June. Didn't know of anyone who'd been down there in the last few weeks. So I'm back to you."

I thought about mentioning Robert Goodwin as someone who spent a lot of time in the park, but I didn't think he could help and I didn't think Reilly would know what to make of his odd style.

"So anyway," he said, "we still don't know a lot. Still don't know who the guy was. No I-D on him. No match with missing persons so far. No match for his prints so far. Only thing we've really learned is it didn't happen where you found him."

"He wasn't killed there on the trail?"

"No. Might have been near there – or not. Could've been anywhere. We do know he was shot, which is no big surprise. Didn't really think he died just from losing his ears. Shot in the chest, at very close range. Probably with a hand gun, fairly high-powered, but we got no bullet."

"How do you know he wasn't shot right there on the spot?"

"Bullet went through his heart and blew a pretty good chunk out of his back. Would have been major bleeding from the exit wound. But there was almost no blood under him or anywhere near him."

"So you're saying he'd been dead awhile when he was left there, and during that time he might have been moved some distance."

"Right."

"Any footprints around him, or anything like that?"

"Oh, all kinds of tracks. Mostly kid-size. And nothing sharp enough to do us much good. Even if we had a suspect, which we sure don't. Only thing we did find was a mess of puke on the trail. Like maybe cutting the ears off the guy's head might've cost some guy his lunch. You didn't see that?"

"No."

"Hard not to. It was right there."

"Where – in relation to the body?"

"Maybe five yards the other side, away from the apartments. You would've almost stepped in it coming up from that side."

"I didn't see it. I guess I was looking at the body at that point and that was all I saw."

"Sure. Okay. We scraped it up and it's gone to the lab. For whatever it's worth, we'll know more or less what someone – we don't know who – had for lunch."

I was thinking of Jesse. I was sure he had nothing to do with the killing, but he had seen the body. Could it possibly be his vomit that was now in a police lab? I also wondered now about his bicycle. He had said he'd almost crashed his bike into the body. I hadn't noticed bicycle tracks at the scene, but neither had I noticed the vomit. I wondered if the police had noticed bike tracks, but I didn't want to ask.

"So that's where we're at," Reilly said. "Pretty much nowhere until we get an ID."

"But someone went to a lot of trouble to move the body to that particular place, in the middle of a trail, and do what they did to the ears. They could've hidden it any number of places in the park where it might never have been seen by anyone, ever, but they obviously wanted it to be seen – and wanted it to look as scary as possible. What do you make of that?"

"No idea. Can't even speculate until we find out who the guy was and what was going on in his life. But let me know if you see anything down there. Like anything looks like a hundred and seventy-pound body was dragged through the woods."

I told him I would keep my eyes open.

He said "Yeah, do that," and then the dial tone buzzed in my ear.

I hung up and checked my email. There was a message from Ronnie saying she would try to get to Albany by ten at the latest.

I forced myself to spend the rest of the day at my desk working on a funding proposal for a housing organization in the lower Hudson Valley. Then I did some vacuuming and changed the sheets on my bed. Then I took my backpack and walked across town to the Price Chopper on Delaware Avenue and bought some groceries.

5

At nine-thirty I was sitting on my front steps. The weather had clouded during the afternoon and now a gentle rain was falling. My tee-shirt was pleasantly damp and cool on my shoulders.

There had been times during the summer when I worried that Ronnie and I were losing touch with each other. I didn't know if seeing her would bring the same sheer joy that it had the summer before when we were together from week to week, sharing things we both loved. I had even found myself thinking of that painfully simple Hemingway story "The End of Something," wondering if when we did get back together something might be missing, so it might just "not be fun any more." Our communications over the last several days had been reassuring, but I wasn't absolutely certain, until she arrived.

Her little blue car pulled to the curb. The door sprang open. She whipped out and raced around the car toward where I sat, and more or less tackled me, knocking me backward onto the top step with my head against the door and with her on top of me, her hair in my face, and then her mouth on my mouth. And then there was her happy laughter. How could Ronnie possibly not be fun anymore?

We got her bag from the car, went inside, closed the door behind us, and hugged. My first Ronnie power-hug in weeks. I had almost forgotten just how really powerful they were.

Finally she leaned back, gazed into my face and said, "I'd been thinking we'd probably have a nice sedate drink and chat and fill each other in on what's happening... But the hell with that. Let's go to bed."

"Good idea," I said. "Drinks can wait."

But we never did come back downstairs that evening.

In the morning we were drinking coffee at the kitchen table when we heard the front door open. Shortly, Jesse appeared.

"My God," Ronnie said. "You didn't tell me. He's all grown up."

Jesse grinned.

"How did you *do* that? It hasn't been *that* long since I've seen you."

He shrugged, still grinning.

Ronnie hugged him.

He looked slightly abashed but the smile lingered.

"Let's take our coffee out on the steps," she said. "I haven't had a chance to sit on those steps with you guys for way too long. But you don't have any coffee, Jesse, and now that you're grown up you're probably a coffee-drinker."

To my surprise, he said, "Yeah, I have some sometimes."

So I poured a third cup of coffee and we all went out to the steps.

The rain had stopped. The top step, sheltered by the eves, was mostly dry, though out in the street the red brick pavement was still wet. The morning air felt freshly rinsed.

Ronnie sat between me and Jesse with her coffee mug tucked between her legs, and put an arm around each of us. "My guys," she said. "What could be nicer?"

"We sure have missed you," I said.

"So tell me what you've been up to. What's happening around here?"

"We've been behaving ourselves mostly," I said. "But we had something weird happen day before yesterday."

Jesse stared silently into the street.

"Jesse, I did tell Ronnie about the thing we saw. Because you know I tell her everything. And you know we can both trust her not to get us in trouble."

"The last thing I would ever do," she said, "would be to do something to get you guys in trouble. But it sounds horrible. If I saw something like that it would totally freak me out."

"Yeah," Jesse said.

"I'd probably need to talk it out with someone I trusted, just to get it out of my head so I could sleep at night."

Jesse said nothing.

"So I think you trust me, and if you want to talk about any part of it, I'm a pretty good listener."

"Maybe," Jesse said. "But not now."

"Okay. But whenever you're ready…"

"I don't know," Jesse said. "Maybe."

"Okay, but what *are* the three of us going to do today for excitement. We need a plan. Maybe a plan with a canoe and some water in it."

"And maybe with some fish in the water," I suggested.

"It might just work," Ronnie said.

We put my canoe on my pick-up and drove north through Troy to Schaghticoke, then east on Route 67 for ten miles to the hamlet of Buskirk. We launched the canoe on the Hoosick River below the Buskirk covered bridge and paddled downstream between wooded shores. Soon we were far enough from any roads so that we heard no traffic sound. The moderate current that had flowed under the bridge dissipated in the first half-mile. The next several miles were flat water backed up from the dam in Johnsonville.

"It's not exactly crystal clear," Ronnie said, "but it's nice. I like it."

"It's the river I grew up on," I said. "Just a bit upstream from here."

"Did you fish in it?" Jesse asked.

"Oh yes."

"What kind you catch?

"Bass, perch, bluegills, carp, whatever came along."

Jessie opened his tackle box and took out the plastic bag of worms we had purchased in Johnsonville. "Could you eat those fish? Or was there PCBs, like now in the Hudson?"

"No PCBs that I know of. Probably some other bad stuff. But we ate them anyway. Sometimes we'd build a fire on the bank and cook them and eat them right there."

"Can we do that?"

"If you can catch something for us to cook."

He flipped the spinning rod, sending a spinner and worm toward the left bank, then began reeling. "Don't worry," he said.

Near the first bend a heron lifted itself into the air from a backwater on our right.

"And there's another one," Ronnie said. "And another. And, oh, still another. There must be a rookery."

"There is. Up in those woods ahead."

"We'll have to check it out sometime," she said.

Off the ledges on the outside of the second bend there was a deep hole, where Jesse caught several perch. As he fished, Ronnie and I watched an osprey circling above the river downstream.

"I don't suppose you have eagles too," she said.

"You see them sometimes, at least in the spring and fall, but I've never seen a nest on this stretch of river. It's not Big Wilder Pond by any means."

"But very nice. And probably more kinds of wildlife than there are in my great big marsh, for all its big flocks of waterfowl."

Further downstream we went ashore where a farm road came down through the woods to a small grassy clearing on the right. There was a ring of stones in the clearing where someone had built a fire. Some dry firewood was piled nearby. We borrowed some of it and built fire. I helped Jesse clean his three perch, leaving the heads on so we could run a sharpened alder stick through the mouth of each and into the back of the cavity under the backbone.

"Like a hotdog on a stick," he said. "How do you know when it's cooked."

"You can let the skin get black – until you can pull it off. Then you can just nibble the fish off the bones."

"Cool," Jessie said.

When the three fish were ready to go over the fire, I said, "For a long time I've wondered where this little road comes down from. If you guys can handle the cooking I think I'll take a walk up there and see what I can see."

"We can handle it," Ronnie said. "Can't we Jesse?"

"Handle the *eating* too," Jesse said. "If he don't get back quick."

I walked up the grassy track through the woods until I came to the edge of a cornfield, where I turned back into the woods and settled myself on a stump. I wanted to give them maybe 20 minutes alone before I returned.

When I got back they were sitting side by side on the bank facing the river.

"Am I too late?" I asked.

"Saved you the little one," Jesse said.

On our way upstream, we stopped again to fish the pool by the ledges, where Jessie caught several more perch to take home to his mother. Back at the covered bridge we tied the boat on the pickup and then drove on east through Eagle Bridge to the Moses Brothers vegetable stand, where we bought some sweet corn and a couple of cantaloupes.

Back on Orange Street, we gave half the corn and one of the melons to Jesse to take home with him. Then we poured some Jack Daniels and sat on the sofa in the living room.

"Did he tell you anything?" I asked.

"Some. I didn't want to sound like an interrogator, so I didn't push him, and didn't get a very clear story – just fragments of a story really. About his buddies somehow being involved."

"Being involved in…?"

"He was adamant that they were not involved in killing anyone. But it sounded like they were there – where the body was found. At some point anyway – probably at night. There was a flashlight."

"Did it sound like he was there with them?"

"It wasn't clear. Either they thought he ought to be there but he wasn't, or he *was* there but didn't want to be. There seemed to be some tension between him and them. Or else it was just the tension *in him* between loyalty to his friends and some other part of himself."

"Did he say anything about who the friends are?"

"No, it was just *my buddies*. Do you know who that would be? Who his buddies are?"

"I don't really know. I've been seeing him lately on the street with guys more or less his age or a little older. All in their early teens I think. Not little kids any more."

"But they would all have been little kids just a little while ago. Do you know if they're the same kids he grew up with – or are they new friends?"

"I don't know. But even if they're kids he's known for years … adolescence changes who kids are. And how they act. It used to be I'd see him here and there with a friend or two and they'd be riding their bikes or throwing a ball in the street – always doing something. Now when I see him on the street he's likely to be with at least three others, and they're never *doing* anything – just hanging out."

"Just being cool."

"But for all I know, maybe they *are* doing something. Like waiting for someone to come along and buy something from them. Or sell something to them. I don't know. It's been bothering me. And now what he told you about his buddies really scares me. If they were there where the body was found, and they were there at night, and he knew about it, even if he wasn't there himself… it's a very different story than what he told me. He didn't just happen into the thing on his bicycle."

"But he did find a way to tell you. A way to tell you and protect his buddies at the same time."

"I'm not even sure now why he did tell me. He didn't re-ally need to tell anyone at all. He must have known the body would be found before too long anyway – being right there in the trail the way it was."

"Oh I think he absolutely did need to tell someone. It was driving him crazy. He needed to share it with someone – with you in particular."

"But not all of it."

"Not all at once, anyway, but as much as he could. He may still find a way to tell you more. And I'll try to spend some more time with him while I'm here, too."

"Having you here has made a big difference. He was sounding pretty much like the old Jesse by the end of the afternoon."

"Catching some fish also tends to make a person feel better," she said.

"Yes it does, but not like having you around does." I slid closer to her on the sofa.

She leaned into me and murmured something I didn't catch.

"What?"

"I said 'Food first.' I was just reminding myself of the official hierarchy of human needs – water, then food, then sex, then fishing. Because when we're together I sometimes forget what's supposed to come first."

We fried some hamburgers and steamed the corn – steaming up the already humid kitchen and ourselves in the process. We ate in the kitchen in spite of the steamy atmosphere. My house really offers no other practical place to eat. Then we retreated to the relative coolness of the front steps.

I told her what I had learned from Reilly the previous day. That the dead man still hadn't been identified, and that, whoever he was, he hadn't been killed where he was found.

"Why in the world would someone move the body to a place like that, where you say it would have been found anyway? Apparently they weren't trying to hide it."

"I think it's pretty clear it was supposed to be found. Otherwise there's no reason for the grisly business with the ears. It was a display intended to present a message to someone."

"But who?"

"As Reilly says, it's almost impossible to guess until you find out who the man was, and learn who his family and friends are, who his enemies might be, and why they're enemies."

"Can you take me to Tivoli Park tomorrow?" Ronnie asked. "I've never been there."

"Sure, we'll do that."

"And not talk about it any more until then."

"Yes."

"And go upstairs now."

"Yes."

In the morning, after breakfast, we walked up Judson and went down the trail to Tivoli Lake, where mist still clung to the surface of the water.

"Not exactly a lake," Ronnie said. "But nice."

"And quiet. And the city's out of sight."

"What's that – over the other side of the dam? You see them?"

We both peered at a little group of shapes moving in and out of the brush. "They look like... Are they really *turkeys*?" she asked.

"Yeah, turkeys. A group I've been seeing off and on since spring, when they were little ones with their mother. They're big enough now so it's hard to tell if one of them *is* the mother – or if they're big kids out on their own now."

"Hard to believe. Wild turkeys in the city. And you even see deer sometimes?"

"A doe with a fawn a while back. Also a family of skunks last week. There isn't much to interfere with the natural world down here."

"What a lovely thing – to have a place like this just up the street from you."

"Yes it is. Part of why I like living where I do."

6

Clouds returned on Tuesday, with showers in the afternoon. I got somewhat wet walking back with Helen from our downtown meeting with bank officials. Helen had an umbrella and offered to share it, but I've never really liked walking around trying to keep a miniature roof over my head, and trying to keep it over two people's heads seems impossibly awkward.

She was talking again about how there were no homes for sale on Livingston Avenue or in the little neighborhood north of Livingston between Northern Boulevard and Tivoli Park.

"I walked around that neighborhood," she said, "and I did see one for sale-by-owner sign with a phone number, on Beverly. But when I called, there was no answer, and then when I went back over there the next day the sign was gone. Someone is just right on top of everything that comes up."

I told her I was going to be seeing my realtor friend Lisa that evening and would ask her what she knew about the situation.

Lisa was an ex-girlfriend. Our relationship had cooled two years earlier, but we still got together from time to time for a drink, some gossip, and usually a sportive argument. She lived on the second floor of a building she owned on Ten Broeck Avenue at the once-fashionable eastern end of Arbor Hill. Her living room was about four times the size of my own and had a row of tall windows that looked eastward over rooftops to the wooded skyline beyond the Hudson River.

"I'm still envious of your view," I told her. "It's still nice to be able to sit comfortably indoors with a martini while looking into the distance."

"Air conditioned too," she said.

"Yes, that too. Nice to be cool without having to go out and sit on the steps."

"Of course you could be cool in your own place. There's not much you can do about your view, but you could have air conditioning if you chose to."

"Which I don't."

"Because you think being comfortable is sinful."

"No, I just think unnecessary energy consumption is... well, unnecessary."

"You do think it's sinful. Like you think martinis are sinful. Like you think I'm a sinful capitalist. And you're secretly attracted to sin."

"Martinis aren't all that sinful, though whiskey is more righteous. But you *are* a sinful capitalist. A sinful profiteering land speculator."

"Thank you," she said. "I do my best. But it's been tough lately. The wages of sin aren't what they used to be."

"Neither are the wages of righteousness."

"You mean righteousness used to be profitable?"

"Well okay, good point."

"Another martini?"

"Yes please. I do still *enjoy* some kinds of sin."

She stood up and took my glass. "As long as someone else pays for it and takes responsibility for it."

"And serves it graciously. The best of all possible worlds."

She stepped into the kitchen and raised her voice. "But what's in it for the server?"

"I'm sure the server can exact some kind of commission."

"Not from you. Not anymore."

"You get someone to argue with. Someone to keep you in training."

"As though I lacked for people to argue with."

"All right. Another person to exchange information with."

She reappeared and handed me my glass, full and icy cold. "You mean you've got a tip for me? Maybe a big investment opportunity in Sheridan Hollow?"

"Actually on Livingston Avenue. It seems that someone is quite methodically buying up property on Livingston and in the little neighborhood north of Livingston, back toward the middle school."

"So what you're really doing is asking me what I know about that."

"As a matter of fact, yes."

"What I know is that someone is quite methodically buying up property on Livingston and in that little neighborhood north of Livingston."

"Any idea who might be doing that, or why?"

"Not really."

"Any suspicions?"

"What are you offering in return? It used to be when I gave you information you'd go to bed with me."

"I thought maybe you'd do it for old time's sake."

"No, but maybe because I'm curious about why you're interested."

"Then I'll try to reward your curiosity."

I told her first about my conversations with Helen Hamilton. Then I told her about the body in Tivoli Park, giving her all the details, right down to the vomit on the trail. Everything except the Jesse connection.

She shook her head. "You do get into the damndest stuff. But don't tell me you actually think there's some connection between a dead man in Tivoli Park and someone buying property on Livingston Avenue. Why in the world would you think that?"

"I don't think that. I don't know what to think."

"But you're looking for a connection."

"They're coincidental. They're connected in time, that's all. And I thought you'd be interested in hearing about something that the media apparently don't even know about yet."

"But they do know. There's an article in today's Albany Times about a body that was found in Tivoli Lake Preserve."

"Oh, okay, I hadn't caught up with that. How much did it say about it?"

"Not much. It didn't mention the ears. And it didn't say it was discovered by the famous sleuth Warren Crow. It was just your basic a-body-was-found-and-police-are-investigating type of article."

"But it did say it was in Tivoli Park?"

"Yes. And I *am* interested. So if you were telling me about it just to bait your hook, well it worked."

"Good. So what can you tell me about the Livingston Avenue purchases?"

"Really only what Helen told you. I haven't been involved in any of those sales myself. Livingston Avenue isn't exactly where my interests lie."

"Do you have that Manhattan phone number that apparently other brokers have called?"

"I know how to get it."

"I don't suppose you could find a pretext for calling it, just to see what you might learn."

"I don't know. I might. It might be interesting."

"Do you have any idea of who might be working here in Albany for whoever the buyer is? Other than the brokers who have that number and call it when they have a listing in that area."

"No idea. There wouldn't necessarily have to be anyone locally, as long as the local agencies have that number. And even if an agent didn't call that number, once the property went into the MLS, a buyer could respond from anywhere. Albany, Manhattan, Kuwait – anywhere at all."

"But if there was no broker, no listing… Helen told me about seeing a for-sale-by-owner sign on Beverly Street that disappeared before she could get in touch with the owner."

"Which doesn't mean anything in particular."

"No, but it could mean someone's walking the streets on a regular basis."

"Possibly."

"Do you know if anyone's doing what Eddie McFadden used to do – walking the streets, knocking on doors, looking for people who're desperate for money and might be willing to sell their homes for whatever he offered?"

"I don't know. No one as crass as Eddie was."

"Which is a good thing – he really was sinful. Taking advantage that way of the most vulnerable people he could find. Both the people he bought from and the people he sold to."

"He certainly was not a likable person, but he was just doing the things he knew how to do to make a living."

"And you think that's okay?"

She was watching me with a sly smile. "You want to fight?"

"No, not over Eddie McFadden. His case is closed, and in the end he got worse than he deserved."

"He certainly did – got his throat cut for trying to take advantage of people who were smarter than him and flat-out evil."

"Anyway, I guess if someone's walking around looking for properties now it's not an Eddie McFadden type. Whoever the buyer is seems to be just picking off whatever comes on the market, and doesn't seem to waste a lot of time negotiating a bargain price."

"But whoever's doing the walking around," she said, "isn't likely to be the actual buyer. Whoever's buying apparently has deep pockets. Or if he's buying with credit it's not local credit."

"Would you be able to find out what prices are actually being paid for those properties?"

"Sure. But most likely they're selling for something close to the asking price. As you said, those deals happen fast."

"So I imagine the listing agents – since they have that phone number – are encouraging higher prices."

She shrugged. "They'd be fools not to."

"But the buyer seems to be willing to let that happen."

"Apparently."

"Which makes you wonder, I said, "why someone wants those properties that much."

"It does make you wonder."

"I'm glad you're wondering."

"And I should know better than to let you get me wondering about something like this. You want another drink?"

"I would, but you know the third drink's likely to lead to an argument."

"It used to sometimes lead to something nicer."

"Yes, and it was more than nice."

We looked at each other.

"I'm sorry," she said. "I shouldn't have said that, but you do take advantage of me, you know. Provoking someone's curiosity like that is kind of like flirting."

"And I'm afraid I enjoy it," I said.

She stood up. "Okay. We'll have one more drink and then I'll throw you out."

7

Tuesday morning I was at my desk, making an effort to catch up with my work, when I was interrupted by a call from Reilly.

"Found out who the body is," he said. "It'll be on the evening news, so thought I'd give you a heads-up."

"I'm interested," I said, "but I'm not sure why you're giving me a heads-up. Why me in particular."

"Like I said before, you're the only guy I know who spends time in Tivoli Park. Plus, you're the one who found the body and I'm still wondering if you've told me everything you know. So I'm staying in touch."

"I *have* told you everything I know. Anyway, who was the guy?"

"Name's Ben Higgins. Looks like we made a mistake thinking it couldn't be a gang killing."

"You're saying he was a gangster?"

"No. But it sounds like he annoyed some gangsters. Guy owned a little so-called grocery down in the South End – beer, cigarettes, lottery, that kind of place. Kids were hanging out there. He didn't like it and gave 'em a hard time. So it looks like they gave him a real hard time in return."

"Is there a reason to think it was actually a gang, not just some neighborhood kids?"

"His wife thinks they were OGK boys. Original Gangsta Killas. *The* South End gang."

"His wife is how you learned who he was?"

"Yeah, she finally called us. Said she and him had a fight and she'd been thinking he'd just gone off to his brother's place in Rensselaer. Said that's what he sometimes did when he was pissed at her. Then she found out no one was keeping the store open, and she called his brother and found out he hadn't been there, and then she saw the AT article, where the description was close enough to make her nervous. So she finally called and reported him missing. Yesterday she identified the body. And she told us about his trouble with the OGK."

"But if his store's in the South End and he was killed by a South End gang, why did he wind up in Tivoli Park? Did he have any connection with the park, or with anything on the north side of town?"

"Not that we know of so far. So that's the question. Why would the OGKs haul his dead ass all the way up there?"

"Unless that's where they happened to catch up with him and they actually killed him there."

"Doesn't make sense. They'd do it on their own turf. If they were going to shoot someone in that neighborhood, it would be someone belonging to West Hill's own Jungle Junkies – that they've been warring back and forth with for years."

"I guess the thing with the ears doesn't make sense either. As you said the other day, gangs don't usually do that kind of thing."

"And if they did go and cut a guy's ears off like that, it would most likely be a rival gang member, not just some storekeeper they're pissed at for trying to run 'em off. So no, it's not a real good fit, but it's what we got right now."

❖ ❖ ❖

That afternoon I checked the Albany Times on line. The story was there. It did not mention the dispute between the victim and the OGK, but it was otherwise the full story as I knew it, including the removal of the ears. This detail, the article said, had not been confirmed by the police, but no other source was cited.

I called Reilly, got his voice mail, and left a message: "Just so you know – It wasn't me who told the press about the guy's ears."

A half hour later, he called me back. "Okay, you didn't tell them," he said, "but who *did* you tell? Who else knew?"

"No one that I know of. I didn't tell anyone. You must have a leak in your own system."

"No way," he said. It wasn't one of ours."

I wasn't comfortable with my lie. Jesse knew, and I had told Ronnie, and Lisa, and also Robert Goodwin. I knew that Jesse and Ronnie would *not* have reported the information to the Albany Times, and there was no reason for Lisa to do it either. But I didn't know what to think about Robert Goodwin.

"If it wasn't one of your own," I said, "then maybe it came from whoever did it – or from another member of the gang, if it was a gang."

"Why would they call it in themselves?"

"Because whoever did it wanted people to know about it. Someone went to a lot of trouble to move the body and cut its ears off. The first Albany Times article didn't even mention the ears. Someone wanted to make sure the next article did."

"You got a point there," Reilly said. Then after a long pause: "So you're sure *you* didn't tell anybody?"

I repeated my lie.

There was another long silence before he finally said, "Okay then," and hung up.

I didn't actually know if Robert Goodwin was the true name of the man I had talked with in the park, but I thought it was time to find out. It seemed unlikely that someone who hadn't wanted to say exactly where he lived would have a listed phone number, but I checked the phone book anyway and found a Robert Goodwin listed with a Livingston Avenue address.

When I called the number, the phone was answered briskly by a voice I recognized. "This is Bob."

"This is Warren Crow, the guy…"

"I know. That I talked with in the park the other day. I was thinking about trying to call you. I just read the story in the paper."

"And I was just wondering if you might have passed along the account I gave you to someone else."

"Good heavens no – though I understand why you might wonder. But no, I didn't. The whole thing is bothering me, however."

"Maybe we should talk," I said.

"Yes. Perhaps you would have dinner with me tonight. Here at my home. With me and a friend, whom I've already invited."

"I'm free," I said. "That would be very nice. At the address in the phone book?"

"Yes, on Livingston. It's the upstairs apartment. The entrance to the stairs is the door on the left. It will be unlocked. Let's say six-thirty."

"Can I bring something?"

"No need. And *please* don't bring the traditional guest's bottle of wine."

"You're a teetotaler?"

"Oh no. Just very particular about wine. And well stocked."

At six-thirty I walked over to Livingston and found the house. Like the majority of houses in the neighborhood, it was in need of paint. The glass in the ground floor door was broken and had been replaced with a piece of plywood. The door was not locked but it took a good yank to get it open. Inside, I found the stairway and the upstairs hallway dimly lit by a single overhead light bulb. But as I reached the top of the stairs, the door to Goodwin's apartment opened and Goodwin himself ushered me into quite a different setting.

The living room was spacious and clean. Much of the wall space was taken up with heavily stocked book shelves. At one end of the room there were comfortable-looking easy chairs and a leather-covered sofa. At the other end there was a desk with a single tidy stack of papers on it, a table with a white table cloth and four straight chairs, and on the wall a large flat-screen TV, which faced the table, not the sofa and easy chairs.

Goodwin was wearing corduroys and an old tweed jacket over a white shirt without a tie. His friend, who rose from one of the easy chairs, was a large, slightly over-weight but powerful-looking African American man in a somewhat rumpled three-piece suit, also without a tie. He was introduced to me as Elwin Thompson.

"Bob's been telling me about you," Thompson said as we shook hands. "And your adventures on behalf of the Neighborhood Housing Association."

"I don't know what adventures he's been telling you about," I said. Apparently Goodwin had learned more about me than I had learned about him. "It's true I do some work with the NHA. But he may have invented the adventures."

Elwin Thompson smiled. "He does tend to invent things."

"But I had no need to invent in this case," Bob Goodwin said. "We're drinking a little gin, if you'd care to join us. It's something I get from a place in Vermont. Hand crafted. Real juniper berries harvested from the ridge above the little distillery, along with other botanicals. Once you've tasted it you'll never want to drink that awful chemically flavored commercial beverage again. And in my opinion it would be immoral to dilute this real gin with Vermouth, which I do not stock. So… on the rocks?"

"All right," I said. "If it's that good."

We sat in the easy chairs and sipped chilled gin, which indeed was superior to any gin I'd ever tasted.

"Since I've now read it in the Albany Times," Elwin said, "I assume Bob did not invent the grisly story he says you told him the other day in Tivoli Park."

"No, I did tell him what I had seen, and the story in to-day's paper is accurate as far as I know, including the detail the police wouldn't confirm – which they suspect reached the press because I told someone about it."

"I've assured him it was not I," Bob said.

Elwin shrugged. "Certainly wasn't me. I *never* repeat what Bob tells me, because I never know what part of it's true, if any."

"This is one story I wish were not true," Bob said. "I've tried to just put it out of my mind, but I can't. And I'm afraid of what the consequences will be."

"The consequences for the man's family are certainly not happy," I said. "But beyond that I have no idea what the consequences will be."

"Bob has lots of worries," Elwin said. "He has lots of interests and worries about all of them."

"So does Elwin," Bob said.

"Not true. I don't have nearly the worries Bob does, because I don't have nearly the investments he has."

"He likes to pretend I'm rich," Bob said.

"He likes to pretend he's not," Elwin said.

"And I have no idea who to believe here," I said. "But, Bob, rich or not, what consequences are you worried about?"

"I'm worried about the consequences for Tivoli Lake Preserve. I'm worried about having too much attention focused on it."

"But if there are wider consequences from this one story," I said, "it will mean even fewer people in the park. It will all be forgotten soon enough but in the meantime people will be frightened away from the place. It will be a place they wouldn't even consider going."

"Oh, people already think it's a scary place. A couple of years ago there was a young woman who disappeared, and a large group was organized to search the whole preserve for her – even drained Tivoli Lake as part of the search. It wasn't that there was any particular reason to think she would be in the park, and of course they didn't find her there, but as someone was quoted as saying at the time, 'It's just the kind of place *they* might *take* someone.' So no, what I'm worried about is that this thing will make the place more visible in the eyes of a city government that has mostly been oblivious to it – which is why it has been preserved."

"But what would be the consequences of their being forced to look at it?" I asked. "Would it really change things?"

"It would change things absolutely if they decided to sell it to someone."

"You think someone might actually want to buy it?"

"Why not? Eighty acres of undeveloped land, next to an I-90 interchange, a mile from the state Capitol – why *wouldn't* someone want to buy it and use it?"

"But for what? For housing? More apartments? I'm under the impression that what's already on the edge of it – the apartments down the street here – aren't as fully rented up as they might be."

"No, probably not residential development. Not now anyway. Unless it's very high end residential."

"But if not residential, what would it be?"

"Oh, there are plenty of potential uses. Maybe just industrial stuff. Maybe just something like a trucking depot, for instance."

"But it's too hilly – and too wet in places. Truckers would want a big dry level area."

"Okay, sure, but maybe something that could make use of the hills and wet areas."

"And what would that be?"

"Maybe something actually more park-like. Like an amusement park."

"Are you serious?"

"Actually yes. I've been thinking about Tivoli Park in Copenhagen? Do you know about it?"

"In Denmark? I guess I associated the name with Italy, not Denmark."

"Well Copenhagen's Tivoli Park, or Tivoli Gardens, is one of the oldest amusement parks in the world."

"You mean Ferris wheels and roller coasters and all that?"

"It has that kind of thing, but not only that. It's a very elaborate and exotic place. With flower gardens, music, cafes, theater, all kinds of entertainment. The founder – the guy who got the right to develop it – is said to have told the king of Denmark that when people are amusing themselves, they don't think about politics."

"The king found that a persuasive idea," Elwin said.

"An irresistible idea for those who govern," Goodwin said.

"So you're joking," I said. "You can't really think the Mayor of Albany would see political advantage in an amusement park."

"Of course he would," Goodwin said. "Maybe not so much because it would distract people. But it would expand the tax base of a city that's hamstrung by the fact that so much of its real estate is tax-exempt. And it would create jobs."

"Maybe a few jobs. Until it went bankrupt. Then the city would be left having to demo a bunch of Ferris wheels and tilt-a-whirls. Anyway, no one would be crazy enough to buy it for that purpose."

"You have no imagination," Goodwin said. "It would be bought by someone with imagination."

I couldn't tell if he was joking or not. Elwin Thompson was grinning at him.

"It's only a rumor," Goodwin said.

"Seriously, you've heard such a rumor?"

"There are always rumors," he said.

"And most of them have no basis."

"Depends on what you mean by basis. Rumors usually reflect what someone's actually *thinking*."

"You guys are scaring me to death," I said. "If you don't stop you're going to persuade me it really could happen."

Goodwin stood up and took my glass. "Maybe a little more gin will help. A little more gin, and then we'll open a nice bottle of wine and eat some paella and be mellow."

During dinner I asked the two of them how long they had known each other.

"We go way back," Bob said.

"A little way," Elwin said.

"In actual years then, how long?"

"Decades," Bob said.

"Maybe one decade," Elwin said.

"Here in Albany the whole time?"

"We've travelled the world together," Bob said.

"Last year for ten days we travelled together," Elwin said. "Otherwise, yes, it's been here and in Troy, where I still live."

"If you'll forgive my curiosity…" but I wasn't even sure what question I wanted to ask next.

"I believe Bob is *enjoying* your curiosity," Elwin said, "but he obviously doesn't intend to satisfy it."

"You then," I said. "Have you always lived in this area?"

"No, I moved up here eleven years ago from the city. I could no longer afford the city, so I moved to Troy. For what I save in housing costs I can take the train to the city any time I want to."

"And how did you meet Bob?"

"We lived in the same building in the Washington Park neighborhood – where I still live."

"Bob, you probably won't want to satisfy my curiosity about this either, but why did you move down here to Albany – and to this neighborhood in particular?"

"I was fed up with the Washington Park preoccupation with their precious little historic locale."

Elwin grinned and shook his head.

"They kept asking me to serve on committees," Bob said. "Here no one asks me to do anything. No one makes any assumptions about who I am or what I do."

"They just wonder why the hell you're here," Elwin said.

"Some people wonder the same thing about me," I said. "Why I live where I do. So I can understand – there's a kind of freedom in not belonging in a place."

"And even more so in a place that doesn't entirely belong to any one group," Bob said. "A place where you're neither an insider nor an outsider. Especially if it's a place on the edge of an 80-acre wood you can wander in."

I asked Elwin, "Do you come to Albany to wander in Bob's 80-acre wood?"

"No, I come to drink his excellent gin and incredible wine and to listen to his lies."

The conversation continued this way – amusing, but revealing very little. At ten-thirty I said, "Well this has been very pleasant but I'd better get home and think about what I have to do tomorrow."

"Such diligence," Bob said.

"But before I go, can you tell me where I can buy some of that amazing gin?"

"Let me just give you a bottle."

"No, please, just tell me where it's sold."

"Deep in the wilds of the Green Mountains. I buy it by the case, and it would be my pleasure to give you a bottle."

So I was in fact given a bottle of what had to be very expensive gin.

On my way out I managed to move along a wall of bookcases slowly enough to see some of the titles. There seemed to be a lot of history – much of it European history – and a lot of philosophy. I thought about asking my host how much of his collection he'd actually read, but I wanted to get home – and I didn't think I'd learn much from his answer anyway.

8

On Wednesday I drove to Poughkeepsie for what turned out to be a long and not very well-managed meeting. It was after seven when I got home, somewhat frustrated and very hungry. I put together a stir fry and while I was stirring I called Lisa and offered to take her out to dinner the next evening and share a juicy rumor. She said she was already committed for dinner but would be home by nine, and if I could promise her the rumor was really juicy I could stop by for a drink. I told her she might not agree about the juiciness of the rumor, but that I would bring some very unusual gin that would make up for whatever the rumor lacked in juiciness.

The next evening on my way to Lisa's I ran into Jesse on Clinton Avenue. He had been standing with several other boys on the corner at the top of Dove Street, but they had dispersed as I approached, and he was alone by the time I reached the corner.

"'Zup," he said.

"I'm on my way to see my realtor friend Lisa," I said. "We're trying to figure out who's buying up property over on the edge of Tivoli Park."

"Why they doin' that?" he asked.

"That's the question – or one of them. There seem to be various questions around Tivoli Park right now. Did you watch the news this evening – the interview with the wife of the guy who was killed?"

"No," he said. "What'd she say?"

"She said the guy'd had some kind of dispute with that gang that call themselves the Original Gangsta Killas. She thinks that's what got him killed."

"Wouldn't know about that."

"You know anything about that OGK gang?"

"Know they're trouble," he said, staring at the sidewalk. "Use to make trouble for uptown kids."

"Ever actually see any of them up here?"

Still looking down, he shook his head. "Come up here now, they in trouble themself."

"So if it really was them that killed the guy you and I saw, I don't understand why they would have hauled him all the way uptown to leave him in Tivoli Park. It doesn't make any sense."

He shook his head again. "Don't think it was them."

"You got a reason for thinking that?"

"Like you say, doesn't make sense."

"Okay. By the way, Ronnie's going to be back in town this weekend. You interested in another fishing expedition if we can talk her into it?"

"Sure," he said. "Interested in fishing most any time."

"So is Ronnie. We ought to be able to work something out."

I presented Lisa with Bob Goodwin's bottle of special gin and told her I'd been instructed never to put Vermouth in it. "And it's good advice," I said. "It's amazingly good gin."

"It might be good advice for someone who thinks a Martini is just an excuse for drinking gin. But I think I'll have Vermouth in mine, thank you."

I made two drinks, one with Vermouth, one without, and we settled in the living room. Since getting home, Lisa had taken off her shoes and changed into shorts, and now lounged on the sofa with her bare feet propped on the leather hassock. I sat in the chair facing her, my back to the darkened windows.

I told her she looked weary.

"Too many meetings," she said. "Too much work."

"Even in this cooled-off market?"

"I don't know – maybe there should be less work, but it doesn't seem to happen that way. Maybe it's just that I push harder when sales are down."

"With your connections I wouldn't think you'd have to push too hard to make a living, even in this market."

"Oh, it's not that I don't make a living. It's just that it isn't as much fun when the market's this bad."

"Okay, sure – selling is fun, and when things are not selling…"

"Then I need to be entertained some other way. So tell me – what's the juicy rumor you promised? That body you found in Tivoli Park's been getting quite a bit of media attention. Is that what the rumor's about?"

"No, it has to do with Tivoli Park, but not with the body, as far as I know anyway. But speaking of the body, you probably didn't see today's evening news. They interviewed the dead man's widow, who is saying the guy annoyed some gang members – didn't want them hanging out in his store. She thinks that's why he was killed."

"Did they say which gang?"

"The Original Gangsta Killas. OGK."

"But his store's in the South End, and that's a South End gang. So how come his body wound up in Tivoli Park?"

"I have no idea, and I don't think the police have any idea either. What his widow is saying may be true, but it certainly doesn't explain the whole thing."

"Okay, so the police are clueless, which is not big news. But what's the juicy rumor? Are you going to tell me or not?"

"Something I heard from this very odd, interesting guy who gave me this gin – someone I've seen from time to time walking in the preserve. His name is Robert Goodwin. I had dinner with him and a friend of his the other night. The two of them told me about Tivoli Park in Copenhagen."

"Ah yes, supposedly built because when people are having fun it keeps their mind off politics, or something like that"

"So you know about that Tivoli Park."

"But it's a far cry from Albany's Tivoli Park. Anyway, you didn't invite yourself over here to tell me about some Danish rumor."

"No, it's an Albany rumor. According to Goodwin there's a rumor that the city might sell Tivoli Preserve for some kind of development. When I asked what kind of development could possibly make sense, the idea of an amusement park was one of the things he came up with."

"That's a joke," she said, "not a juicy rumor. The guy's gin is much better than his rumors. But who *is* he? And why are you interested in such a crackpot?"

"I'm interested in him because I haven't been able to figure him out – and because he's interested in what happens to Tivoli Park."

"What makes him think anything's going to happen to it, other than having stuff dumped in it?"

"Well, I have no idea if he really heard a rumor about an amusement park, but I wouldn't be surprised if he did hear some kind of rumor about the city maybe selling the land to someone. And he did say some sensible things about why the city might *want* to sell it."

"Sure – if they could get a decent price for it, and start collecting taxes on it. But seriously, who would buy it, and for what?"

"I don't know. When I resisted the amusement park idea, he told me I have no imagination. And maybe that *is* my problem – because something weird is going on in that place and I can't imagine what it is."

"Help yourself to more gin," she said. Maybe it will help you with that problem."

"More for you too?"

"I'm going slow. Don't need my imagination charged up tonight."

I took my glass to the kitchen and poured another drink.

"Put the bottle in the freezer if you want," she said from the living room. "And I'll just leave it there for when I want to lure you over here – or lure someone else who might have juicier rumors."

I put the bottle in the freezer and returned to the living room.

"Goodwin himself has plenty of imagination," I said. "In fact it was more like he was trying out different ideas than reporting specific things he'd heard."

"In other words he was just bullshitting – is that what you're saying?"

"I guess, but he's a puzzling guy. He says interesting things that could be true or not, and it's hard to know which. In fact his friend Elwin said he himself never repeats anything Bob Goodwin says because he's never sure what part of it is true. He also suggested that Bob is rich, but pretends not to be."

Lisa lifted her martini glass. "This is a rich man's booze."

"And the wine he served was a rich man's wine. Or else he's just a connoisseur who has very few responsibilities and just barely enough money to afford certain very nice things. I don't know."

"It sounds like he doesn't *want* you to know. Whether he's hiding his wealth, or hiding his lack of wealth."

"Exactly."

She laughed. "If he really is rich – and really thinks someone might want to buy that land – then maybe his interest is speculative. Maybe he's thinking about making an offer. It's what I would think about if I believed those things."

"I don't know. But speaking of real estate speculation, did you learn anything about who's buying houses in the Livingston area?"

"Nothing significant. I did learn that when agents call that Manhattan number with a new property, they get an answering machine that doesn't tell them who or what they've reached but invites them to leave a message. Their calls are then returned by an unidentified woman who says she's been asked by a potential buyer to make a certain offer on the property in question. If there's then a verbal agreement on a price, the agent is told to send a proposed contract to an attorney at a Manhattan address."

"And when the sale is closed what name goes on the deed?"

"Livingston Properties, Inc."

"Mean anything to you?"

"No, and I haven't talked to anyone who'd ever heard of it before the last couple of months."

"Do you have an address for it?"

"It's the attorney's New York address. And at the closings, the full payment is simply made from the attorney's escrow account. No mortgage is executed."

"Know anything about the attorney?"

"Nothing."

"Is it possible to find out who controls the corporation?"

I guess you could get the names of the initial board members from the Department of State – and the corporate address that's registered with them – but none of that is going to tell you much. However, the interesting thing is that there's now an alternative. Brokers are getting calls from someone else – I got one this week – asking to be notified of any listings in that neighborhood. And this one's nearer home. The call was from an attorney in Troy – someone I don't know, though I know people who've dealt with him. If I had a listing in that neighborhood, I would call him, but I don't. I'll keep my ears open, though."

"Me too – and while we're at it let's also keep our ears open for any rumors about Tivoli Park."

"I won't plug my ears, but I have no idea where I would listen for such a rumor."

"Any possible sources in city government?"

"No one I could just walk up to and say, 'Hey, is it true you guys are going to sell Tivoli Preserve for an amusement park?'"

"But is there maybe a secretary or someone you could sort of gossip with? Tell them you heard a certain rumor, and see how they react?"

"Oh, I suppose. There's someone in Development and Planning that I worked with a few years ago in a different connection. I might find an occasion to chat with her, but I'm not going to ask anything stupid like the amusement park question."

"No, don't ask about the amusement park thing. Maybe just mention a vague rumor that someone wants to buy that land for *something*…?"

"If I find the occasion…" She yawned and stretched.

I stretched and stood up. "I'd better head home."

9

Thunder was rumbling ahead of me in the west as I walked back up Clinton. There had still been no rain when I got home, but during the night a real downpour drummed on my bedroom window. In the morning there were puddles in the street, but the sky had cleared and the sun was shining.

After one cup of coffee, I went to Tivoli Park and jogged down the trail from Livingston Avenue toward the pond. The birds were singing, the air was fresh-washed and cool, the sun was shining through the still-wet leaves. My legs were happy to be jogging downhill. But my mind was wrestling again with the puzzling fact that whoever had killed the South End resident named Ben Higgins had left his body up here in the woods on the northern edge of the city. I was picturing the body as I had seen it, with the bloody shirt and severed ears, when I was jolted back to the present by the realization that

I was actually seeing the thing again, recreated in front of me here in a different part of the park.

I stopped and stared at what was now undeniably another body – on its back at the point where the trail that I was following was joined by the trail that comes in from behind the Green Tech Charter School on Northern Boulevard.

I moved closer cautiously. I could see that this time it was a woman, a young woman with long dark hair. She was unquestionably dead. She was half naked. Her t-shirt had been pulled up to expose a pale belly streaked with blood. Her face, too was bloody. And her ears were gone.

I turned and went back up the trail. The obvious thing to do was to call the police again, but I was worried about what they would make of the coincidence. Would they believe it was just happenstance that I was the one to report both bodies, or would they want to make something more of it? I considered *not* reporting what I had just seen – letting someone else find it and report it – so there would be no coincidence and I would be free of any suspicion. But that would leave me out of the loop, with no further first-hand knowledge of a set of circumstances that I was starting to feel did somehow involve me.

It was just seven-fifteen when I reached my house. I made the call and told the voice at the other end of the line that I needed to report a murder and that it was important that I talk with Detective Reilly because he was already investigating a related murder.

I was asked where the murder had taken place, and whether I was at the scene.

"No, I'm not at the scene. I'm calling from my home phone. The body is in Tivoli Park – at the place where the trail down from Livingston Avenue meets the trail coming in from the Northern Boulevard side."

This obviously meant nothing to the person I was talking to. I was asked for my name and phone number and told to wait for a call-back.

Reilly called in about two minutes. I told him what I had found.

"Shit," he said. Then, after a pause: "You're at home?"

"Yes, on Orange Street."

"Yeah, well, I'm home too. Haven't even had a cup of coffee yet."

"Sorry. It's not a good way to start a day."

"You got coffee there?"

"I do."

"Well pour me some, and I'll pick you up in ten minutes."

I was sitting on my front steps with two travel mugs when he pulled up. I got in beside him and gave him one of the mugs. He drank most of it as he drove the few blocks to Green Tech Charter School, and finished it as we were getting out of the vehicle at the trailhead behind the school.

I followed him up the narrow trail between dense thickets still wet from the night's rain. Looking back over his shoulder, he said, "You want to explain why you're the one finding all these bodies?"

"Only two bodies."

"Yeah, well, two is enough. And you got both of 'em."

"I guess it's just that I spend more time in the preserve than most people. It's certainly not what I come here to look for."

He looked back at me again but said nothing.

When we were within sight of the body, even Reilly slowed his pace, as though not wanting to disturb the person on the ground ahead of us. He approached the body along the grassy edge of the trail. Then he stood and stared down at the dead young woman for what seemed like a long time.

I moved closer and looked at her also. There was blood on her t-shirt. And blood where her ears should have been. Also on her mouth and smeared sideways from her mouth onto one cheek. Her bare legs extended at awkward angles from her naked hips. On one leg a pair of dirt-smudged red shorts clung to her knee. There was a streak of blood on the inside of the thigh above it. She was wearing running shoes.

"This one wasn't only shot," Reilly said, still staring at her as he pulled a cell phone from his pocket. "Or maybe not shot at all."

He flipped the phone open, glanced at it, selected a number and made his call. In a moment he was giving instructions to someone on how to find us. "Tech guys'll be along," he said, closing the phone. "So you got no idea who she is?"

"No idea."

"Take a good look."

I moved up to where he stood and looked more closely. She was a slender young woman – probably twenty-something – with an olive complexion and long straight black hair. Her face was turned to the side as though she was trying to avoid looking at something unpleasant. I could imagine that the face would be quite pretty if it were animated, which it absolutely was not. I had a feeling I had seen her somewhere, but didn't know where.

"No, I don't know her," I said.

"Okay. You got any more coffee in the car?"

"The other cup is mostly full."

I followed him back to the car. We got in and I gave him the other travel mug.

He took a large swallow of coffee, then wiped his mouth on the sleeve of his denim shirt. "So tell me what's your thinking on why someone is always leaving dead people for you to find."

"You don't really think someone cares who finds them do you?"

"I'm trying to figure out what to think."

"So am I, but I'm starting from the assumption that whatever someone is doing here has nothing to do with me."

"I'm not starting with any assumptions at all," he said.

"No assumptions about gang involvement this time?"

"Nothing's ruled out."

"The only starting points seem to be the obvious questions. Why are they left here in the preserve? And why do both of them have their ears cut off – what's the message supposed to be?"

Reilly grunted. "Most likely the message is we're dealing with a lunatic here."

"Something awfully methodical about it though."

"Lunatics can be very methodical." He took another swallow of coffee and stared straight ahead through the windshield. "So tell me about your morning. You were just out jogging?"

"Yes."

"And you were coming down the trail from the head of Judson?"

"Yes."

"So you'd been in the park what, maybe five minutes? Did you notice the time when you found her?"

"It would have been a little before seven."

"And you didn't see anyone else?"

"No."

"When was the last time you were in the park – before this morning?"

"Two days ago – Wednesday morning."

"Same route?"

"Yes."

"And there was nothing unusual?"

"Nothing."

"See anyone at all in the park?"

"No. It was early – I think I was back home before seven. I don't usually see anyone at that hour."

"I need to talk to anyone who goes there like you. Can you tell me how to find any of those people?"

"There are a few people I see there occasionally. We don't generally introduce ourselves, but I'll start asking, and give you any names I come up with."

I knew I really needed to tell him about Bob Goodwin, but I didn't want to do it without first telling Goodwin I was going to do it.

"You do that," he said. "Get me some names. Call me on my cell. You still got that number?"

"Was it on your card?"

"Yeah. You need another?"

"I'm not sure." I couldn't remember what I had done with the card he had given me the week before.

He shook his head, pulled the notebook from his shirt pocket, removed another card from the back of the notebook, and gave it to me.

When the technicians arrived, Reilly took them back up the trail toward the body. I walked home, started another pot of coffee, and then called Goodwin from the kitchen phone.

He answered on the first ring. "This is Bob."

"This is Warren Crow. I've had another bad morning in the preserve, and I think I need to fill you in." I told him about the body of the young woman.

There was a long silence. Finally he asked, "So it was just like the other one?"

"Not really, but she'd obviously been attacked."

More silence.

I recounted my conversation with Reilly. "He wanted names of other people I've seen in the preserve. I didn't want to give him your name until I'd told you what was going on."

Still more silence.

"He's not asking for names of people who might be walking around the park killing people. He just wants to talk to anyone who might have seen something. He doesn't have much to work with at this point."

"Of course. I don't think I've seen anything useful, but I guess you should give him my name."

I told him I would do that. Then I told him I had really enjoyed dinner with him and Elwin the other night. He said he had enjoyed it too. Then we were both silent – any possibility of casual conversation overwhelmed by the far-from-casual reason for my call.

"Well, I'll see you." I said.

When the coffee was ready, I poured a cup and took it up to my desk. I fished Reilly's card out of my pocket and called the cell number.

Reilly answered with a flat "yeah."

I told him about Bob Goodwin as someone I saw occasionally in the preserve.

"You knew his name – why didn't you tell me before?"

"I felt like I just needed to fill him in on the situation before you got in touch with him. Now I've done that."

"That's not how it's supposed to work."

"I didn't think it would do any harm, and might save you some time."

"What'd you tell him?"

"Only what I'd seen, and that I had taken you to the place."

"It didn't occur to you I should be the one to decide what he's told?"

"No, it didn't. I would have told him sooner or later anyway. I thought it might as well be sooner."

"Well, I can't talk now," he said, "but give me the guy's phone number. And, look, I need to straighten out some things with you. I'll call you in a while."

It was late afternoon when he called and asked me to meet him at the police station on Henry Johnson Boulevard. I was happy to get out of the house at that point, and glad to have a chance to finish whatever I had to finish with Reilly before Ronnie arrived for the weekend in just a few more hours.

I found him staring at a laptop that sat on the papers sprawled on his desk. I sat down opposite him and waited. Eventually, without looking up, he said, "Okay, since you prepped this Goodwin guy before I talked with him, maybe you can prep me. What do you know about him?"

"So you did talk with him?" I asked.

"Didn't say that. Asked you a question."

"I know very little about him. He's just someone I see in the preserve."

"You know where he lives?"

"On Livingston. A second-floor apartment."

"Second floor. So maybe you've been there?"

I couldn't deny it. If he had talked with Goodwin he might already know I had been there.

"I didn't even know his name until after the first body was found," I said. "But after that, a couple of days ago, I wound up having dinner with him at his place. He is an unusual kind of guy, and I haven't really figured him out."

"I never figured you out either," Reilly said. "Why did you have dinner with Goodwin?"

"Because he invited me."

"Why did he invite you? You don't usually invite someone for dinner just because you saw them walking in the park."

"We'd only just had a brief conversation in the park before that time."

"A conversation about the body you found?"

"Only in a very general way," I said. But I was on thin ice – earlier I'd told Reilly that I had not said anything to any-one about the condition of the man's ears. Now I didn't know what Goodwin might tell him, or might already have told him, about that conversation in the park.

"We talked about it in more detail the evening we had dinner," I said.

"Was this dinner before or after the AT article – not the first report but the more detailed one?"

"It was that day, right after the second article was published."

"Was that the reason you got together?"

"Not specifically."

"So what all was said about it? I mean once you all agreed it was a terrible thing and all that, what else was said?"

"We talked about how the news could affect the way people think about Tivoli Park. It was something Goodwin was worried about."

"Why?"

"He said he was afraid if a lot of people started seeing the preserve as a dangerous place, the city might be tempted to sell the land. And he didn't want to lose it as a natural preserve."

"He really thought they could sell it? Why would anyone buy it?"

"He seemed to think there could be interest in developing the land. He claimed to have heard rumors to that effect."

He stared at me. "No way."

"That's what he said he'd heard. But I have no idea whether he was serious or just trying out an idea on me."

"You mean seeing if you'd believe it?"

"He does that sort of thing."

He shook his head. "All right, what *do* you think about that idea? Is there any way it could be true?"

"It's possible. Deals like that have been known to happen."

"Not in places like Tivoli Park."

"Okay, but something *is* going on in Tivoli Park that we don't understand."

"You mean something besides someone dumping bodies there? Used to be a place people dumped trash. Now it's a place where they dump bodies. Doesn't mean there's something going on there. Just the opposite – it's a place where *nothing* is going on."

"But it's really not like someone is just dumping bodies there. It's like someone is leaving gruesome displays there.

And maybe someone is leaking information to the press to make sure everyone knows about those displays and where they are. There has to be something going on."

"Sure, but *where* it's going on doesn't necessarily mean anything except that it's an empty place where you can dump stuff. Why do people do certain things in vacant lots and abandoned buildings? They do it because those places are *empty*. Like Tivoli Park."

"Okay, I have no answers – just a lot of questions. And speaking of questions, can I ask if you've learned anything about how the young woman died? Or anything at all about her?"

He closed the laptop and stood up. "Buy the paper. You can read what we tell the media, when we tell them."

"All right."

But I do have one more question for you," he said. "Did you tell Goodwin about the condition she was in?"

"I told him she'd obviously been attacked."

"So outside of us in the department, it's you and him who know. That means if the media get it before we tell them…"

"It's Goodwin and I who know, *and* whoever did it or was part of doing it. I certainly have no reason to tell the media, and I can't imagine Goodwin has either. I don't know about the others."

Reilly shrugged. "By the way, thanks for the coffee this morning. That was helpful."

10

Ronnie arrived around seven. I'd made a sauce and was prepared to cook spaghetti if she hadn't eaten when she got here, but she had picked up something at a place she'd discovered off I-88 between Oneonta and Cobleskill.

"The food was okay," she said, on her way into the house, "but what I really like about the place is the young couple who run it. They just seemed to be having so much *fun*."

"How young?" I asked, shutting the door behind us.

"Oh well, probably a little older than me. But it's this sort of Ma-and-Pa place, and they're young compared to how I think of a Ma and Pa being. But hey…" She came into my arms and kissed me hard and laughed. "You probably haven't eaten. I should have called and told you I was stopping."

"Mostly just hungry for your company. But now that you're here we can take a walk and I'll buy a sub, and one for you if you can eat more. The people at Subway have a pretty good time too."

"I can always use a walk," she said. "And I can always eat more."

Since a Subway shop had been opened by a local woman in the little plaza at the corner of Henry Johnson and Livingston, the place had become one of my regular sources of lunch, and sometimes dinner.

We walked down Orange and turned left and went up Henry Johnson. We didn't say much on the way, but having Ronnie striding along beside me changed the feeling of the day. We bought two subs, then crossed the street and bought a cold six-pack.

Back on Orange Street we sat on the front steps with our subs and beer and talked about her field work, which had to do with the concentrations of different botanical species in relation to the Ph of the water and other factors in different parts of an extensive wetland. I liked hearing about her work and I liked picturing her wading around in her wetland, and I had no desire to talk about my own very different activities in Albany.

But eventually she asked if there was any recent news about the body in Tivoli Park, and I had to tell her about the second body – and about the day's several uncomfortable conversations with Reilly.

"So he thought you weren't being straight with him? But why *wouldn't* you be?"

"He still thinks I'm holding out, and actually he's right – I haven't really been straight with him from the very beginning of this thing."

"You mean because of Jesse – not telling him that it was actually Jesse that found the body. But that didn't make any difference, and this one today you really did find."

"Yeah, but I sort of complicated the situation for myself by talking about this guy Bob Goodwin."

"The guy you told me about on the phone – but why does he complicate things? He's not a potential suspect is he?"

"No. I don't think so. But he is a puzzle, and I guess I just don't want to share my puzzle with Reilly. I'm afraid I have this tendency – as you've sometimes pointed out – to want to solve puzzles for myself, by myself."

"Well sure, and I don't really care if you don't fall all over yourself to share everything you know with some dumb cop. As long as you share everything with me."

"Reilly is not dumb, but I'd absolutely rather share with you."

"In just a little while," she said, placing a hand on my knee. "But tell me how Jesse's doing."

"I saw him just once during the week. I ran into him on Clinton Avenue, and we talked a little bit about the theory that the storekeeper, Ben Higgins, was killed by gang members who were pissed because he wouldn't let them hang out in his store."

"So he's at least talking about it. Did he say what he thought about that theory?"

"He said he didn't think it was the OGK gang that did it."

"Did he say why?"

"I had already said it didn't make sense for a South End gang to bring their victim up here to the north side. He agreed it didn't make sense. I couldn't tell if he might also have other reasons for thinking it wasn't them."

"You're still worried about him?"

"Yes. And I did tell him you'd be here for the weekend and I asked him if he'd be interested in another fishing trip. It sounded like he would be."

"But you haven't seen him today… Does he know about the second body?"

"I don't think so. Unless it was on the six-o'clock news – but I don't think Reilly was going to let that happen. Not today, if he could help it."

"Speak of the devil," Ronnie said.

Jesse was coming from his house next door, walking slowly, hands in pockets, studying the sidewalk, not looking at us but definitely heading toward us.

"Hey, Jesse," Ronnie called. "Are you ready for some fishing tomorrow?"

He looked up and grinned.

"Well, come sit down with us, and we'll make some plans."

He sat down on the other side of Ronnie. She punched him lightly on his shoulder. "Okay, what kind of fish do you want to catch?"

"Big ones," Jesse said.

"But big is relative. Twelve inches is a big brook trout, but a little pike, or a just-barely-legal bass."

"I've caught those big pike," he said, spreading his hands wide. "But I don't like 'em to eat. Too boney."

"Okay then – trout or bass?"

"I like bass," he said.

"Big mouth or small mouth?"

"Don't care how big their mouth is."

"Okay, I know a place. And it's a place Crow likes, so he's not going to complain, even if we don't let him fish."

Saturday morning, we got up early, loaded my canoe on my pickup, and gathered up Jesse and his fishing tackle. A few hours later, in the middle of the Adirondacks, we turned off Route 30 at the south end of Big Tupper Lake, followed a blacktop road for several miles, then turned down the gravel road leading to the lower dam on Bog River. Before reaching the dam, however, we arrived at what looked like a traffic jam.

The turn-around at the end of the road has parking space for no more than half a dozen cars, but at least two dozen vehicles were parked back along the side of the narrow road.

"Oh man," Jesse said. "*Everybody* here. Place got to be fished out."

"Don't worry," Ronnie said. "It's like this every weekend, but these cars belong to paddlers – they aren't here to fish."

"Why not? Come all the way up here... way to the end of this scrabbly little dirt road... and they not even going to fish?"

"Most of them will be paddling ten or twelve miles up the flow to campsites around Lows Lake – that is, the ones that aren't up there now, already camped. A few of them might do a little fishing, but not very seriously. Most of them wouldn't know how."

"What *else* they going to do? Just paddle around, paddle around, that's all?"

Ronnie laughed. "Pretty much. Just paddle around, relax, feel the breeze in their face, or lie around camp and listen to the breeze in the trees."

"Man!" Jesse said, shaking his head.

"But for guys like you who *do* know how to fish, there's plenty of bass. And all those paddlers will be way off up the flow – you won't even know they're around. You'll have the fishing to yourself. But of course the fish aren't guaranteed. We didn't tell the bass you were coming. They might have made other plans."

"Hope they go along with *my* plans." Jesse said.

"It's between you and them," Ronnie said.

By the time we stopped for lunch in a vacant campsite, Jesse had caught four bass, including two very nice keepers, and was feeling quite cheerful. After he had chewed his way through three sandwiches and a bag of potato chips, I thought it was as good a time as any to bring up the subject of the second body.

"So, Jesse," I said, "I guess I should tell you there's more weird stuff going on in Tivoli Park."

"Rather not hear that kind of stuff."

"But it's going to be in the news sooner or later. People will be talking about it. Another body turned up in the preserve. And this time it actually was me that found it, without any help from anyone else. I just thought I should tell you. Who- ever killed the first person must have killed this one too. So I'm pretty sure you were right about OGK not being involved – this one didn't look like it had anything to do with any kind of gang conflict. It was a woman this time. She'd been beaten up."

Jesse sat very still.

"When we talked last weekend," Ronnie said, "while Crow was taking a walk and we were cooking your fish over the fire… I got the feeling you were worried about your buddies somehow getting in trouble because of that first body that was found. Like maybe they had seen stuff they shouldn't have seen – or knew something they weren't supposed to know. I don't suppose they'd know anything about this other body though."

"Don't know what they know," Jesse said. "But they sure don't want me talking about it."

I decided to probe just a little further. "If there's someone who's making them do stuff…"

He gave me a quick look; then picked up his spinning rod from the ground beside him, stood up, walked to the shore and whipped his red and white lure forcefully out over the water. "Just don't want to talk about it," he said.

We left it at that. The rest of the afternoon we concentrated on making sure he filled his limit with five good bass.

It was after six o'clock when we got back to Orange Street. After we had filleted the fish on a cutting board over my kitchen sink, Jesse went home with half the fillets for himself and his mother. The others we put in my refrigerator for our own supper. Then we opened a pair of beers and retreated to the front steps.

"Pity we had to leave the north country and come back into this heat," Ronnie said. "It would be nice to be back in that campsite under the pines. You think there's any chance Jesse will ever agree to sleep in a tent?"

"Sleep in a tent and have to listen to those loony birds, as he calls them?"

"Yeah, I know. But it's hard for me to imagine *not* liking the sound of loons calling – the sound of a peaceful wild place. It's hard to imagine actually feeling safer in a place like this where kids are liable to be shot down on the street – and are afraid to talk about whatever it is their friends are up to."

"No question but what Jesse would be safer if he lived in a different kind of place."

"And you… Do you really feel safe living here? I mean I know you *like* living here, but do you feel *safe* here?"

"I do. And I actually am safe here. It's a much safer place for me than it is for Jesse. I live here but I'm not connected to the things that make it dangerous for him."

"You mean because you're white?"

"And I'm older, and I'm not involved in the dangerous stuff that goes on. People see me walking around the neighborhood, they know I live here, they know I mind my own business. I'm not a threat."

"Not a threat, but it might be worth someone's while to put a knife against your throat and take your wallet."

"I suppose. But I spend a lot of time on the streets in this neighborhood – and some other neighborhoods like it in other cities – and nothing like that has ever happened, so I don't even think about it as a possibility. What about you – do you think about it? Do you feel safe here?"

"I don't feel threatened. But I certainly don't feel the kind of safety that I do in my little cabin on Fisher Lake. I feel actively protected there – sheltered."

"I guess I do too. It's a special place."

"It makes me feel like I live in a happier world just to know it's there, even when I'm *not* there."

"Yes, me too."

"But of course I don't really want to be sheltered all the time."

"And I'm glad. People worry way too much about safety. Most people's goal seems to be to eliminate every last bit of risk from life. Which of course is impossible – but spending all your time trying to avoid risk is no way to live. I'm glad you're willing to risk a visit to my little house, where the only way to be comfortable in this heat is to sit out here next to the street, unsheltered."

"I've heard some people do have air conditioning..."

"People are obsessed with avoiding not only risk but any kind of physical discomfort."

"Well limiting energy consumption is a good thing, but I wouldn't say physical comfort is a *bad* thing."

"True. I'm just stubborn about the air conditioning issue."

"Well then, here's a different idea. Suppose we go inside and take off all these hot clothes."

"Could be risky," I said.

"Certainly hope so," she said.

11

In the morning, as the coffee was brewing I went upstairs to my desk and checked the Albany Times web site, where I found a brief news item, with a photo of a smiling young woman. She looked familiar in a way that the dead body had not.

ANOTHER BODY FOUND IN TIVOLI PRESERVE

ALBANY -- Police are investigating the second apparent homicide victim found in Tivoli Park. Friday morning the body of 23-year-old Beth Ellsworth was found in the park west of the Green Tech Charter School on Northern Boulevard by an early morning jogger.

Police spokesman Arnold Williamson said Ellsworth was a resident of the West Hill neighborhood, living within a few blocks of the park. She was reported missing by her mother because she did not return home Thursday night.

Williamson said the cause of death had not been determined but the body showed signs of physical abuse. He said detectives are canvassing the neighborhood in search of leads, including who Ellsworth might have been seen with that day and evening. Anyone with information is asked to call detectives at the number below.

I went back to the photo and studied it and gradually pulled into focus what it was in her face that seemed so familiar. Then I called the number that appeared in the article and spoke with a Detective Burns.

I told him I was the one who had found the body. "I didn't know who she was then," I told him, "and I still don't know, but now that I've seen the photo in the Albany Times I do recognize her as someone I've seen jogging in the preserve."

"When? How recently?"

"Not recently. Earlier this summer."

"Just one time?"

"More than once. I think at least twice. I think each time I saw her she was smiling, and it was a good smile. It's what I recognized in the photo."

"Was she with anyone?"

"I don't think so. I don't remember anyone being with her."

"She was jogging?"

"Yes. Or running – actually running at a pretty good speed. And enjoying it I think."

"What time of day?"

"I don't remember, but morning is when I'm usually there, usually between six-thirty and seven-thirty, but occasionally at other times. Sometimes in the afternoon."

"But you don't remember which time of day you saw her."

"No."

"Did you say anything to each other?"

"No."

"Do you remember anything else about her?"

"I'm afraid not."

"Okay, if you do remember anything else, please call us. And give me your phone number, if you would."

I gave him my number. Then I went down and rejoined Ronnie at the kitchen table. As she poured coffee, I told her about the Albany Times article. I had hardly finished when Reilly called.

"Following up on what you told Burns," he said.

"All right."

"You didn't recognize her body but you recognized her photo?"

"That's right."

"When you were looking at the body you didn't even wonder if it was that woman you'd seen jogging in the park?"

"No, I didn't recognize the body. I'd seen her alive just briefly, in passing, and the body looked very different. And I guess I was focused on what had been done to her."

"Where in the park did you see her?"

"She was coming along the road that parallels the railroad."

"In which direction?"

"Coming from the west, running."

"Each time you saw her?"

"Yes, as far as I can remember."

"And how many times was that?"

"At least twice that I can remember."

"The trail where the body was – which side of where it joins that road did you see her?"

"She was west of where the trail comes in."

"Every time?"

"Yes."

"So after you saw her she might have turned up the trail toward where we found her?"

"That's right," I said. "Did you find anything indicating she was actually killed right there?"

"Look, I'm the one asking questions," he said. "You're the one who found her body and then it turns out you remember seeing her in the park before. You're the one needs to ask yourself is there anything else you didn't remember."

"I don't know what else there could possibly be. I'll certainly call you if I think of something."

"Damn well better." He hung up.

Ronnie had been staring at me. "That's awful," she said now. "I mean of *course* it is, but the feeling didn't really hit me until I heard you talking about seeing her alive. A live person instead of a corpse."

"Very much alive as I remember her."

"Did he tell you... the cop, did he tell you if it happened in the park?"

"No, he wouldn't tell me, but it seems likely it did this time. With the first one it was really unlikely that a middle aged South End storekeeper would have a reason to be in the preserve, but this one, I know she did spend time there..."

"But both of them were treated the same way. I mean they both had..."

"Yeah, the business with the ears. It has to be the same person who did it to both of them."

"Or maybe..." she said, "it could be some kind of gruesome gang thing. It could be different members of a gang doing this to, you know, to prove themselves. Like taking scalps or something."

"I suppose. But I don't think there's any history of that kind of thing."

"It doesn't really seem like something *anyone* would do."

"Unless they're totally insane. Or they're some completely cold-blooded person trying to send some kind of message, but no one seems to have any idea what the message could be."

"Whoever it is," she said, "or whatever it's about, it's connected to something that's got Jesse really uptight."

"Yes."

"Has he stopped going down into the park? He must have."

"I don't know. I haven't asked him, and he hasn't said. But I'm guessing he's avoiding the place."

"And what about you? Are you going to avoid it now?"

"It wouldn't feel right to be scared into staying away."

"I suppose not."

"I'm sure *you* wouldn't be scared into staying away," I said.

"Not if I lived here, I guess, but I don't live here. And when I go back to Ithaca, I wish I could just think of Tivoli Park as that lovely place where you and Jesse can get out of the neighborhood and enjoy a little part of the natural world."

"That's my wish too, but I'm stuck with whatever the hell is going on here."

"And I guess, back in Ithaca, I'll just have to think about something else – like a Labor Day outing to Little Wilder Pond."

"For sure," I said. "In only a few weeks."

12

The first letter to the editor appeared in the Albany Times Monday morning. I read it as I finished my coffee before heading off to the meeting I'd scheduled with Helen Hamilton.

To the Editor: Now there's been a second murder in Tivoli Park, and it sounds like the police have no clues – no way of finding this vicious murderer and locking him up to protect the community, and it's not surprising. Anyone can do anything they want in a place like that without any fear of consequences. It's a piece of wilderness where the only law is the law of the jungle. But it's not out in some wild place, it's right here inside the city, and it's time the city did something about it. If the city is going to own it and call it a park, then they better do something to bring some law and order into it. It's part of the city. They can't go on acting like it's not their responsibility. It's in the city and it's the city's property. They can't pretend it isn't.

-- Luther Adams, Latham

Crossing Clinton Avenue on my way to the NHA office on Second Street, I tried to imagine what Reilly's reaction to the letter would be. Whatever it was, he wasn't likely to spend much time worrying about it. Even if the powers-that-be decided the police should begin patrolling the preserve frequently enough to "bring some law and order into it," his responsibilities as a detective wouldn't change. He would not be one of those charged with patrolling that "piece of wilderness" – though he would certainly welcome any useful information such a patrol might bring back to him. And he would be happy not to have to rely on an odd-ball civilian like me to tell him what goes on in the place.

As I rounded the corner from Judson onto Second Street I was confronted with the sight of two police cruisers, blue lights flashing, halfway down the block, and for a moment I had a chilling memory of a similar sight in more or less the same location when Jonah Lee had been murdered in the NHA office. But quickly the memory was eclipsed by the immediate scene, which was not immediately in front of the office but across the street. Two uniformed officers stood on the sidewalk trying to talk to two women, who were ignoring them completely while shouting loudly at each other. One of them was angrily stabbing an index finger at the face of the other, who was just as angrily waving an arm toward the second story of the house in front of them.

They were still carrying on as I went down the steps to NHA's basement office, where I found Helen in front of her computer, coffee cup in one hand, mouse in the other. Without looking up, she said, "Good morning, Warren. Welcome to our peaceful neighborhood."

"What's going on out there?"

"Someone called the cops on someone else's kids."

"What were the kids up to?"

She shook her head. Either she didn't know or it was none of my business. As it was, I had no idea whether the kids were five-year-olds making too much noise or twenty-five-year-olds selling drugs – or for that matter thirteen-year-olds making too much noise *and* selling drugs.

"Coffee's brewed," Helen said.

I got myself a cup and sat down at the end of her desk. "Looks like you're checking the MLS again," I said. "Anything new on the market?"

"Not the kind of thing we're looking for. Not *where* we're looking for it. But I've been talking to people." She let go of the mouse and rotated her chair toward me. "Including someone on Livingston who just sold her house – for sale by owner, no realtor. And then another person who did sell through a realtor."

"The one that was sold by the owner, did someone knock on her door?"

"No, but someone called her – a lawyer in Troy. He asked what her asking price was. She told him, and he said that sounded about right, and then he said he'd just do up the paperwork and cut a check and they could get together and finish the deal. And in three days it was done."

"Did you get the name of the attorney?"

"She said his name was Thompson."

"Did she say anything about him?"

"She said he was very nice and kept his word – brought her papers to sign and a check for the full price. And even though he knew she hadn't paid her taxes this year, he didn't subtract anything for that. She was one happy lady, I'll tell you."

"Had she already moved out of the house when the guy called her? Or could she get out on such short notice?"

"That's another part of what made her so happy. She was living in the house and still is. She'd been planning on moving in with her daughter. She told the lawyer she would need more time to get her stuff out, and he just said 'take your time.' He said for the first month he wouldn't charge her anything, and after that he would just charge her a little rent to make it official and she could stay as long as she wanted."

"How much rent – do you know?"

"Way less than we have to charge for a single-family place. Just three hundred a month. So obviously it isn't a slumlord buying up property. It's got to be a speculator, who's happy to keep the place occupied until he's ready to cash it in, which probably won't be any time soon."

"Looks that way. What about the other person you talked to, who sold through a realtor – any idea if the same Thompson handled that sale?"

It sounded like a different kind of deal. There *was* some negotiation on that one, though not a lot. The buyer did offer less than the asking price, but pretty quickly agreed to split the difference. The realtor and a lawyer for a title company handled the closing."

"And is this seller still in the house?"

"No. The family was out before the closing. And right after the closing the house was boarded up."

"With both these houses, do you know what name went on the new deed?"

"The first one I was telling about, the name was actually the lawyer's name, Thompson. With the other one it was some business name the seller couldn't remember."

"With the first one, was the rent going to be paid to the lawyer, do you know?"

"It sounded that way."

"And whoever bought the other one maybe doesn't have anyone local working for them. Except to board up the place. They probably don't want to have to do *anything* with the property until they eventually cash out."

"I wish buying property could be that simple for us," she said. "I'm still trying to explain to our lenders why we want to sell a house on a community land trust ground lease – trying to explain that to a couple of potential homebuyers too. In fact I'm still trying to understand some things about it myself. I've got a list of questions for you."

We spent a half hour going over her list, and as usual I was impressed by how clearly she framed the questions and how quickly she understood my responses.

Back home at my own desk I went online and looked for a Troy attorney named Thompson. I found there was in fact an Alan Thompson, Esq., and called the number listed for his office. The phone was answered by Thompson himself. I told him I had a house on the north side of Albany that I wanted to sell, and asked if I could drop in and talk with him.

"What's the address?"

I had thought about working up a fictional Livingston Avenue address, but decided to play it safe. I gave him my own Orange Street address.

"Sorry, but I'm not interested in Orange Street."

"I suspected you might not be," I said, "but I thought I'd check. Anyway I *am* interested in talking."

"And the nature of your interest?"

"I'm doing some ownership research in that area."

He laughed.

"It's funny?"

He cleared his throat. "Sorry, no. But I don't see how I can help you with that."

"I'd just like to compare notes."

"I'm not sure what that means," he said.

"I'm not either, but I'd like to try to find out."

"Well you're welcome to stop by if you want to."

"Got a few free minutes sometime today?"

"Tied up 'til five."

"I'll be there at five."

"Make it five-thirty."

I got to his second floor office on River Street a little after five. The door was open. He was on the phone but waved me in and quickly wound up his call, then stood up, smiling, to shake hands. He was as large as Goodwin's friend Elwin Thompson and looked somewhat like him.

"Is Elwin Thompson by any chance your father?" I asked.

"My uncle. Folks do seem to think we look alike, but no he's not my dad. Have a seat."

When we were both seated, he said, "So tell me why you're coming to Troy to research property ownership in Albany."

I told him about the purchase that Helen had described.

"Okay," he said, "one of my Santa Clause deals."

"You're representing Santa in the Albany real estate market?"

He laughed. "Might as well be with that kind of deal. Got to say it's a lot of fun to give people just what they need and want that way. Wish all my work was like that."

"I wish all my work was like that too. How does a person *get* that kind of work? Where do you apply?"

"Wouldn't you like to know," he said.

"Yes I would."

"And of course I can't tell you."

"So Santa insists on confidentiality?"

"I don't blab about any of my clients – whether they're Santa or Satan."

"I think I have an idea who this client is," I said.

He shook his head. "You're not going to tease it out of me."

"Even if I name the guy?"

He moved thumb and finger across his mouth as though zipping it shut. "If you think you know who Santa is," he said, "then go talk to him."

"I guess I'll have to," I said.

From Thompson's office I drove on up Second Avenue to 112trh Street, crossed the river to Van Schaick Island, then made my way to Peebles Island State Park. The island lies in the mouth of the Mohawk River, whose waters divide around it to complete their final rushing descent to the Hudson. Like Tivoli Preserve, Peebles Island is undeveloped, but a lot more people go there than go to Tivoli. It is a good place to walk and a good place to let the sound of moving water rinse irrelevant stuff from your thoughts. I walked around the perimeter of the island, then sat where I could watch the water pitch over the ledge on the east side of the island. I spent an hour there, and felt better when I left.

13

Another article on the Tivoli murders appeared in the Albany Times the next morning. It was very brief.

NO EVIDENCE MURDER VICTIMS KILLED IN TIVOLI PRESERVE
Albany – According to police spokesperson Arnold Williamson, it has been determined that the first body found in Tivoli Preserve was killed elsewhere and brought into the Preserve at a later time. Williamson also said it has not been determined whether the second victim, found in the Preserve on Friday was killed in the Preserve. According to Williamson it is believed that the second victim, identified as Beth Ellsworth of the West Hill neighborhood, was not killed at the point where she was found, although detectives have not ruled out the possibility that she was killed at another point in the Preserve.

There was also a letter to the editor responding to the letter that had been published the day before.

Letter to the Editor: Regarding the recent letter from Luther Adams, of course it's a wilderness. That's what a preserve is supposed to be – and it is a preserve, not a park. It is a little bit of wild nature that is preserved, so modern city people have at least some chance to see what the natural world is like. Let's not change that. Let's not give it up just because some urban violence has happened to spill into it. The preserve itself doesn't breed violence. What breeds violence is poverty in the surrounding neighborhoods. Or to put it more generally, what breeds violence is the inequality and injustice of a society that is ruled by the wealthy 1% and their powerful corporations.

-- Marion Peters, Albany

I answered some email, went downstairs, fried some eggs, then called Goodwin. I asked him if he had seen the latest letter to the editor. He said he had not. "I'm slow getting to things some mornings," he said. "I'll check it now."

"I think you'll like this one. It's a pretty good response to yesterday's letter – if you happened to see that one."

"I did. In fact I was thinking about responding to it myself."

"I haven't been over to Tivoli yet this morning," I said, "but I'm getting ready to head that way now. If I were to drop in on you in a few minutes could I beg a cup of coffee from you?"

"Certainly. Except I'm a tea-drinker. I don't think I've got any coffee at all."

"Tea would be fine, and I don't really need anything. I just wanted to chat for a few minutes about the various strange things that are going on."

He did serve tea. We sat at his dining table. His TV had been muted but I had an excellent view of a group of life-size people on its huge screen. They were sitting around a table, apparently engaged in a heated argument.

"I apologize for the tea," Goodwin said. "I'm afraid it makes me seem like some effete English gentleman."

"Not at all," I said. "I don't drink tea often, but when I do it's usually during a wilderness canoe trip, where it just seems like the right beverage. It's a traditional outdoors drink – and not only for English gentlemen."

"I wouldn't know about that, but I'm glad it's acceptable."

"Anything would be acceptable. I just do appreciate your letting me drop in this way, and I hope you won't mind me sharing my confusion over all these questions that seem to be piling up around this whole Tivoli situation."

"It *is* a very disturbing situation," he said noncommittally.

"I'm hoping maybe you can help me figure out how to think about it all."

"I doubt if I can help, but I'm happy to listen."

"I'm not sure how much you know about what's going on in this neighborhood, but I think maybe you know a good deal more than I do, and I'm hoping you can explain some things."

"I don't know what things you're referring to."

"There seem to be investors who are buying up property in the area. Two separate investors, seemingly competing with each other."

"I'm afraid I pay very little attention to that sort of thing," he said. "I don't even know the names of any of my neighbors, much less what's being bought and sold around here."

"But I do think you care about what happens to the neighborhood, and I do think you know who's buying property."

"Why would you think something like that?" he said carefully.

"Because one of the people buying property is the nephew of your friend Elwin Thompson."

"My goodness. Really?" He peered into his tea cup.

"Actually, he's buying with someone else's money – on terms that are quite favorable to the seller."

"And how do you know this?"

"I talked with him. He's enjoying it. It's what he calls his Santa Clause work."

He shook his head, frowning. "I do know Alan Thompson. He's a very professional young attorney. He's not a real estate speculator."

"Yes, he's acting in a professional capacity, purchasing property for another."

"Surely he didn't tell you that. He would respect a client's confidentiality."

"I learned about one of those purchases through a friend of the very happy seller. And the fact that Thompson's name is on the deed is a matter of public record." When I talked with him he did not deny the transaction. And he acknowledged it in a way that suggested it was not the only such transaction he was involved in. But he did quite properly refuse to tell me where the money came from – even when I told him I thought I knew whose money it was."

"Warren, I really don't understand what you're doing."

"When I told Alan Thompson that I thought I knew whose money it was, he said, 'If you think you know, then go talk to him.' So that's what I'm doing."

"You think it's me."

"I do"

"But it's not."

"I didn't expect you to admit it. I know you're a hard guy to pin down. As your friend Elwin suggested, some of what you say is fiction. He also suggested that you're rich."

"And you think Elwin is a trustworthy source?"

"I don't know what to make of either one of you."

"I don't know what to make of you, either," he said. "Why are you here? I mean why do you care who's buying property in this neighborhood?"

"I'm trying to understand all the things that are going on here. And what I really want to know is why you... or let's just say why *someone*... is doing it. Because it pretty clearly is not being done for any of the reasons that people usually buy property. It's not being done by someone looking to turn a profit. It's not being done for the reasons that someone *else* is buying property in the area."

He was staring again into his tea cup. "What's your theory then?"

"My theory is that someone like you is buying up property to prevent the thing that someone like you is afraid will happen. That is, to prevent the loss of the preserve to development, and this whole edge of the neighborhood along with it. And I really want to know who that someone is because I think whoever it is must know something about that *other* party they're competing with."

"I guess at least I persuaded you the other day that the preserve is threatened that way."

"You got me thinking about it. But it's the purchases of property in the neighborhood that have persuaded me there really is a threat – not only to the preserve but to the neighborhood around it."

He looked up from his tea cup and smiled at me but said nothing.

"I'd really like to help prevent that from happening, but I need information. I'd really like to know what you know about the other buyer. *Why* are they buying?"

"I can't tell you that, but if I was going to guess why they're buying, I'd say, yes, they're planning some kind of large scale development for the area."

"That's what most people would guess under the circumstances. I was hoping you could tell me something more specific."

"Sorry," he said.

"Anyway," I said, "I hope you're able to fund a lot of purchases by Alan Thompson. If the word gets around about how well the buyers are treated, you should have a lot of opportunities."

He stood up with his cup and saucer and turned away from me.

I said goodbye and went on down into the preserve and jogged until I'd worked up a sweat, which didn't take long – the day was heating up. I then walked up the trail to Park View Apartments and went on home and spent the rest of the day and evening working on a grant proposal that I had promised to write and that, as usual, I'd put off for too long.

14

I finally finished the proposal late the next afternoon. After I emailed it to my client I called Lisa and asked her if she still had the gin in her freezer. She said she did. She also said she was busy with work that had to be done by the next day.

"I've been pinned down that way too," I said. "And I don't have any juicy rumors. But I did learn some interesting things from Helen Hamilton about a couple of those home sales in the Livingston area. And I learned a little more from the Troy attorney who closed one of those deals in his own name. And then I talked with the guy I think funded that deal."

"Okay," she said. "Interesting. I guess I could spare a few minutes to have a drink with you tonight. Come on over if you want – maybe eight or so."

On my way down to Lisa's at eight o'clock I spotted Jesse standing alone on the corner of Clinton and Swan, hands in his pockets, not going anywhere. I hoped he would stay there and at least give me a chance to say hello, but when he saw me coming he moved off briskly down Swan into Sheridan Hollow. It was beginning to feel like no one wanted to talk with me. I was glad that I could at least go and complain about the situation to Lisa.

"People won't talk to you because you're too nosey," she said, handing me a glass. "You're always nosing into everyone else's business."

"Unlike you – who have no interest at all in what those people are up to."

"Only a professional interest."

"Because it's all about real estate, right?"

"Right. But tell me – what's this about you talking to that Troy attorney? I hear he's pretty cool."

"Alan Thompson. I went up to Troy and talked with him, and yes, he is pretty cool. Helen Hamilton had told me about someone who'd sold her house to him. Paid her asking price *and* covered some unpaid taxes. No negotiation. Closed in three days in Thompson's name. *And* she gets to stay in the house – apparently for as long as she wants – with minimal rent. So I went to his office and asked him about it."

"And he wouldn't talk to you."

"Actually we had quite a jolly conversation. He referred to it as his Santa Clause work and said he wished all his work was like that – just giving people everything they wanted. But he wouldn't tell me who he was working *for*."

"Surprise surprise."

"I told him I thought I knew who it was, and he said well then I should go talk to that person."

"And?"

"And so I did. The guy who buys expensive gin."

"Oh. And he wouldn't tell you anything either."

"Anyway he wouldn't admit he was the one funding the purchase – those purchases, however many there are."

"If the word gets out that Santa's buying, there could be quite a few of them. Is he that rich?"

"I don't know. He of course wouldn't admit anything at all. He explicitly denied that he was behind it, but he seemed to have a pretty good idea of what's going on. He didn't seem surprised when I said there was also someone else buying property and that I thought he was buying to block that other effort. In the end it seemed like he was not so much denying that he was doing it as just saying he didn't want to talk about it."

"At least not with nosey Warren Crow."

"I don't know if there's anyone he does talk to about this stuff. In some ways he just seems like a very secretive person."

"You said Helen Hamilton told you about a *couple* of sales. Am I right that one of them was the other buyer. That corporation, Livingston Properties?"

"Yes, Helen talked with that woman too. She's really on this thing. She does not like the idea of a speculator buying up her neighborhood."

"And she talks to you."

"About certain things – this kind of thing. And the other sale looks like a much more cold-blooded kind of speculation – not at all a Santa deal. The buyer paid less than the asking price – made a low offer, then split the difference. Closed in the name of the corporation. Had the house boarded up immediately. And is out of there, leaving one more empty boarded-up house in the neighborhood."

"And you think maybe your fancy gin guy... What's his name?"

"Bob Goodwin."

"You think he maybe knows something about what's going on there?"

"Knows, or suspects, or is guessing – I don't know. But he pretty clearly sees it as a threat to Tivoli Preserve. He does at least have motivation for an effort to block it."

"And you do at least have an interesting story here. Something is certainly going on in the neighborhood. But does it necessarily have anything to do with Tivoli Park?"

"What else is there about that neighborhood to invite speculation? It's not as though the buildings give it the kind of historic significance that your neighborhood here has. It's just another northside working class neighborhood. But it's the *only* northside neighborhood where someone's buying."

"Okay," she said, "it has to do with Tivoli Park. And I too would like to know what it is about that big piece of overgrown wasteland that someone thinks is valuable. Would you like another drink?"

"Only if you do."

"Okay, I'll join you. And let's just brainstorm all the things we can think of that could possibly be developed there."

While I refilled our glasses, she went into her bedroom and came back with a laptop. She now sat on the sofa with it, looking eager. When Lisa is looking eager she is one of the most attractive women I know, second only to eager Ronnie.

"Let's make a list," she said. "You start."

"Okay. Amusement park."

"Come *on*. But all right, it's a brainstorm. How about high-end housing."

"How about low-end housing."

"Get serious. Shopping mall."

"Horse farm, riding stable."

She stuck out her tongue at me. "Okay, zoo"

"Fish farm."

"Sports stadium," she said. "For our big-league teams."

"College campus."

"Railroad yard. The place *is* next to a railroad."

"Trucking depot," I said. "It's next to an interstate too."

"Conference center."

"Product distribution center."

"Bio-fuel power generation plant."

"State office facilities."

"Computer chip factory."

"Potato chip factory."

"High tech research center."

We went on this way for several minutes, until finally Lisa said, "I don't think this is getting us anywhere."

"I guess we just lack imagination, like Goodwin says."

"But all we're *doing* is imagining. We could go on all night this way imagining different kinds of things. But even if we do imagine the *right* thing, we'd have no way of knowing *which* was the right thing."

"That's the trouble with brainstorms," I said. "Nothing gets sorted out."

"So it's back to plain old work – one-step-at-a-time work."

"There's always Google."

"Well what are you going to Google," she said. "Tivoli fish farm?"

"I guess I need to start with Livingston Properties. Check the Department of State, try to get some names, and just stay with it – follow up on everything I find and see if it leads anywhere."

"I'll email you the little bit I've got. That telephone number. And I'll try to find out more about which realtors actually dealt with that buyer. And I really will find an excuse to talk with my friend at Development and Planning."

There was some of the old excitement of working together on a puzzle. Part of me didn't want to go home. We got to our feet at the same time, and I gave her a quick hug.

"Better go Google," she said.

I went home and did in fact spend several hours on line. When I went to bed I didn't feel that I had made any real progress, but did have a handful of things to follow up on later.

15

In the morning I decided not to go jogging in the preserve, but instead took my first cup of coffee up to my desk. After waking up my computer, I went to the "Opinion" section of the Albany Times website and read the letters to the editor. Even if no one in city government was actually thinking about selling Tivoli Preserve, it seemed that other people were. One of the letters was the following.

Letter to the Editor. Apparently the police don't think the murder victims found in Tivoli Park were actually killed there, or at least they don't want us to think so, because they don't want to be forced to patrol the place all hours of the day and night. There's no way to tell if they're right. Everyone is talking about it but no one really knows what's going on. But even if it is true that bodies are not being killed there but are just being dumped there the way all sorts of trash used to be dumped there, it's still a terrible thing to have going on in the city. So maybe it is time the city should think about selling the place. The city has owned it for a long time. But think about it – it is not being maintained as a park. And, with all due respect to the Haywood Burns Environmental Education Center, it is hardly being used at all for educational purposes. And it's not bringing in property taxes to help pay for parks and schools elsewhere in the city. Why not sell it to a private developer who would pay taxes and create jobs?

-- Charles M. Schakowsky, Albany

However, Charles Schakowsky didn't seem to have any more idea of what kind of private developer would want to buy it than Lisa and I did.

I had just left the Albany Times website and was getting ready to resume my Googling when Reilly called. He wanted to know if I had ever seen "a really big guy in Tivoli Park."

"Not that I can think of," I said. "How big are you talking about?"

"Well he wears about a size fifteen shoe, which means he's gotta be really big, or else he's just a big-footed freak."

"I don't remember seeing any sort of big-foot in the preserve. But I'll keep my eyes open. I assume you found a big footprint over there somewhere."

"At a place on the dirt road where it looks like there was some kind of scuffle. And there were prints from the running shoes she was wearing, and these really big prints."

"Was there blood?"

"Not that we've found."

"So she wasn't killed there."

"All we can say is she wasn't cut there. She might've been beaten and strangled there, and died there. Or not. She might've been raped there. Or somewhere else."

"So she was raped?"

"You don't need to know."

"Anyway, it sure looks like a different kind of motive," I said. "Different from the first one."

"Yeah. If she still had her ears on her I'd say it was a different guy did it. And even with the ear thing, can't be sure it was the same guy."

"You mean it could be a different guy trying to make it look like the first guy?"

"I wish you hadn't told that Goodwin character about the ears."

"You mean you wish someone hadn't told the press about the ears," I said. "I'm still sure it wasn't Goodwin who told them."

"Whatever."

"By the way, did you see the latest Tivoli letter to the editor? Today's letter?"

"I got better things to do. But I guess it would be someone else complaining we can't maintain law and order in the jungle?"

"This one actually says, well, since you *can't* maintain law and order there, the city should sell the place."

"Yeah, right."

"You remember Goodwin claiming he heard a rumor about the city selling the preserve?"

"I remember you saying he did. But when I asked him myself, he said, oh, he was just joking. You should have known that, he said – because who'd ever want to buy the place? I told him yeah, Crow's kind of naïve that way."

"You mean like two years ago – when I thought there were people trying to buy property in Sheridan Hollow, of all places, and I thought that was why Jonah Lee got himself killed."

"Okay, even naïve guys get lucky sometimes."

"It wasn't luck. I spent a lot of time researching property transactions in Sheridan Hollow."

"Okay, but this is different. Back then you were looking at actual sales of particular properties, and there was a real connection with what Jonah Lee was doing. But this thing now is just one big stupid rumor."

"But what I'm doing now is looking at actual sales of properties surrounding Tivoli Park. Sales not to people buying homes for themselves, but to speculators, who seem to be ready to invest quite a lot of money in the area."

There was a period of silence, followed by a sigh. "All right, I need to know everything you've got. And then I need you to let me decide what's relevant and what isn't – and not go off on your own on this."

I told him I was in the process of looking up some details and when I had them put together I would email him all the information I had.

"I'm not holding my breath," he said. "But make sure you do it – all of it. I'm investigating two murders here and I don't have time to fool with you."

I emailed Lisa to tell her about the conversation with Reilly. I figured Reilly would want to know the source of any information I passed on to him. Much of that information had come from Helen Hamilton, who had gathered it through her own persistent leg work in the neighborhood, but part of it had come from Lisa, who had access to certain things as an insider. I was hoping for more of that insider information – particularly the information she'd said she would send about other recent sales in the area bordering the preserve, which would require much time and effort to gather by other means. I told her she should let me know what I should not attribute to her, and I would find a way not to.

I sent the email and then went downstairs and scrambled some eggs.

Lisa replied at noon:

Meant to get this to you last night. I did go to the records office yesterday and sweet talked my little friend Billy Seymour into helping me find the recently filed deeds for those properties, plus one he'd received but hadn't filed yet. But there's nothing illegal about that. It's public information. Or just tell your cop friend you know this hot babe who can get information out of anyone.

She then listed the addresses of nine properties that had sold either to Livingston Properties, Inc., or to Alan Thompson. Four of the first five had gone to Livingston Properties. Three of the more recent four had gone to Thompson, so he had four altogether. "Local team's catching up," she noted.

She also sent the Manhattan phone number that agents had been calling when they had new listings in the area. I called the number and reached an answering machine. I hung up, turned back to the computer and went to the website of the NYS Department of State's Division of Corporations, where I searched for Livingston Properties, Inc.

As I'd expected, I didn't learn a great deal. The date of incorporation was May 29, only a little more than two months earlier. A Seventh Avenue address was listed, but it might not be – in fact might never have been – the address of the corporation's actual base of operations. The site did not list a "registered agent." I could submit a written request for a copy of the certificate of incorporation, which would indicate the initial board members, but I couldn't access it directly on line. It could take weeks to get a copy, and even then it might not tell me who the current board members were and, even if it did, I wouldn't know for sure who they really answered to.

I sat and thought about how much I didn't know. Then I printed Lisa's email, and set out on foot to look at each of the properties she'd listed. In particular I wanted to be able to estimate what the four Alan Thompson properties would have sold for.

Three of them were on Livingston Avenue – wood frame houses in need of paint and various other types of deferred maintenance. The fourth was on Beverly Avenue and was a better looking house. None of the houses was boarded up. Two of them appeared to be occupied. I took my time. I walked completely around each house, looked at the condition of foundations and sills, siding, windows and doors. I peered into windows where I could. As much as it was possible to see from the ground I noted roof conditions.

I figured the Livingston Avenue homes would appraise in the $90,000 range, the one on Beverly for more. It seemed reasonable to guess that the generous Santa Clause had paid something like $400,000 for the four of them. And reasonable to guess that a greedy Santa might be willing to sell the four for $600,000.

When I got home, I called Robert Goodwin and told him I was still trying to figure out who the other buyer was and what he was up to.

"Surely you don't think I can give you more information," he said.

"Maybe you could, but I don't think you will. You certainly haven't told me much so far. But I'm calling to tell you what I'm thinking about doing – and to ask if you know of any reason why I shouldn't do it."

"All right, I'll listen – if it relates to the future of the preserve."

"I'm convinced that it does. I want to contact whoever it is that's representing Livingston Properties, Inc. I want to pretend to be representing the owner of those Santa Clause properties that Alan Thompson now owns, and I want to suggest that those properties could be purchased if the price is right."

"But they absolutely cannot be."

"I know that but I doubt that the guy representing Livingston Properties does."

"No, don't do it," he said. "You don't know what you're getting into."

"That's why I want to get into it – to find out what it is. Of course you could save me some trouble if you'd just tell me whatever you know about it."

There was silence – until eventually he said, "You won't get very far. It won't take them long to figure out you don't really have anything to sell. You'll just annoy someone who is best not annoyed."

"And you know who that someone is?"

"No, I just know there's got to be that kind of someone."

"All right. But there's one thing you could do – you could call Alan Thompson and just let him know what I'm up to. If someone calls him to ask if he really is prepared to sell… you could ask him to just string that person along for a bit."

"I have no influence there. He owns the properties."

"Okay, and I have no influence with you. Just a suggestion. Anyway, just so he knows – if you do talk with him – the price I'm thinking of asking for the properties, as a package deal, is $600,000."

"That's ridiculous," he said.

"Why do you say that? I'm assuming that if he were going to sell them at all he would want a substantial profit."

"It's just a completely unreasonable price."

"So you do know what properties – and how many of them – we're talking about."

He was ready with an answer, but he offered it a little too quickly and didn't quite hide the fact that he was flustered. "Well from talking with his uncle Elwin, I got a general idea."

"Oh, okay, you got it from Elwin. I guess those Thompsons do confide in each other."

He was silent.

"Well, I'll be in touch."

"I hope you'll be careful," he said before hanging up.

I then called the Manhattan number again and this time left a message. I gave my name and said I was representing the owner of some Albany properties that would interest the party I was calling. I also said I was going to be in the city the next day and might be able to find time to meet with the party to discuss what I had to offer. I didn't know what someone would make of the idea of someone from Albany travelling to the city to peddle real estate, but I hoped whoever it was might agree to meet in an effort to figure out what I was up to.

For the rest of the day I answered the phone as "Orange Investments." By five o'clock I was losing hope of getting a response, and was thinking I probably needed a more patient strategy – though what I really wanted to do was to just go to the city and talk to someone face to face.

But at five-thirty I did get a call.

"Mister Crow?" It was a woman's voice.

"Yes."

"Mister Lucas would like to know what properties you were referring to in your message."

I gave her the four addresses. Then I waited for several long minutes, until finally a man's voice said, "All of those properties were sold recently. Are you saying they're back on the market?"

"They could be back on the market."

"At what prices?"

"It would be a package deal."

"The four properties? For how much?"

"At least the four properties, possibly more. For a price that will depend on what kind of arrangement we agree on."

"You're not a realtor then?"

"No, I am representing the owner, but I'm not a realtor. And you…? Your role is… Realtor? Attorney?"

"Let's just say I'm like you – I'm representing the interests of Livingston Properties, Inc. Period."

"Okay, that's all I need to know, besides your name and where and when I can find you tomorrow."

He said his name was Eliot Lucas. He gave me a Seventh Avenue address that was the same as what the Department of State had listed for the corporation. "Office is upstairs," he said. "But meet me downstairs, street level, in Herm's Coffee Shop. Let's say eleven o'clock. Place'll be mostly empty. I'll be the bald guy at the back table."

"I'll be there," I said.

After hanging up, I Googled the guy. I found Eliot Lucas mentioned in two news stories as an attorney associated with someone who was being tried for fraud. Then I found a report of his disbarment in New York State. But that was all I found.

Before going to bed I emailed Lisa's list of properties to Reilly. I noted that there were two different buyers and that both of them were buying properties as soon as they went on the market. I did not mention that I had talked with one of the buyers and was about to go to the city to talk with a representative of the other one. If he took an interest in what was going on with these properties he could do his own research.

16

I was up early, relishing the opportunity to ride the 6:10 train from Rensselaer down the Hudson to the city. It is one of only two train trips I ever take. The other one is the trip from Sept Iles, Quebec, northward along the Moisie River and its tributaries into Labrador. I love both trips for the opportunity to sit in comfort and watch a river unwinding beyond the window – while travelling into worlds that are as different from each other as they are exciting. Unlike the numbing process of air travel or the wearisome routine of long-distance highway travel, rail travel is still fun. And being able to step off a train at Penn Station in the very heart of a great city is still a wonderful experience.

Before nine o'clock I was wandering down Seventh Avenue looking for an interesting place to have breakfast. I peered through the windows of several places and settled on a deli where I could see a couple eating bagels and cream cheese that looked good. It turned out that the bagels were not as good as I'd hoped, but that was all right. I got to spend an hour lounging with coffee at a front table watching Manhattan pedestrians hurrying by. At ten I walked on down Seventh Avenue and peered into Herm's Coffee Shop. There were four people scattered among maybe eight tables. None were bald. I continued south a few blocks, then made my way west through Chelsea to look at the river.

I got back to the coffee shop about ten minutes before eleven. There was still no bald man, so I walked around the block. When I returned and peered in the window again, I could see that there was indeed a short, stout, bald man at a back table.

I went in and introduced myself. He leaned back in his chair and stared at me in silence, as though I was an unexpected stranger intruding on his coffee break.

"I'm assuming you are Eliot Lucas," I said.

He motioned to the chair across the table from him, and I sat down.

"So tell me what's your game," he said, his voice surprisingly gentle, as though he was just asking about my health.

"I'm working for the man who bought those four properties and who is interested in reselling them."

"Alan Thompson," he said.

"Yes."

"And what's he asking?"

"Six hundred."

"He's starting way too high."

"To make it worth his while I think he would need to get something like that."

From behind the counter, where she was washing dishes, a middle aged woman asked, "Nother coffee over there?"

"Please."

"And why didn't Thompson just call me himself if he wanted to deal?"

"I believe he doesn't want his funding source to know about this contact he's asked me to make."

"So he's speculating with someone else's money."

"Of course. Isn't most speculation highly leveraged?"

The woman brought my coffee from behind the counter, set it in front of me and turned away, ignoring the splash she'd left on the Formica table top.

"Cut the crap," Lucas said, his voice still gentle. "No way is this guy working with regular bank financing. Tell me where the money's coming from, and why. Who's this so-called funding source, and why are they buying up property in that poor little rundown neighborhood on the edge of a wasteland?"

"That's the question, isn't it? Why would anyone? Why would Livingston Properties want to? Or more to the point, why was Livingston Properties created in the first place?"

"Which is not something you need to know."

"Okay, but this is how I see it. You and I could work something out that would be profitable for both of us. But we can work it out only if we can trust each other, which means we have to be willing to share some information about our respective sources of funding – not everything about them, but those sources can't stay completely hidden either."

He studied me in silence.

"Neither of us wants to go into it blind," I said.

"What makes you think I want to go into it at all."

"I don't necessarily think you do. I think you haven't decided yet."

He shrugged. "So what I hear you saying is you think Livingston Properties has a deep pocket and could pay inflated prices for Thompson's properties – the ones he has now and maybe ones he picks up in the future – and you think Thompson would settle for a modest profit, and you and I could take something on top of that."

"That would be one scenario," I said.

"And another would be...?"

"I would be willing to go around Thompson. Arrange the purchase of what he's already got and then leave him out altogether. I live right there. I could manage the Albany end of things for you. Negotiate lower prices..."

"And what's in it for me? You're talking about replacing me." He sounded amused by the idea.

"No. Partnering with you. You need a local partner. With me on the Albany end we could buy for less, take a nice commission for ourselves – and Livingston Properties would be rid of the Albany competition it has now."

"And you think Thompson and his backer would just let that happen?"

"They wouldn't like it and they'd try to stop it. But that would be my problem. They're in Albany and I'm in Albany, and I can deal with it."

"Why should I believe that?"

"As I said, trust is important."

"So maybe you should tell me just what you'd be dealing with up there. Why is someone trying to beat us to those properties?"

"Because they don't want you to have them."

"Well yeah. But why?"

"They don't actually have a use for them. They just want to lock them up to keep them from being used – and Tivoli Preserve from being used – the way your people want to use them."

"And they know what that use is?"

"It obviously involves development of the preserve. The properties we're talking about are obviously important as the interface between whatever is developed there and the city."

"And what would that be – what would be developed. They think they know what that would be?"

"For some people it isn't so much what replaces the preserve, it's the loss of the preserve to any kind of development. So I think they know all they need to know. And I think I do too – except for one thing."

"You do know all you need to know, believe me. And more than you oughta know. But okay, tell me about this one thing."

"The mutilated bodies being left in the park."

"I don't know anything about any mutilated bodies being left anywhere." He studied the inside of his coffee mug. Then, without looking up, he said, "So you're a cop?"

"No. I just don't want to wind up as one of those bodies. I want to make some money on this thing, but not at that cost."

"Yeah, I didn't really make you out to be a cop. You're talking way too naïve to be a cop."

"Just an innocent Albany guy trying to make a buck – and stay alive."

"And it didn't occur to you I already got a guy making a buck in Albany?"

"No way of knowing that without talking with you," I said. "Now I guess I know."

He stood up. "You don't know nothing, Pal."

I walked west through Chelsea again and found a small Lebanese restaurant, where I consumed a large plate of stuffed grape leaves with plenty of lemon juice, and a bottle of Almaza beer, before walking back to Penn Station.

When I got home, it was not yet five o'clock. I emailed Lisa, telling her I'd been to the city, had talked with a guy representing Livingston Properties, Inc., had learned a few things, and was interested in debriefing with her when she had time.

She responded almost immediately: "Will call when I get home from work. Got a date later. –L."

It was only five-thirty when she called.

"So you went down and confronted the beast," she said.

"Not exactly. I talked with a guy who works for the beast, guy named Eliot Lucas."

"And what's his role with Livingston Properties? Attorney?

"He only claimed to be a *representative*. I did Google him before I went down to meet him. Apparently he's a disbarred attorney."

"And what was your strategy in talking with him?"

I told her about my strategy of offering Alan Thompson's properties for resale, and about the conversation that had ensued.

"You actually proposed the two of you scam Thompson, direct all sales to Livingston Properties, and skim something off the top of all sales? Did he think you were serious?"

"I don't really know. Like me he was fishing. He wanted to learn what he could about what I knew, so like me he had reason to string the conversation along."

"What did you think in the end? That he was already double-dealing – skimming from Livingston Properties?"

"I'm not sure."

"So did you really learn anything at all?"

"Not much. But it pretty well confirmed that the purchase of those properties has everything to do with someone's plans for development of the Tivoli land."

"Which is where we were already at. Didn't really need to be confirmed."

"And I no longer have any doubt that the bodies in the preserve have everything to do with an interest in development of the place."

"But the important thing we still don't know – development of *what* in the place."

"No, we don't know. Lucas wouldn't give it away. I have some ideas, but they all seem so… well, so improbable."

"Like the ideas that came up in our brainstorm the other night?"

"I'm thinking of one that didn't."

"You were holding out on me."

"No just screening out the most improbable."

"You're not supposed to screen anything when you're brainstorming."

"I know. I'm not very good at not screening."

"This is true. You're a secretive calculating bastard. And sinful too. Look, I have to get ready to go. We'll talk later."

"I'm going to Ithaca for the weekend," I said. "Be back Sunday night."

"Aha!" she said.

I didn't bother to offer the excuse that it was a work-related trip.

17

My excuse was a Saturday afternoon housing symposium that was being sponsored by Ithaca Neighborhood Housing Services. I expected it to be interesting – and it was – but I would not have driven all the way to Ithaca for such an event if Ronnie hadn't been there.

When I got to her apartment at five-thirty she announced she was taking me to Collegetown for dinner. "I'm in a barbecue mood, " she said. I know a place that does incredible barbecue, and if we leave now we can get a booth before it fills up."

It was a little place on Dryden Road. We got the last available booth and were immediately handed menus by a young woman who greeted Ronnie by name. Ronnie grinned at her and said, "Saranac Pale Ale – two of them."

"So you come here often?"

"Not that often. I don't go out a lot in Ithaca. My boyfriend lives in Albany."

"But people know you here. Sometimes I think people know you everywhere."

"No, that's just my friend Louisa. She's in my program, and we hang out and talk sometimes, so she knows a little bit about you and now she gets to check you out."

Louisa reappeared quickly with our beers. When she had left, Ronnie said, "You couldn't see it, but she gave me a thumbs up. You passed."

"I don't think I've been graded that way in quite a few years."

"Oh I'm sure you have. You just don't know it. It was only last summer that *I* was checking you out."

"And I was checking *you* out. Although the first time I saw you, you had a canoe on your head and I thought you were a guy. But by the time I'd watched you lift it off and you'd smiled at me, I was in love with you."

"Well it took me much longer before I decided I was in love with you. You remember your first night at the lake – you and Raymond were standing out on the dock talking?"

"And you were sitting in your canoe just off shore in the dark, eavesdropping."

"Checking you out."

"And then offering your services as a guide."

"But it wasn't until that next weekend when I took you to the ponds that I decided."

"As I recall it was the sight of the moose cow and calf in the marsh that triggered your affection."

"Oh but I think I decided before that. It was when we were both up to our asses in mud dragging the boat through that beaver-flooded spruce thicket. Which I admit was a sort of calculated test. But then we were getting it done together and you seemed to be having fun, and I was having fun. And I wanted more of that. From then on I was checking you out *because* I was falling in love with you. Also because of that, I started worrying that you might think I was a spoiled rich girl."

"I certainly never thought you were spoiled. But I didn't know how to think about the fact that your family was rich and owned the eighteen thousand acres."

"And as you know, I didn't have any idea how to think about it either. And of course neither did Mom. Which was fortunate, because it's why she hired you – to help her figure it out. Otherwise everything would be different now."

"And how is your mom?"

"Pretty good. Busy as always with all her nonprofit in-volvements – and working with the state on the land deal. She's also been down here a couple of times this summer. Stays at the Statler. Takes me to Moosewood for dinner."

"And your sister – how is Kelly?"

"Not so good. Next time I'm in Albany I need to get up to Clifton Park and see her – if she's there instead of at the lake. I do worry about her. It's nothing new, but she's still trying to figure out if she belongs in Clifton Park or at Fisher Lake. And if she really belongs with Jeff. It's all been up in the air for too long."

Louisa appeared at our booth and eyed our half-empty bottles. "You guys going to eat, or just drink beer and gab?"

"I'm starving," Ronnie said. "I think we'd better have two big slabs of ribs, with your good fries and your excellent col-lard greens. If that works for Crow."

"Works perfectly," I said.

After Louisa had departed, Ronnie said, "Okay, tell me how our boy Jesse's doing."

"I wish I knew. He mostly avoids me."

"Maybe we need another fishing trip."

"It's the one thing we can do with him that feels good, but I'm afraid it still won't get him to open up with us about what's going on in his life. I mean he wouldn't even talk about it on Bog River when he should've been loosened up by catching bass hand-over-fist. I think I just need to give him some space and not press him on it for now."

"But I don't like thinking about you and him that way. I can't help wishing you could both be in some better place, someplace where there isn't a ton of bad stuff going on around you and keeping you separate."

"It's his own place though, even with the bad stuff."

She picked up her bottle, took a swig, and then studied the label. "Saranac is such a lovely name, and it has such good as-sociations, even if the brew actually comes from Utica."

"Better that the brewery's in Utica. That way the village of Saranac Lake doesn't have a big brewery in the middle of it."

"Are you teasing me? Are you suggesting I only want to deal with the nice stuff, not the nitty-gritty stuff it comes from?"

"Of course not. You're the one who wades through the nitty-gritty of marshes and flooded spruce thickets. I was seriously being glad Saranac Lake doesn't have a big brewery in the middle of it. And I'm glad you prefer marshes to breweries."

She smiled, but only briefly. "Well I do know your neighborhood is Jesse's place, and your place too. But I'm afraid it isn't my place – and that's a kind of problem I still don't have the answer to."

"The problem of the little cabin on the lake and the little house in the city."

"And the little apartment on the edge of Collegetown. I mean it's wonderful to see you on weekends, and it's especially wonderful to see you here on my turf this weekend. But part of the reason it's wonderful – and it's only a part – is that it's *only* weekends."

"So we're not doing the weekday nitty-gritty together."

"Yeah. Do you realize we've been lovers for a year and we've never had a fight – even though we're both pretty strong-willed people, and really pretty different from each other."

"We haven't wanted to spoil the weekends with anything unpleasant."

"So the weekends *are* wonderful, and in some ways it's a great way to live. We each have our own lives in our own places with our own work, and then when we get together it's all about *being* together. But there's something… There's something…"

She stared at her beer bottle and was silent for longer than I was used to having her be silent. Then I realized she was actually blinking back tears. "Not really the time and place for this," she said.

"Later then. It really is time to talk about it."

Later, snuggling against me in the single bed we shared in her tiny bedroom, she said, "Some happy news from home. Skinner and Pat are expecting a baby this fall. They are really happy."

"That's wonderful."

"And I am really envious." She lifted her head and looked at me closely. "Don't take that the wrong way."

"What would the wrong way be?"

"Oh, well, I'm not jealous, and I'm not envious of either of them for living in that old trailer, with their log house still not finished inside, and not enough money to finish it this year. All kinds of ways I'm not envious, but..." She pressed her face back into the hollow of my shoulder.

"But you're envious of them for having a baby," I said.

"It surprises me that I am. But it's not really all about the baby. I mean... well this takes us back to what we were talking about at dinner."

"Skinner and Pat are sharing the nitty-gritty."

"I don't really know how it works for them, but yes, they have each other every day."

"And a baby is one of the things that come out of that."

"Oh, is *that* where they come from?" She laughed and wriggled more closely against me.

"Maybe I should say it's where *families* come from."

"Does this subject scare you?" she asked.

"It used to."

"It used to scare me too." She was quiet for a minute, then abruptly raised her head again. "Oh! Oh dear."

"What?"

"I was actually forgetting you've been married – you've lived with someone full time, and it wasn't..."

"Sometimes I forget it too – mostly I'd rather forget it – because, no, it wasn't fun. And it wasn't very long before both of us knew it wasn't *going* to be fun, even though we went on for a while trying to make it work – or telling each other we *ought* to try. That was the worst part, thinking of years and years of just going on that way."

"Now you're really scaring me."

I tightened my arm round her. "No, come on. That marriage was a mistake. Trying to make a mistake work is grim. But you and I are not a mistake."

"Okay. We're definitely not a mistake. And we do have fun. And now it's time for me to shut up – and *have* some fun." Her hand began to move slowly up the inside of my thigh.

In the morning we had bagels and coffee in Collegetown, then bought more bagels and coffee to take with us, and set off in Ronnie's Prius along Cayuga Lake to visit her research site in the Montezuma marshes fifty miles to the north.

"Headed north this way with you," she said, "It's hard not to think about just going on all the way to Fisher Lake."

"I would like nothing better," I said.

She glanced sideways at me and raised an eyebrow. "We could."

"Soon, but..."

"I know you have things to get done."

"I have work I'm behind on, as usual, but it's not that. I'd be ready to push it off a few more days and take some time to be with you up there – or in Ithaca for that matter. But it's not the work. It's just all the unresolved stuff in Albany. I don't even know what there is I can do about it right now. All I can do is keep picking at it. Anyway I can't turn my back on it and not think about it."

"So tell me about it. Tell me the latest. We've talked about everything else this weekend, but not that."

So I told her everything I'd learned about the homes being purchased on the edge of the preserve, and about Alan Thompson and the Santa Clause properties and Lisa's list of properties, and my conversation with Bob Goodwin about those properties, and then my trip to the city and my meeting with Eliot Lucas.

By that time, we had almost reached the marshes.

"You want to go get some more coffee or something," she said, "and talk some more before we get into the muck?"

"No, it was good to be able to fill you in. But now let's get wet. If wading in the mud together made you fall in love with me, I want all of it I can get."

We spent several hours in the wide marsh with a wide sky overhead and a breeze whispering quietly in the sedges. When we talked it was only about what was growing where, next to what, how tall things were, and how deep the water was and what its temperature and Ph were, all of which she was measuring and recording systematically.

Later, over burgers in a Seneca Falls restaurant, she said, "So you've learned a lot but really you still don't know what's going on with Tivoli Park."

"I still don't. It's driving me crazy."

"But you think all those things are related? Including both the buying up of property and the killings?"

"It's hard not to think so. None of it was happening two months ago. What's happening now is too much coincidence to explain as *mere* coincidence. There has to be a reason why these different people are suddenly focused on a place that no one's paid any attention to for a century."

"But it sounds like you think whoever's responsible for the killings is doing it to force the city to sell the land."

"Yeah. Whoever's responsible."

"And that would be whoever this guy Lucas works for."

"Or whoever Lucas's employer works for, or collaborates with, or shares an interest with…"

"But some party does want to acquire the land," she said, "for some very specific reason, even if you don't know what it is."

"However, that one party may represent the interests of a lot of different people and may be a long way back behind what's happening in Albany now."

"Wherever it's coming from, what's happening in Albany affects Jesse."

"It did. But I hope it was a one-time situation for him. I hope it's now water over the dam."

"I wish it was water over the dam for both of you."

"I do too."

"But there's that part of you that doesn't want it to be that way – that wants to solve the puzzle, not just let the whole thing go on over the dam."

"Sure, but a bigger part wants to hang out with Ronnie Wetherby."

"Really? A bigger part?"

"Right now it's way bigger."

"I'll ignore that image, but only for a little while. By *now* I guess you mean this weekend – this Sunday afternoon. But how about Monday morning. Do you turn back into a detective at the stroke of midnight?"

"I'm kind of hoping you'll share your bed with me again. Then you can check me out in the harsh light of a weekday morning."

"That would be lovely, even if you have to get up at four o'clock and get on the road, as I expect you will."

"No, I want a regular weekday morning, with coffee and some kind of breakfast at a regular workaday hour."

She was grinning. "Is there maybe something we could argue about over breakfast – just to get some practice, so some day we might even be able to have a real fight?"

18

I got home just before noon on Monday, made a sandwich and took it to my desk to check email and voicemail and decide which of my deferred obligations I should deal with first.

The voicemail included a very brief message from Reilly.

"Another one. Call me."

The last thing I wanted to hear.

I called but he was not at his desk. I left a message saying I'd been away for the weekend and had just got home. A half hour later he called back.

"Another woman," he said. "Like the last one. Young. Attractive. Beat up bad. Just checking to see if you've been down there lately and if you saw anything. Since you're the one usually finds them."

"Not in the last four or five days. Where was this one found? And when?"

"On the dirt road where the trail down from Judson comes in. Our patrol found it last night."

"You've started patrolling? On foot?"

"You kidding? We've got a car swinging through couple times a night. Probably try to do it more often now."

"With this one, was it the same with the ears?" I asked.

"Yeah, the same."

"Have you identified her?"

"We're not saying anything about it yet."

"How much do the media know?"

"Only that another body was found in the park. That's all. And please keep it that way."

"Any more of those extra-large footprints?"

"Thunderstorm last night. No tracks now."

The voice of another person – I assumed a colleague – said, "Reilly, we need you." And the line went dead.

I then set to work trying to catch up with the more urgent tasks that I'd been putting off since the middle of the previous week. But by six o'clock I needed to get out of the house and move around. I put on my running shoes and shorts and headed for the preserve.

The sun had disappeared behind thunderheads that were building in the west. It was still hot but if the clouds moved in, there was hope for some cooling. I jogged down the trail from the head of Judson, past Tivoli Lake, to the intersection of the trail with the dirt road.

Yellow crime scene tape was strung around the whole intersection. I could see nothing significant inside the tape. There were tire tracks where a vehicle had pulled off the dirt road toward where I now stood – presumably from a police vehicle. There were footprints on the sandy surface of the road, presumably made by police feet since the thunderstorm. There was no sign of disturbance in the vegetation on the far side of the road.

I went around the tape to my left and jogged westward, keeping an eye out for anything out of the ordinary. Again the only footprints were those I guessed were made by the cops. At no point did the footprints appear to have left the road and gone into the woods.

I began to wonder if the police had carried out any kind of search away from the road and trails. In the case of the first murdered woman, Reilly had said they'd found the site of a scuffle on the dirt road, but that was all. It seemed likely that once she'd been subdued she could have been dragged into the woods somewhere, before eventually being brought back to the road or trail. If she'd literally been dragged, there would be a fairly obvious trail. If she'd been carried, the trail would be less obvious, but maybe still visible.

I assumed the police would have looked for such evidence, but I doubted that any of them had great skill as woodsmen. I slowed my pace and began to look for places where a person could have gone into the woods without having to struggle through heavy brush. Near the place where I had seen a doe and fawn earlier in the summer, a game trail crossed the road, not heavily used but discernable. I explored it for a short distance on each side of the road but saw no evidence that anyone else had followed it.

A little further on there was just the suggestion of an opening between dense thickets. Again there was no real evidence that someone had passed that way, but it was the sort of place a person might have tried if he needed to find a way into the woods. And on the very edge of the woods I did find a few garlic mustard stems that had been broken – which of course could as easily have been caused by a deer or raccoon as by a person.

I worked my way in, not really expecting to find anything, and guided less by any specific signs than by the assumption that someone carrying a body would want to get out of sight of the road as quickly as possible and would therefore go straight into the woods perpendicular to the road. After several hundred feet I was ready to turn back when I realized that ahead of me to the left was a place where vegetation had been broken and compressed. It was not the tidy little oval imprint that a deer leaves behind after bedding down. It was a much larger area and there was more damage to the undergrowth. Several large clumps of cinnamon fern had been flattened. Foot-high tree seedlings had been mashed down and broken.

I stood still and stared.

There was blood on the ferns.

Beyond the ferns there was a pale twist of a shape – like a twist of apple peel – half hidden in the leaf litter. I circled to the other side of the area to get a better view.

It was a human ear.

Once again I returned to Orange Street and called Reilly. Once again he picked me up at home and we drove to the area behind the Green Tech Charter School – this time stopping not at the entrance to the foot trail but at the nearby gate at the eastern end of the dirt road. Reilly unlocked the gate and we drove up the dirt road and parked where I had gone into the woods, and once again I led Reilly to something ugly I'd discovered.

He sidled around the perimeter of the site, peering at it, then brought his phone from his pocket and called for crime scene technicians. I hoped that if he had questions for me – as he certainly would have – we would retreat from this place and go back to the car to talk. But he continued to stand, staring at the site.

"I'm having a real hard time believing this," he said. "Explain to me how you found this place."

"I was jogging and just keeping an eye out for a place where someone might have taken a body into the woods."

"You mean it was like you were looking into the woods, and back in there somewhere you saw this bent twig. So you said to yourself that looks exactly like the way our perp would bend a twig. I don't believe it for a minute. Add it to you being the one who found the first two bodies, and what the hell am I supposed to think?"

"In this case, today, I poked into a couple of places where it looked like someone could possibly have gone into the woods, and I stumbled into this. Just a matter of chance."

"I don't think so," he said. "I think there're two ways of explaining it. Either someone you're not telling me about is feeding you information, or you're the guy yourself, the guy who's doing this. You just know too damn much."

There was nothing jocular about his statement. He was serious. I felt like I'd been slapped in the face.

"You're saying I'm a murderer and rapist."

"I'm just saying there's only two believable explanations for why someone would know the things you know."

He was staring hard at me and I felt I had to meet his gaze and could not afford to look away, much as I wanted to.

Finally he said, "Okay, of course I'm not really saying you're the one did this stuff. I am saying you're holding out on me. And we got to change that. Even if I have to take you in and hold you."

"You can't hold me." I was being attacked and I was angry. "You can't arrest someone for finding dead people in the middle of public trails and reporting them to the police. And you can't arrest someone for finding evidence that a competent police search of the area should have found in the first place."

"Now you're fucking pissing me off." His face was getting red. "If you think we don't have plans to search the whole area, you're a fucking idiot."

"Three murders and you're just now getting around to planning a thorough search of the area?"

"Listen to me, asshole. Now is the *right* time for a methodical search. And the *wrong* time to have some asshole jump in on his own and stumble into something and screw it up. For all I know you've stomped all over this site."

"I haven't touched it," I said. "I haven't been any closer than where we're standing now. And I've brought you to it. What the hell more do you want?"

"I want you to tell me everything you know and then stay the fuck out of my way. If I have to throw you in jail to get you out of the way, I will."

"And what do you plan to charge me with?"

"If I have to I can lock you up as a material witness."

"Bullshit! You can't hold someone as a material witness unless you've got a reason to think he's going to take off on you – which I'm not. You know where I live. You've got my phone number. And I'm not a witness. I haven't witnessed any crime."

"We'll just let a judge sort out the legal shit while you cool your ass in jail."

"That's ridiculous. You're not going to embarrass yourself that way."

He pounded a fist into his palm. "You're driving me fucking crazy."

"And you're driving me fucking crazy. I have not withheld information from you. And I *have* given you significant information that you've made no use of."

"Like what?"

"Like the real estate transactions in this area that I reported to you."

He started to say something but then he straightened up abruptly, staring into the vegetation on the far side of the disturbed area. "Duct tape!" he said.

Following his gaze, I could make out a section of silver tape tangled in a clump of cinnamon ferns.

"Had she been restrained with duct tape?" I asked.

"Get yourself back out to the road," he said, "and when my guys come along, bring them in here."

When I got back to the site with the crime scene technicians, Reilly had worked his way around to the far side of the site, beyond the piece of duct tape, which he was studying intently.

Pointing at the tape, he said to the technicians, "Blood and hair on it. Make sure the photos show that. And we got possible fingerprints there."

"We're on it, Detective," one of them said.

Then to me, Reilly said, "Okay, you've created enough problems for one day. Get the hell out of here."

With frustration churning in me, I walked back to where the trail came down from Livingston Avenue. Then I ran hard up the trail to Livingston and on down Judson toward my house – managing to burn off some, but not all, of the frustration.

After a shower, I sat at my desk and struggled to sort out the feelings the encounter had left me with. I was still angry at Reilly's charge that I was holding out on him, and still stung by the suggestion that I could actually be the one doing the killing, raping and mutilating, even if he didn't entirely mean it. And I was angry that I had let him make me feel defensive. I was also frustrated by his lack of interest in the real estate transactions as evidence relating to the question of why someone seemed to be working methodically to turn the preserve into a conspicuously scary place.

But then I was also feeling guilty. It was true I hadn't told Reilly everything I might have. I hadn't told him about my conversation with Alan Thompson. I hadn't told him about my suspicions that Bob Goodwin was funding the purchase of some of the properties. I hadn't told him about my trip to New York and my scheming interview with Eliot Lucas. In fact there was a lot I hadn't told him.

I hadn't told him certain things for the same reason he wouldn't tell me certain things. Neither of us wanted the other to interfere with what we wanted to do ourselves. He of course had a right to proceed that way. I did not.

19

I spent all of the next day at my desk diligently trying not to think about Tivoli and what was happening in and around it, until after six o'clock. Then I did walk up Judson and jog a quick loop around the preserve – without seeing any dead bodies or blood or severed ears. I left the preserve by way of the trail that comes out behind the charter school. Then I bought a big sub at the Henry Johnson Subway, which I took home and ate on my front steps before going back to my desk.

Sometime after ten o'clock an email came in from Lisa, with the word *rumor* in the subject line. The message was:

Finally talked with my friend at Development and Planning. Told her I'd heard something about someone maybe wanting to buy the preserve, and could there possibly be any truth in it.
She said what are you talking about?
I said I'm serious, I heard it could really happen.
She got a funny look on her face.
I said WHAT?
She said If someone asks me, I'm supposed to ask them what they heard, but not tell them anything myself.
I said do you know anything you COULD tell?
She said she wasn't sure.
I said well I'll tell you what I've heard if you'll tell me what you've heard.
She said not here.
So we're having lunch tomorrow.
We'll see. There's still some of that gin left if you want to drop by tomorrow evening.
    --Lisa

The next day there was a brief article in the AT reporting the death of the second young woman. She was identified as Beatrice Furrilo, a SUNY Albany student, but no other details were given. It would seem that the police had waited as long as possible to release even that much information, and the media hadn't yet had time to learn anything on their own.

I again spent the day diligently at my desk. At six-thirty I went down to the kitchen and fried a hamburger and opened a package of sauerkraut. It wasn't really enough but I would eat more later.

I left the house and walked down the long slope of Clinton Avenue and went up Ten Broeck and rang Lisa's doorbell.

"Rumor and gin," she said, opening her door. "It'll bring him in every time."

"I'm afraid so. It's an irresistible combination. Especially if it's a rumor cleverly extracted from deep within city government."

"So make us a drink. Mine with Vermouth."

I made the drinks and we sat by her tall windows, where we could see the low evening sunlight just touching the wooded crest of land beyond the river to the east.

"So you had lunch today with this person?"

"I did."

"And you learned something?"

"I heard this person's story. Which could possibly mean something."

"And now you're going to hold it behind your back and tease me."

"But of course."

"Okay, it's probably just some silly story anyway. Who cares."

"You're right. It's probably just too silly. I won't waste your time with it. So tell me about your weekend in Ithaca. How is your lovely friend?"

"It was a great weekend. And my friend is great. And she doesn't tease me the way some of my friends do."

"Really? She never teases you? Does she know how much fun she's missing?"

"I'm just going to sit here," I said, "and enjoy my gin and admire the view from your windows, and wait for you to get bored."

"Oh all right," she said. "This person, whose name is Jean, heard something from a guy whose name she didn't know, who works for some company she also didn't know the name of. He'd been meeting with Jean's boss, and when he came out of the boss's office he said to her, 'So what do *you* think about this idea of a casino in Tivoli Park?'"

"A casino – he actually said that?"

So she said to him, 'What casino? I don't know anything about any casino. And he then said, 'Oops, I guess I shouldn't have said that.'"

"You believe this story?"

"There's more. She went to her boss and told him what the guy had said. And according to her he looked like it really freaked him out... was how she said it. But then he told her, no, the guy was just making it up, and was just trying to see if *she* had heard any such thing. And then he told her, if she heard anything like that from *any*one else, to be sure to tell him."

"So something's going on," I said.

"As we already knew."

"And it maybe involves a casino."

"Which I suspect is something you've thought of, and is maybe the thing you said you'd *screened out* of our brainstorm."

"Yeah."

"You screened it out because it would require a change in the New York State Constitution."

"Among other things," I said.

"Yes, and it would take a while, but the governor's already proposed that the constitution *be* changed to legalize gaming. And it's going to happen. Because there's already a race to see who'll get the revenue and the jobs. Massachusetts is already ahead of New York, and New Jersey and Connecticut are way ahead."

"Anyway, it makes sense that some people are trying to get out ahead of state government and be ready if and when it's legal."

"Or maybe someone's talking with some Indian tribe," she said, "which wouldn't require a constitutional amendment – thought it would involve the feds, which could take even more time than a constitutional amendment. But maybe you should check with your friend Raymond – see if he's heard anything."

"I think I will. But also... is there a way to learn more about this guy who mentioned the idea of a casino in Tivoli Park?"

"Not that I know of. I think Jean truly didn't know who he was – or else she's cleverer than I think she is."

"Where do you stand with her now? Were you able to give her something in return for what she told you."

"I told her I had a friend in the police department who said the police were convinced that the Tivoli Park murders were an effort to get the city to sell the preserve for some kind of development – and that one of the ideas they're working on is that someone with an interest in casino development is behind the whole thing."

"I like it," I said, "even though it's way out ahead of where the police actually are. You think she'll take that to her boss?"

"Already has, I'm sure. Soon as she got back to the office."

20

The next day the Albany Times featured an article entitled "Cops Search for Answers in Tivoli Park." There was no indication that the police had found any answers, but the questions were thoroughly dramatized. Both women had been "brutally raped, beaten, and mutilated." All three victims had had their ears "slashed from their heads." I was sure that neither this phrasing nor the basic information had been volunteered by a police spokesman, and I wondered again who was feeding it to the media. It was also reported that residents of the adjacent neighborhood were "increasingly frightened," and one of them was quoted as saying she was "outraged that the police can't seem to do anything about it." The police spokesman, however, was quoted as saying the police were "combing the area for clues and patrolling the park at frequent intervals."

Finally, in its concluding paragraphs, the article reported the one thing I'd hoped it wouldn't. It stated that according to an "unofficial source," two of the bodies had been discovered by Orange Street resident Warren Crow, "who was also involved in the investigation of the so-called Neighborhood Housing Association murders two years ago." It then briefly

summarized that two-year-old piece of Northside Albany history, pointing out that the crime in that case "had its roots
outside of Albany," and concluding with the question: "Is it
possible that the Tivoli murders are also a product of outside
forces?"

I considered calling the Albany Times and asking to talk
with the author of the article, so I could try to find out who
the unofficial source was. But I decided that any kind of response from me would just play into the hands of the press.
They wouldn't have to tell me who the source was and I'd be
giving them an opportunity to ask questions. The only strategy that made sense was total silence on my part.

But maintaining silence was going to require an effort.
Soon after finishing the article, I got a call from a TV reporter
who wanted me to do an on-camera interview – if possible,
she said, at the entrance to Tivoli Park. I told her I was sorry
but there was nothing I could say or wanted to say, or that the
police would allow me to say.

"What do you mean they won't allow you to? Aren't there
things called freedom of speech and freedom of the press?"

"Anyway, I don't want to. Sorry."

After hanging up, I turned off my phone's ringer. I would
screen my calls, at least for the morning.

I then called Bob Goodwin, who said, yes, he'd read the
article too and was indeed concerned. I asked him if we could
get together and talk about it. He said he had commitments in
Troy, but we arranged to get together at his place at the end of
the afternoon.

I then called Zera, who said, no, Raymond wasn't up yet
but was probably awake and she would take the phone to him.
I apologized for calling at that hour and asked if I could drop
by his place later if I brought lunch from Subway's. Like me,
he has a weakness for Subway's subs.

At noon, Mabel the cat sat on Raymond's big kitchen table and
oversaw the unwrapping of the sandwiches, then sniffed each
in turn. Raymond broke off a piece of salami for her and low-
ered her to the floor before pouring coffee for me and himself.

"I'm here to pick your brain," I said.

"You still worrying about Jesse?"

"Well, yes, I am, but there's something else I wanted to ask you about. It's this whole Tivoli Park situation I stumbled into. I've been puzzling over it."

"I've been seeing stuff in the media about more bodies," he said. I knew his scanning of the local media was intermittent at best, so he probably hadn't seen that morning's article and we wouldn't need to talk about it now.

"There's also some very puzzling stuff going on *around* the preserve." I filled him in on Livingston Properties and the Santa Clause properties and my talks with Thompson and Goodwin. "As I see it, the only possible explanation is that someone has a major interest in developing that land and therefore wants to control the surrounding land as well. Lisa and I've been speculating about what kind of development could possibly be driving all this stuff."

"If you and Lisa can't figure it out…"

"No one wants to talk about it, but Lisa did get a little something from a woman who works in the Department of Development and Planning. How much do you know about the process for developing a casino away from a reservation?"

"Always thought that was an interesting way to name that department," Raymond said. "First comes the development, then you plan what to do about it."

"Very realistic approach," I said.

"Anyway, that's what she heard? A casino?"

"Nothing definite, but the idea did seem to make city people perk up their ears. And I'm just trying to figure out if it's even possible."

"If you're asking me, I guess you're not talking about casino development the way it's done in places like Vegas or Atlantic City or any of those places where they've decided to let people shed their money without help from us Indians."

"I'm talking about our own state, which our own governor says should become one of those that won't need help from you Indians."

"Which of course means amending the constitution."

"And that means approval of the amendment by both houses of the legislature in two consecutive sessions, and then approval by the voters state-wide. It won't happen over night. But in the meantime we've still got you Indians."

He looked at me thoughtfully. "Okay, but I only know a little bit about that depressing subject."

"Your little bit is a probably lot more than I know."

"I guess you know about that Wisconsin Mohican deal down in Monticello that the feds vetoed. Hard to believe someone's going to pull off something like that here when it didn't even fly in Sullivan County, where there's already a year-round race track with slot machines, and where the governor and an influential senator threw their weight behind it."

"But it almost succeeded down there and if things were just a little different it *might* succeed up here."

"Things would definitely be different here," he said. "This is nothing like the southern Catskills, where you've got a history of resort hotels offering all kinds of entertainment, and where gambling already has a toehold – and where there's a lot more land available than just Tivoli Park."

"But what if it was a New York State group wanting to do it, instead of some group from Wisconsin? What if the Oneidas wanted to open another casino, for instance?"

"I think they've pretty much got what they want right there in their own territory. They might want to expand Turning Stone, but not go a hundred miles down the Thruway to Albany." He took a bite of his submarine sandwich.

"Then what about your friends the Mohawks?"

"It's sure not the kind of thing they're thinking about," he said around a mouthful.

"They wouldn't be tempted by the possibility of a casino in a bigger market?"

"Oh some of them might. They certainly don't all agree. Some of them wish the Akwesasne community didn't have the gambling stuff it's already got, and some of them just can't get enough of it. But the ones who run things are working on consolidation right now – bringing their casino and their bingo palace closer together."

"But once that's done, isn't it possible that the ambitious ones might look further afield?"

"The ambitious ones – in other words the greedy ones – probably want to stay close to the business opportunities they have right there in Akwesasne. There are all kinds of import-export opportunities when you have an international border running through the middle of your reservation. Especially if you deal in booze or drugs, or of course cigarettes."

"Yeah, okay – especially if you've got all of Canada full of nicotine addicts who can't afford to smoke legal cigarettes any more."

"Right," he said, "But the other thing is... Albany is not really that tempting a market."

"Unless being within a few hours of New York, Boston and Montreal makes it the center of a really big market."

"New York already has Atlantic City. Boston's already within easy reach of a couple of world-class casinos in eastern Connecticut. And Montreal has its own grand government-owned casino on Isle Notre Dame. So an Albany casino would really just have the Capital District market – which might be enough to interest some little group looking for a way into the business but not enough to interest a group looking to go big-time."

"But we're still the state capital. We still have a bunch of trains running back and forth to New York."

"Yeah, and Trenton is the capital of New Jersey and it has a bunch of trains running back and forth to New York, but New Jersey's casinos aren't in Trenton, they're in Atlantic City."

"So maybe the point is that casinos don't have to be either centrally located or in a big tourist destination. Turning Stone isn't. Akwesasne certainly isn't."

"Okay, sure, on that modest scale it could happen. But who's going to push it?"

"Actually our mayor's been talking up the advantages of bringing gaming to Albany."

"But that's been in connection with talk of the downtown convention center that's been on the drawing board for years."

"And probably will never happen. But I think what he cares about is the jobs and revenue, not where the thing is located. And the city already owns those eighty undeveloped Tivoli acres, so if someone was to come to the city with a proposal..."

"Yeah it would work for the city – if there really is someone."

"Or hurt the city, depending on your point of view. Any casino proposal's got to be complicated politically. And just how complicated would depend on where it's coming from."

Mabel had reappeared on the table and was stalking my sub. I picked up the sub. Raymond picked up Mabel. "You're thinking these murders have something to do with this whole thing?" he asked, returning Mabel to the floor.

"Did you see that letter in the Albany Times the other day suggesting the city ought to sell the preserve to a developer?"

"I don't read those things. But you're not saying someone's actually calling for a casino, are you?"

"No, I'm just saying that a series of mutilated bodies winding up in the preserve is a pretty good way to get people stirred up to pressure the city to sell the place."

Mabel appeared on the table again and sat down where she could keep an eye on both subs. Raymond removed a piece of salami from his sub, gave it to her and returned her to the floor. "Sounds like you might be sticking your nose into something dangerous again," he said.

I told him about my trip to the city and my conversation with Eliot Lucas.

"Definitely sounds like you're sticking your nose into something dangerous."

"I'm going to be really careful," I said.

"You're too stubborn to be really careful," he said.

"Not that stubborn. But, by the way, you haven't told me yet about Zera's trip to Honduras? I knew there was some kind of Caribbean connection in her past – but *Honduras*?"

"Yeah, the *edge* of Honduras. Her family's from a Garifuna community on the coast. You know about the Garifuna?"

"No, I guess not."

"Pretty interesting. Descendents of African slaves who wound up living with Indians on a Caribbean island after a slave ship was wrecked. Sort of merged their West African culture with native Caribbean culture. Got bounced around by the competition between England and Spain in the seventeenth century, and wound up on the coast of Central America, where they've been living in communities on the beaches ever since. And *only* on the beaches. So, for centuries they didn't have much to do with the dominant Hispanic culture, and therefore kept their own culture."

"Does sound pretty interesting."

"Sometime we'll have to have you and Ronnie over for dinner. Zera can show you photos. And maybe teach Ronnie to do the Punta. She's tried to teach me – with no luck at all. Probably wouldn't have any luck with you either."

21

I arrived at Goodwin's apartment a little after five o'clock and found him sampling another micro-distillery product from somewhere in Vermont – this time a twelve-year-old rye whisky.

"Not quite my favorite beverage," he said. "But interesting. You must have a taste."

He poured me a rather large taste. We sat in the easy chairs next to the book shelves and sipped expensive whiskey. I wanted badly to launch more questions at him, but my earlier efforts had accomplished nothing and I didn't have a fresh strategy, so I sipped in silence and waited.

Eventually he said, "What is happening out there is exactly what I feared."

"And you were certainly right to fear it. It's giving the city a powerful motive to unload the preserve. If there's someone willing to buy it."

"Yes." He was gazing sadly toward the windows that looked out over the park.

"And clearly there is someone who wants to buy it – at least if the necessary arrangements can be made for the kind of development this someone wants to do."

"Mmm," he said. "You haven't told me what you learned in the city last week. Did you learn anything about this someone?"

"Not really. I'll tell you about my conversation with a man named Eliot Lucas, but first tell me if you made that call I asked you to make to Alan Thompson."

"I did seriously consider it, but it would have been extremely awkward."

"All right. You might still ask him, though, if he's had any inquiries about those properties from a guy named Eliot Lucas or from Livingston Properties, Inc."

He nodded. "But tell me about this person."

I gave him a summary of my conversation with Lucas. When I'd finished, I said, "That's the little I know, but I'm wondering if maybe you yourself know something about him."

He shook his head, but only slightly, as though it didn't matter whether he knew anything about Lucas – as though what mattered was something beyond Lucas.

I told him then what Lisa had heard from her friend Jean. He continued looking toward the windows. He did not look surprised.

"For the murders to make any sense," I said, "it would *have* to be something like a casino. Something that could generate huge profits and that might involve some kind of underworld connection."

He said nothing.

"Do you agree?" I asked.

"It's a reasonable inference."

"And if someone can strike a deal with the city – at least get an option on the land contingent on the legal hurdles being negotiated – then the murders will stop. And eventually we'll lose our preserve. But the underworld connection will never become visible. So the only way to stop the whole thing is to *make* that connection visible."

He turned and looked at me, frowning. "Is it that simple?"

"I'm not saying it's simple at all. I'm just saying the little bit I know how to say about the situation."

He studied his whiskey, slowly turning the glass one way and another. Finally he said, very quietly, "Do you believe in evil?"

"Ah, I don't know. I'm not sure what you mean by evil. If evil is just people doing bad things to other people and to other living things, then of course I believe evil exists – it's all over the place."

"All right. Of course those bad things happen, but I mean something more than that. I mean the force that generates those bad things."

"A force other than human motives? Something other than greed, anger, hatred…? I assume you're not talking literally about Satan stalking the land and recruiting people to do bad things."

"Or just licensing them to do bad things," he said. "But no, that's not what I mean. I don't believe in Lucifer any more than I believe in Jehovah. But neither am I just talking about isolated human acts." He studied his whiskey some more. Finally he said, "I mean something like weather. Evil is bad weather. Weather that can become so bad – like a hurricane – that it affects everything. It does terrible things to everyone concerned, no matter what they try to do about it."

"I guess that makes a kind of sense," I said. "It's certainly hard to think of the Holocaust as no more than the sum total of Hitler and his subordinates doing bad things."

"That's right. The moral weather in that time and place was very very bad. The Holocaust could not have happened in good weather. "

"So you're suggesting that some kind of bad moral weather is affecting Tivoli Park?"

"I'm not saying it's comparable to the Holocaust, but yes, some kind of bad weather."

"But bad weather is something we can't do anything about – except stay indoors, close the windows, hunker down, and wait for it to go away. There's no way we can intervene, no way to change it."

"I know," he said, "it's not a helpful metaphor that way. But I'm afraid it describes how I *feel* about it."

"But you *have* intervened," I said. "You *are* changing the way people in the neighborhood will be affected. Maybe even the way the preserve itself will be affected. You're putting a lot of money into buying houses for God's sake – to change what's going to happen here."

He raised his eyes from his glass and looked at me, then nodded – a single brief lifting and lowering of his head – before looking down again.

I was certain he'd just affirmed what I'd said, but I wanted unequivocal affirmation. I wanted to say, "So you're finally acknowledging you're the one doing it." But I was afraid that if I put it into words he would need to deny it. Instead, I said, "And I'm really glad you're doing it, and I want to help."

He was silent.

"Not that I have the wherewithal to help buy up houses."

He shook his head. "I don't need help buying real estate. It's easily enough accomplished, but that kind of thing can only do so much. It's a little like building a levy so when the storm comes the town won't be flooded. But if it's a really big storm it will overwhelm the levy and the whole town will be flooded anyway."

"Okay, I like your metaphors but I think they're getting in our way now. I want to talk about the specific, actual people that are behind all this stuff."

"But you don't know who they are."

"And that's exactly what I want your help with. I think you know more than I do, and if you'd share what you know, I might be able to help do something about it."

"But what I don't understand," he said, "is why you're so determined to get into it personally – so passionate about it. I mean I know you were the one who found two of the bodies, and I understand that makes it a very immediate kind of thing for you. But really… you've reported what you found to the police. Isn't it up to them now? What can you or I do that they can't do better?"

I wanted to tell him the police were just not getting it done – that they had no imagination, that they were treating the whole thing as though it was just a series of the sort of street crimes they were familiar with. But I knew that was not entirely true. And that complaining about the police would only highlight the relevance of his question about why I felt so strongly about it all. If I was really going to answer that question I would have to tell him about Jesse. I still had not told anyone outside of Raymond and Ronnie about Jesse's involvement, and I did not intend to.

I found that I was now the one studying my whiskey in silence.

Finally I said, "There is someone I care about who is innocent but is involved in this and could be terribly hurt by it. That's really all I can say."

He was looking at me steadily and, I thought, sympathetically. And nodding. "That does make it hard," he said.

My first thought was that somehow he *did* know about Jesse. But then it occurred to me that maybe his situation was similar to mine – that his unwillingness to talk about what he knew was due to the involvement of someone *he* cared about who could be hurt by whatever was going to happen.

"Yes it does make it hard," I said.

He continued nodding.

I went back to studying my whiskey.

"Are you still walking in the preserve?" he asked. "I am."

"I still go jogging down there, but more and more I dread stumbling on something else awful. It's no longer a restful place to wander around."

"May I give you a bottle of this interesting old whiskey? It's as good a way to distract oneself from dreadful things as I know of."

"Oh, thank you, but no. I've really enjoyed the incredible gin you gave me, but you can't go on giving me ultra-expensive bottles every time I visit you."

"I can if I want to," he said. "And I'll feel terribly rejected if you won't take it."

So I walked home with another ultra-expensive bottle.

After leaving the bottle in the cupboard under my sink, I walked on southward, through Washington Park and then to the Price Chopper on Delaware Avenue, where I bought a frozen pizza and some other odds and ends.

Back at home, while the pizza was in the oven, I allowed myself to be distracted by another shot of twelve-year-old micro-distilled Vermont rye whiskey.

First thing the next morning, I checked the AT's Opinion section on line, and found a letter to the editor responding to the previous day's "Cops Search for Answers in Tivoli Park" article. The letter-writer said he didn't care who the murderer was or whether he came from inside or outside Albany. What mattered was keeping the park safe for innocent people. Either the police needed to "do whatever it takes so that "thugs won't dare go near the place," or else the city needed to sell the place to a private developer who would "do something with it that would do away with any kind of cover for any kind of thugs." Or else, if the police can't do what it takes and no one wants to develop the place, the writer said. the city should "eliminate the cover" by clear-cutting the entire preserve, "so the place can be patrolled with helicopters if necessary."

It was hard not to be reminded of Viet Nam and the US strategy of defoliation that made it possible to find and kill Viet Cong from the air. Of course if Raymond were to read this letter he might point out that deforestation had also been key to making all of eastern North America safe for Europeans. The only problem with Tivoli Park was that the city of Albany had failed to keep the place safely deforested.

I went downstairs and refilled my coffee cup before returning and checking my email.

There was a note from Lisa with the subject line reading, "stirring the rumor pot."

Having fun with this. Fed another "rumor" to Jean at D&P. Told her my friend in the P.D. told me they were looking into someone buying up property on Livingston. Said they seemed to think it was the same people who were trying to get Tivoli for a casino. Jean was VERY interested. I'm sure it's now bouncing around various city offices, lighting them up like a pinball machine (or so I like to think). Stay tuned. –L.

I was delighted. I repied:

You are brilliant. This will really shake things up and I hope finally shake a useful response out of someone. I owe you at least a gallon of gin (and some Vermouth). Please keep on having fun.

There was also an email from Ronnie, whom I was planning to see again in Ithaca the next day, which would be Saturday. Ever since leaving her apartment Monday morning I'd been especially eager to get back there. It felt like we had begun a discussion that needed to be continued. At the same time, it now felt like the week in Albany hadn't been long enough and there was a whole lot here that needed to be continued. Not that I was about to change my plans. Her note said: *"Tomorrow! I've been thinking up stuff we might be able to fight about if we get tired of sex, barbeque, and wading in the muck. But those things come first. So hurry!*

22

Much of Friday was taken up with preparing for and sitting in a meeting with a Schenectady group.

I got home at six. I opened a cold Sam Adams and took it out to the front steps, leaving the door open behind me in the hope that at least a little of the hot indoor air would escape.

As I was finishing the beer, Jesse appeared at the corner of Robin, coming from the direction of Clinton. I thought he would probably head straight for his own house, but instead he came my way on a long diagonal across the empty brick pavement of Orange Street. His head was down. He wouldn't look at me, but he came straight to my steps and sat down beside me. He was holding an envelope.

He began to tap the edge of the envelope against the step he was sitting on, still not looking at me.

"What's up Jesse?"

He looked up quickly, then down again without speaking. The tapping rhythm quickened. Finally he handed the envelope to me. "Sorry about this," he said.

The envelope had my name on it. I asked if he knew what was in it?"

"Nuh-uh."

"But you know who gave it to you to deliver."

He shrugged.

I opened the envelope and took out a single sheet of looseleaf notebook paper on which someone had scrawled:

Stay out of Tivoli, stay out of stuff not your business or something bad going to happen to your friend Jesse.

My skin prickled and the hair stood up on the back of my neck. For a long moment I felt paralyzed and wasn't sure I could breathe.

Jesse looked up at me. "Guess it's bad," he said. "Like I said, I'm sorry."

He did sound sorry. In fact he sounded and looked desolate.

I crumpled the paper and stuffed it in my pocket. "But you don't know what that note said…"

"No."

"But you might know who wrote it…"

"No. One of my buddies… he had it. Just said someone told him give it to me and tell me to give it to you. Don't know… Hope it's not big trouble for you."

"It'll be okay," I said, still struggling to think of what to do. "It's something… well, it affects both of us. Your Mom too. What time does she get home?"

His eyes were wide. "Not till like ten o'clock. Why you asking?"

"I need to talk with her. Really with both of you together. I'll watch for her around ten and then I'll come over for a minute or two. I hope that'll be okay."

I expected him to object, but he didn't. "Don't come till I can tell her you're coming" he said. "I'll call you when she's home and I've told her."

"Okay. Have you had supper? I'm going to go in and scrounge up something if you're hungry."

"Mom always leaves me something in the fridge," he said, standing up and turning toward his house.

I went up the steps and into my hot stuffy indoors. I didn't really have any idea of what to do about supper. I wasn't hungry. I went upstairs and sat at my desk and tried to think. My first thought had been that Jesse's mother needed to know that he had been threatened. But maybe it wasn't really such a good idea to tell her. Maybe I should just get out of town and stay away for however long it took to avoid even the appearance of interfering in "stuff not my business." But there was no guarantee that even that would keep Jesse safe. The whole situation was heating up, and I hated the idea of just going away and doing nothing – letting whatever was going to happen go ahead and happen, and do whatever it was going to do to Jesse.

I picked up the phone and called Ronnie.

"I hope this call doesn't mean you can't come tomorrow," she said.

"I hope it doesn't too." I told her about the note, quoting it word for word, then told her what I was wrestling with.

"You have to bring him here," she said. "Would his mother let you do that?"

"I don't know. Where would he stay?"

"He could stay here in the apartment and I'll just sleep at a friend's place – one or another friend's place. Or on the floor here. I'll work something out. And maybe if he's up for it I can give him some work to do, data entry stuff, to help keep him busy."

"I'm not sure how long a time we're talking about."

"We're talking about our friend Jesse – not some tenant with a lease that's going to expire on a certain date."

"Thank you," I said. "I'll see what Jesse and his mom think of the idea."

"I hope he didn't do something bad," Mina Johnson said. She was sitting rigidly upright on the sofa in their living room, with Jesse hovering by the window to her left, and me in a chair across from them. She was frightened by my request to talk with her, but she was certainly not one to cower. She faced me squarely with her head up, her eyes never leaving my face.

"No, it's nothing like that," I said. "It's someone else who's threatening to do something bad to Jesse. Threatening me, really, by threatening to hurt Jesse if I don't do what they want. I don't know if they really would do anything – probably not – and I'm not even sure if talking with you about it is the right thing to do."

"If there's anything could happen to my boy I need to know about it."

"That's what I thought you'd feel. So I think I should just show you this note I received. They sent it to me by way of Jesse but he hasn't seen it, doesn't know what it says."

I had refolded the note and put it back in the envelope. I took it out now and gave it to her. She studied it for a long moment, then looked hard at me.

"I don't understand. What's this about Tivoli? What is it you been doing? What they want you to stay out of?"

"I'm not sure what they *think* I'm doing, but I was the one who found two of the dead people in Tivoli Park, and reported them to the police and tried to answer their questions. And I've learned about some other things going on around there – someone buying up property around the park – and I've been trying to figure out what's going on."

"And they want you to stop."

"It looks that way."

"And if you stop they won't hurt my boy."

"That's what the note says."

"But you telling me you're not *going* to stop? Even if it hurts my boy?"

"I don't want to do anything that would hurt Jesse."

"So you got to stop doing whatever they telling you to stop."

Her eyes were unrelenting. I felt pinned to my chair. "It's easy to stop going to Tivoli Park," I said. "And maybe that's all I'd need to do. But other things are more complicated. The police are probably going to have more questions for me as they go on investigating those murders. They may want me to testify. Whoever this note is from may not like that. I don't know who they are or how dangerous they are…"

Jesse stirred for the first time. "Can I see it – the note?"

His mother hesitated, then handed it to him, but without taking her eyes off my face. He read the note quickly, then crumpled it in one hand, making a fist.

"What do you think, Jesse?" I asked. "You don't know who wrote that thing, but you might have some idea about the kind of people behind it – and whether they're dangerous."

"Not good people," he said. "Trouble for anybody they think messing with them."

His mothers eyes turned to him for the first time. "You know these people?"

"Some of my buddies know 'em."

"Your friends are mixed up with that kind of people?"

"It's okay, Mom. My friends are okay. This didn't come from them."

"All right," I said hurriedly, "here's an idea I wanted to suggest."

Mina's eyes returned to my face.

"I have a good friend who lives in Ithaca. She's a good friend of Jesse's too, the one we go fishing with sometimes. I called her this evening and told her about this business. She said why didn't I bring Jesse to Ithaca to stay with her for a while… until we're sure things are going to be okay around here."

I was addressing Mina, but I was aware of Jesse physically coming to attention where he stood by the window.

"Stay with Ronnie?"

"She said she had some computer work you could help with. And she lives right near the Cornell campus, where you know she's a graduate student. She could show you around. You'd have a chance to poke around and get the feel of the place – see if maybe you'd like to go there someday."

"Yeah, right," he said. But he was excited.

"This is only if you're okay with it," I said to Mina. "If you get too lonesome for your boy, I promise to bring him back whenever you say."

She looked steadily at me, saying nothing, thinking. Finally she said, "He went with you that time last year for a weekend. He had a good time and I think it was good for him."

"In fact that was when Jesse and I both met this woman whose name is Ronnie for the first time."

She turned to Jesse. "You want to do this?"

"Like to try it," he said.

She turned to me. "When you thinking you'll go?"

"I was already planning to go to Ithaca to see Ronnie tomorrow – leaving first thing in the morning. If that works for both of you…"

"Okay," Mina said.

"I better go pack," Jesse said.

23

He was in my kitchen before seven AM with a suitcase. He had made the effort to dress up a bit – maybe because his mother had told him he didn't want to be walking around a big university looking like a homeboy. He wore pressed khakis and a blue and white striped shirt with a button-down collar. It heightened my feeling that he'd grown into a different person from the kid I used to know.

By seven o'clock we were swinging onto I-90 headed west. The wooded edge of Tivoli Park lay off to our left, not far beyond the interstate. But in a few moments we'd be leaving the place behind.

Jesse sat quietly and a little stiffly beside me in his dress-up clothes. He'd been avoiding me for some weeks and we'd become shy with each other. I hoped we'd now be leaving behind the problem that had come between us, but it was going to take a while to find out.

I-90 soon joined the New York State Thruway. We picked up a toll ticket – although, since we were going only as far as I-88, this section of the Thruway would be free (the state having bartered away some toll receipts in return for federal dollars to build the lightly used interstate connector).

Half an hour down I-88 we stopped for breakfast at the little restaurant beyond Cobleskill, whose young proprietors Ronnie had described as just "having so much fun." And they were still having fun. When Jesse ordered just eggs and toast, the woman said, "Well, let's see. How far you traveling today?" When he said, "Ithaca," she said, "Oh, that little breakfast will never get you to Ithaca. Can't you think of something to go with those eggs?"

Jesse grinned. "A little ham would go good."

"That's better," she said. "And maybe we could give you a stack of pancakes instead of just toast. Would that be okay?"

The grin widened. He nodded, then pointed at me. "Better make him eat a good breakfast too. Don't want him giving out on me."

When we left the place, both of us were well filled and well cheered. We still didn't talk a lot, but what talk there was – mostly about what we were seeing from the car – felt easy.

At Bainbridge we left I-88 and headed west on route 206 through country that had seen better days and, unlike the country I grew up in, remained relatively unaffected by tourism or gentrification.

"That barn getting ready to fall down," Jesse said. "Can't see how it's still standing."

"I'm afraid a lot of barns are falling down these days. The barn I grew up milking cows in looks about like that one. No one's taking care of it so it'll fall down pretty soon."

"Milking cows? You a *farmer* then?"

"My father was a farmer. I was the kid who got stuck doing the milking, and a lot of other stuff – until I escaped and went off to college. And not long after that my dad sold the cows."

"He didn't want to be doing it all his self?"

"No it wasn't that. He just couldn't make any money at it any more, like most of the other farmers around. So now most of the cows are gone and most of the barns are falling down."

"Where those cows *go*? I mean we still got milk."

"Yeah, now instead of a lot of little farms, there are just a few really big ones, with maybe a couple thousand cows, or more – good sized businesses. Need computers to manage operations like that. The world is changing really fast, in the country as well as in the city."

"Don't see it changing so much on Orange Street," he said.

"Maybe not, but I don't think you're going to spend most of your life on Orange Street."

He was quiet, turning his eyes, if not his thoughts, back to the countryside. After a while he said, "Where you went to college – that was Cornell, where we're going, right?"

"Right. I was an undergraduate there. Now Ronnie's a graduate student there."

"You like it there?"

"Eventually. But at first I was scared to death. There were times when I wished I was just back milking cows, where at least I knew how things worked and what I was supposed to do."

"But you a real smart guy. You figured it all out pretty quick I bet."

"It took me a year to get to where I didn't worry about it all the time. Then the second year I went too far the other way. I turned into a smartass who drank way too much beer, and other stuff, and just barely kept from losing my scholarship and my work-study job. After that I kind of straightened out and got interested in some of my courses and eventually turned into a more or less serious student, and actually got where I liked the whole thing."

"A guy like me, though... be pretty tough to make it in a place like that."

"What do you mean, *a guy like you*?"

"Black kid from the neighborhood, don't know much, not much of a student..."

"Well I was a white kid from a poor family on a failing hardscrabble farm in the Hoosick Valley, and a mediocre student in Hoosick Falls Central School. Knew next to nothing about how the world worked outside the Hoosick Valley – probably a lot less than you know now."

"Yeah but you..."

"Okay, I'm smart. Smart enough to learn. Now you want me to tell you again what I keep telling you? *You* are a smart guy, Jesse."

"Yeah, you keep saying it, but how'm I supposed to know if it's true."

"If you're saying I can't tell the difference between a smart person and a dumb person, then you're telling me I'm *not* smart. Is that what you're saying?"

He thought about this for a while, then finally shrugged and smiled.

As we worked our way westward over the long ridges between I-88 and Ithaca we began to see signs on people's lawns expressing support for or opposition to the practice of hydrofracking.

"So this is where they want to do that fracking stuff," Jesse said.

"And where some people don't want them to do it. So I guess you know about it, how it works?"

"Don't really know how it works. They drilling for gas and they pump this chemical stuff down in the hole to break up the shale rock and let the gas come up out. But New York State hasn't said they can do it yet. Because some people think it's going to mess up their own water."

He seemed to know as much about the subject as I did. "You think those people are right?"

"Don't know. But the ones want to do it, they're going to make a lot of money at it, so they're gonna try to do it no matter what."

"You're right about that," I said. "But right now they're arguing about it. Let's see which side is winning the argument. Let's count the signs for and against."

After about fifteen minutes of counting, we had the pro-fracking people slightly ahead of the anti-fracking people. At that point Jesse said, "Not going to do *this* all day."

"Yeah. And counting signs isn't going to change anything. Maybe we should be trying to learn more about what the effects of fracking really are."

"Don't know if I want to do that either. Have to be some kind of scientist to do that."

We were both quiet for a while. Then I said, "What do you suppose your buddies are doing right now back in Albany?"

"Hanging out."

"But that's not *all* you guys do, is it?"

"Do a lot of stuff. But I guess you want to know if we do any bad stuff."

"No, I'm not trying to check up on you, and I don't care what you guys do – I mean I do care, but I'm not going to hassle you about it. What I really want to know isn't what you do but what you *know* – what you and your friends might know about some of the bad stuff that's going on."

He was looking straight ahead down the highway, completely unresponsive for so long that I was sure he just wasn't ready to talk about these things.

But finally he said, "Well, there's some stuff we do. I mean sometimes we smoke a little green, or whatever you want to call it. But not a lot. And some of the guys selling a little of it."

"Does that worry you – the selling?"

"Yeah, sort of worries me."

"You're afraid they'll get caught?"

"Not so much that. It's what they're getting into with the guys they're getting it from."

"Good thing to worry about," I said.

"Yeah well, some of 'em think I'm chickenshit for not doing it. I mean even my buddy CJ sells a little, just in his spare time."

"Sounds kind of funny to talk about someone pushing drugs in his spare time, like it's just a hobby or something."

"Isn't no hobby. He's got some places down on Sheridan, near where all those people park their cars to go up the long stair, where he can spend an hour after school and make pretty good money."

"He's taking a big risk, but I guess it's better than doing it *in* school."

"Be crazy to do it in school. They're real serious about it in school. Big trouble if they catch you."

"Anyway, you're smart not to get involved with the older guys who're supplying the stuff."

He was silent.

"I don't suppose those older guys have had anything to do with what's been happening in Tivoli Park."

He was still silent.

I plunged ahead. "Okay, I think you have a pretty good idea that what I'm really interested in is how you guys came to know about the dead guy behind the Park View Apartments. Because I don't think it was just you stumbling into it on your bike."

He sat very still, gazing away from me out the window, still saying nothing, and I was sure I'd pushed too hard too soon. But then, without turning away from the window, he said,

"Yeah well, I owe you. You did like you promised. You told the cops you found it yourself. So… time I told you something I guess. There was five of us that was being kind of scouts, because we knew our way around Tivoli, and these two older guys hired us to show 'em around, and then they got us to be like lookouts that night while they did something that they didn't tell us what it was. But where I was being a lookout I saw them carrying something from a car behind the apartments. It was creepy, but then I was real curious to know what it was. Anyway the next morning I walked back in there and found the thing, the body. That's how it was. I thought someone ought to know about it, but it couldn't be me telling them. I had to stay out of it."

"Had you been seeing these two guys around the neighborhood?"

"Not until like a few days before."

"Would they be easy to spot after you'd seen them once?"

"The big guy, yeah. They call him Tank and he's *really* big, like he could've played in the NFL or something. The other guy – Switch they call him – he's just ordinary looking. Doesn't stand out like Tank. Hard to describe."

"Black? White?"

"Kind of in between. Maybe Puerto Rican or something."

"How's he talk? Sound Hispanic?"

"No, just ordinary. Talks kind of quiet but real fast. He's the one in charge, and if he tells you do something you better do it fast. Tank, he just does the carrying and stuff."

"Have you been seeing them around these last few weeks – since that one time?"

"Not much. Couple times. Probably just come up from the city certain times. That's where they from – what they say anyway."

"How did you guys happen to get hooked up with them?"

"Some guys told 'em about us, told 'em we knew the park. Guy's who told 'em were, you know… where my buddies were getting the stuff they were selling. Told us these guys were Crips from the city, wanting to start up a Crips gang in Albany. Couple of my buddies thought it'd be cool. Started calling us the West Hill Crips."

"That as far as it went – just using the name that way?"

"Pretty much. But it was dumb. That's a big-time gang all over the country, the Crips. Nothing' like us."

"Did these guys have any more jobs for your buddies after that one time?"

"Don't think so. But I been kind of keeping my head down lately. Still hang with CJ and a couple of the guys. But a couple other guys, I been kind of... I don't know... They getting into certain stuff that's more'n I want to mess with."

"You think it might have been Switch who wrote that note to me?"

"Don't know but that's what I'm thinking."

"Okay, one more question. Can you think of any reason *not* to think these guys are the ones who're leaving bodies in Tivoli Park?"

He shrugged. "I saw 'em the first time carry that big bundle into where the body was. Don't know anything about the others. But Switch... he could be doing it, so I don't know."

We were getting close to Ithaca. "I better pay attention here," I said, "Or I'll miss my route. But thanks for telling me this stuff. We'll be at Ronnie's in maybe fifteen minutes and then we can forget about Tivoli Park for a while."

Ronnie and I were sitting in the kitchen of the two-bedroom apartment she had arranged to use until the graduate students who were its regular tenants returned for the fall semester. Jesse was in one of the bedrooms, from which the sound of a television continued to come. Earlier he had called his mom on Ronnie's cell, which had a 518 area code and wouldn't be traceable to Ithaca. All was well for the present.

"TV's still going, but I bet he's asleep," Ronnie said.

She opened the door, slipped in, turned off the TV, and slipped back. "Dead to the world," she said.

"And I am very grateful. He seems pretty much his old self. And being here is going to be good for him in all kinds of ways. I just hope it isn't going to be too awkward for you."

"We'll work it out. Any problems, we'll just have to get you back down here. But right now it's time to relax. I bought us a present." She opened a cupboard and produced two glasses and an unopened bottle of Jack Daniel's.

I got some ice from the refrigerator and poured us each a drink. "I think I'd just like to sit here and look at you," I said, "and drink bourbon, and not think about anything else for a long time."

"Okay, but I'll probably haul you off to bed before you have too many drinks. Also I'm dying to know what the two of you talked about on the way down. Did you learn anything?"

"Quite a bit. More than I know what to do with right now."

I gave her a quick summary. "And some of it is stuff that really has to be passed on to the police. But I haven't begun to figure out how to do that and still keep Jesse out of it."

"Yeah, awkward. But I'm sure you'll work out something with your friend Reilly."

"My friend Reilly is not at all happy with me right now – even less happy than when I last told you about all this. He's already convinced I'm withholding information from him. This will make it even more complicated to figure out what to tell him and how to avoid not telling him some other things."

"Any chance Jesse will come around to being okay with talking to the police himself?"

"I doubt it. Anyway I won't encourage him to. If he could just pass on what he knows about these two guys Tank and Switch, which would have to include seeing them carry a large object into the park the night of the first murder… If he could just leave it at that, it would be okay. But the cops would have all kinds of questions about how he happened to see what he saw, and who his friends are, and how they all got involved with those two guys."

"Okay, you certainly can't ask him to do that. But the good news is he was finally ready to tell *you* about it."

"Just getting out of Albany made that possible. And you're the one who made it possible to get out of Albany."

"And now the bad news is this all made it possible for him to transfer his burden to you. I think your idea of just having a little bourbon and not thinking about it tonight is a good plan. So let's have one more drink and then go check out my friend Jessica's bed."

"Now that I think about it," I said, "the bed is a better way to not think about it than the bourbon. Let's check it now."

She stood up. "Okay, but first, actually, I have another present for you."

From a shelf behind her she produced a cell phone and handed it to me.

"I know you don't like cell phones, but I would really like being able to call you wherever you are – like out on your front steps, where you spend half your time. I'd like it especially with the way things are now. And I'm hoping maybe you'll at least like the ring tone I downloaded for you. Took me a while to find it."

She took her own cell from her pocket and selected a number. In a moment the gadget in my hand came alive. *Caw, caw, caw,* it said.

"Crow's cell." She was grinning.

"How can I resist," I said.

In the bedroom Ronnie opened a drawer in the nightstand beside the bed, which turned out to contain an interesting collection of vibrators and dildos. "More gadgets," she said.

"You're a nosey girl," I said.

"But of course. Think we'll need any of these?"

"Don't think so." I was getting out of my jeans. She gave me a vigorous push and toppled me onto the bed, then dropped on top of me.

In the morning the three of us spent an hour exploring the campus.

"Didn't think it was so *big*," Jesse said.

"And you've seen just one part of it," Ronnie said.

"How you get 'round it all, if you don't have a car?"

"A bike helps," she said. "probably should have told Crow to bring your bike." She took a folded paper from the back pocket of her jeans. "A campus map helps too." She unfolded the map and showed him where we were and where we'd been, then handed it to him. "If you want to poke around some, go ahead. We'll just go chill on that bench over there."

He studied the map and his surroundings for a minute or two, his eyes shifting back and forth from map to surroundings. Then he pointed and asked, "That the library over there?"

"That's it. Olin Library."

"Okay, think I'll go look around. Won't be too long."

Jesse headed off and Ronnie and I settled ourselves on the bench.

"So what are you thinking," she said. "Can you spend another night?"

"I really really want to, but I'm thinking I just have to get back and try to figure out how to deal with this situation."

"Any thoughts since last night on what you're going to do?"

"I'm going to talk with Raymond before I do anything. That's as far as I've got at this point. Talking with Raymond is always a good way to get pragmatic."

"True. Good idea."

"But leaving you and Jesse... You know what it feels like? It's like now I have this little family in Ithaca, and a big need to stay with them."

"A family?"

"Well sort of."

"It's not like he's our son. He's got a mother in Albany, who no doubt is missing him right now."

"Sure. It's just a new feeling I have. I've been thinking a lot about the conversation we had last weekend. It's a new feeling about you, about us, really."

She had turned toward me on the bench and was studying my face. "You mean we're dealing with some nitty gritty together?"

"Yeah, call it that."

"And is it, um, an okay feeling?"

"It's a little scary but really very good."

She hunched herself closer on the bench, leaned into me and kissed me hard on the mouth.

"That's a very good feeling too," I said.

"Oh yes," she said. "But anyway, don't worry about your family here in Ithaca. We'll do okay."

"You always do okay," I said. "You did okay even when you were sharing your little cabin at the lake with your wayward friend Nicki when she was completely at loose ends."

"Easier at the lake than it will be here if Jesse and I have to move back into my little apartment – which will be in three weeks. And the other thing that happens then is Labor Day.

Sure would be nice if you and I could still manage to get to the ponds that weekend." She was looking at me questioningly.

"One way or another," I said. "My goal is to have Jesse home and us at the ponds by Labor Day. Just can't possibly let this situation go on longer than that."

However, I still had absolutely no idea what I was going to do about it.

24

I got home around ten in the evening. I opened all the windows, then opened a beer and went upstairs to check my email. There was a message from Lisa, sent that morning, with a subject line reading, "rumor mill."

Happened to be talking with an old colleague Friday night whose sister is an Albany Times reporter. Told him about these rumors about someone wanting to develop a casino in Tivoli Park. Asked if he'd heard anything. He said no but thought it was an interesting idea and maybe he'd ask his sister if she'd heard anything. So I told him about the Livingston home purchases. Wanted to know if it was another rumor. Told him no I'd checked and had a list. Wanted to know if it was a list I'd share. Big-hearted Lisa said oh sure. Today he emailed me saying his sister would love to see the list. Just sent it to her.
Only one gallon of gin?

I thought about checking the Sunday AT online, but decided that could wait. I shut down my computer, turned off the lights, and went to bed in my overheated bedroom, and thought about Ronnie.

In the morning I went to Washington Park to jog. I was going to avoid Tivoli Park completely until things were straightened out. When I got home, I called Zera and asked her to ask Raymond if he would stop by Orange Street on his way down to his place in the hollow.

He arrived mid-morning and we took our coffee cups out to the front steps.

"I've got a problem," I said.

"Figured you'd get yourself in trouble," he said.

"Yeah, well, you know me too well. But it's not like someone's trying to kill me."

"Not yet. That's good."

"But in some ways it's worse than that. A lot has happened in the last few days." I told him the whole story. The threatening note, the arrangement with Ronnie, the drive to Ithaca with Jesse, and all that he had told me.

"So now the problem is how do I tell the police about Tank and Switch and what some kid named Jesse saw them doing the night of the first murder. How do I do it without putting Jesse in the position of betraying his friends, and maybe even getting himself in serious trouble?"

"But if he agreed to talk with cops and tell them this stuff, he'd be okay."

"Yeah, probably okay with the law, but not with his friends."

"So you don't think he'd do it."

"I don't think he'd volunteer, and I don't think I'm going to force him by reporting what he told me."

"But neither are you going to just sit on information about guys who may be the killers the cops are trying to identify."

"Yeah."

"So… you got any thoughts about what to do?"

"All I can think to do is to tell Reilly what I've heard and claim it's something I overheard from kids on the street, or at the Gander Bay Bar, or something like that. But Reilly's already convinced I'm withholding information. He'll be suspicious as hell, and I want to work out something as believable as possible before I talk with him. I thought maybe you could help me do that."

He reached behind his head with his left hand, gathered up his ponytail and held it for a time, gazing off down the street toward Sheridan Hollow without saying anything.

"I mean I thought maybe I could try a couple of stories on you and you could tell me what's wrong with them."

He let go of his ponytail, and after a while he said, "Or maybe I could try a couple of stories on you. See, I do talk with kids on the street, and I do have a beer at the Bay now and then. And now that I'm thinking about it I'm starting to remember hearing those names, Tank and Switch. Even some rumors on the street that they might be the ones dumping bodies in Tivoli Park. Even that someone saw them carrying a large object into the park."

"You mean you really *have* been hearing that stuff?"

"I'm telling you, aren't I? You're hearing it from me."

"And I was ready to believe you. It certainly is more believable coming from you."

"Yeah, you'd try to say too much, you always do. Better if they hear it from some mostly silent enigmatic Indian."

"I am sure glad I have one of those as a friend," I said. "I'll tell Reilly I heard something like that from my enigmatic Indian friend, and he should call you."

"Always happy to cooperate with the police," Raymond said. "But now you got to tell me everything Jesse told you about those two guys, all the details. Doubt if my sources got all the details right."

Reilly was behind his desk, which was even messier than usual. He himself looked even wearier than usual. But he definitely liked the information that I told him I'd got from Raymond.

"Good, I'll talk to the guy," he said. "I remember him from two years ago. The guy who saved your ass."

"I learned a lot from him back then about what was going on in Sheridan Hollow. And he seems to know a lot about what's going on now."

"Yeah, okay. Sounds like he knows more than *you* ever gave me."

I stood up, ready to leave and feeling extremely grateful for what Raymond was doing.

"Hold on," Reilly said. "Still gotta talk to you."

I sat down again.

Rubbing his forehead, he stared at the drift of papers on his desk.

"Always happy to talk," I said. It sounded glib and I regretted it.

"Yeah, right." Finally he leaned back in his chair and looked at me "One time, I think you mentioned some rumor about a casino in Tivoli Park."

"I mentioned rumors about development. I don't think I said specifically development of a casino, but yeah, I've heard that. Are you saying you've heard it now?"

"Not me, no. But the chief has. Heard it from someone in the Mayor's office for God sake. They also said they heard we were investigating it as something connected with the murders."

"What did you tell them?"

"I told the chief it was bullshit. But he didn't exactly agree. He said, 'well, it's an interesting coincidence. Maybe you *should* be looking into it.'

"So I said, 'well, okay, first step would have to be asking the Mayor if there's any truth in it.' He didn't think that was such a good idea. I said, 'I don't see how anyone thinks they can buy the place from the city without having a little talk with the mayor right up front.'

"And the chief said, 'If the mayor knows something he's not talking about, it's because he doesn't want to talk about it, and if he doesn't know anything about it, you can bet he's got his own people looking into it right now.'

"So I said, 'If he knows something he doesn't want to talk about then he doesn't want us looking into it. And if he's got his own people looking into it, then we're liable to get in their way if we're trying to do the same thing.'

"So the Chief scratches his head for a while. Then he says, 'Well be careful but learn what you can and keep me posted.'"

"Pretty awkward," I said.

"So I hate to say it but I'm back to talking to you – *carefully* of course. Now refresh my memory – where did you hear that rumor back then?"

"I'd heard it back then from Robert Goodwin."

"Okay, my favorite non-sources – you and Goodwin. You think maybe he started that rumor himself? Or maybe you did?"

"It's quite possible that he did. I can tell you absolutely that I didn't."

"He say anything to you about it since he mentioned it back then?"

"No."

"Anyone else mention it?"

"A friend of mine said she heard it from a friend of hers who heard it from a friend of his. I guess that's how rumors work."

"Yeah, well, thanks for nothing." He swiveled his chair a quarter-turn away from me, pulled his cell phone from his pocket, and began poking among the papers on his desk. "Time to call your friend Raymond," he said, "and talk about what's happening out there in the *real* world."

Early that evening I bought a large bottle of what, until recently, I would have considered top-of-the-line gin. I took it to Lisa's door but found her just leaving.

"Gotta date," she said. "Is that for me?"

"Down payment," I said.

"Okay, but you're still going to owe me for the rest of your life."

"All right. Just keep up the good work."

I walked home and called Ronnie on my new phone and the two of us spent some time filling each other in on the day's events.

"So Raymond came through for you."

"He did. I haven't heard yet how his talk with Reilly went, but I'm assuming it accomplished pretty much what we wanted. It amounted to a kind of good-source-bad-source routine we played out with Reilly."

"You being the bad source."

"Yeah, the guy who only wants to talk about rumored real estate transactions, not about who the actual killer might be. Whereas Raymond talks about the real world, and Reilly was hungry for it."

"Cool."

"How's Jesse doing?"

"Really well. I think he's about ready to get in touch with the Cornell Admissions Office."

"That may be the best thing that comes out of all this."

"He really is a smart kid. But you knew that. By the way, I just emailed you a couple of photos for his mom."

After we'd hung up, I printed the photos – Jesse in front of Olin library, Jesse at the kitchen table working on Ronnie's laptop. I took them next door and knocked. I thought Mina might not be home yet and I was getting ready to slip the photos under the door, when I heard her voice from inside. "Who is it?"

"It's Warren. Thought you'd like to see the latest from Jesse."

The door opened immediately. I gave her the photos. "I know he misses you," I said, "but I think he's kind of getting a kick out of being there for a while."

She studied first one photo, then the other, then looked up at me and smiled. I think it was the first time I'd ever really seen her smile. I went home and called Ronnie back to tell her about it.

25

The next morning there was an Albany Times article on real estate speculation in the vicinity of Tivoli Park. It wasn't a very long article but the link to it was prominently posted on the AT homepage. The byline was Elizabeth Hollings.

WHO'S BUYING PROPERTY AROUND TIVOLI, AND WHY?

It didn't identify individual properties, but it reported the total number of sales that had "come to the attention of this reporter." The number matched the total number of properties on Lisa's list. It described the general locations of the properties accurately – "the part of Livingston Avenue adjacent to the park, plus Beverly Avenue." It noted that there appeared to be "more than one party buying," but that there was no doubt that all were purchased by "investors, not individual homebuyers."

It then observed that "Tivoli Park has been much in the news of late as the site where the bodies of three murdered people have been found."

And it noted that in recent days there had been "a growing buzz of rumor and speculation – no doubt fueled at least in part by the murders – about the future of the preserve, and in particular the possibility that someone was trying to buy it as the site for a casino."

The Mayor was quoted as saying that, although he thought a casino could be a great economic resource for Albany, there had been no discussion with any potential developer of Tivoli Park. Asked if there were any circumstances under which the city *might* consider selling the preserve, he said he couldn't think of any. But he then went on to emphasize that the city "faced severe financial straits," and that "under such circumstances various options might be considered that wouldn't otherwise be on the table."

The article concluded, "Although little information is currently available, it is impossible not to speculate that the coincidental things going on in and around and relating to Tivoli Park are not *mere* coincidence."

I was about to send a congratulatory email to Lisa when a note from her arrived in my inbox.

Yes Elizabeth Hollings (today's AT) is the one I sent the list to. She could have done more with it but it's a start. She'd probably love to interview you. What do you think?"

I replied:

You're the one she should interview. You're the author of this story. But let's talk about how we should follow up. Got time for a drink this evening?

I was headed downstairs to refill my coffee cup when the phone rang behind me. I went back to my desk and answered it and was greeted by Reilly's voice.

"Jesus H. Christ," he said.

"Is that your way of saying good morning?"

"It's my way of saying this Tivoli Park thing is driving me batshit crazy. You see the Albany Times article this morning?"

"I did."

"Well the chief saw it too. Got a message from him already asking what we know about those properties on Livingston. Thank God I had that list you sent me, so at least I could tell him something the Albany Times didn't know."

"The specific addresses? Something they didn't print, anyway."

"Whatever. But now I need to know where you got it."

"Like I told you when I emailed it, a realtor friend of mine checked recent deed filings and made the list. The information is public."

"But why did she do that? And why did she share it with you?"

"It was something we'd both been interested in. Because why would anyone want to buy up property around the park – and be willing to pay fairly healthy prices – if they didn't think something significant was going to happen there. As far as we can tell now, the two buyers are competing with each other to buy everything that comes on the market in that area."

"But what made you look into it in the first place?"

I couldn't resist the temptation to needle him. "These are questions I expected when I sent you the list. Didn't think it would take you so long to get to them. But anyway... I'd been talking with Helen Hamilton at the Neighborhood Housing Association, who's been shopping for homes in Arbor Hill and West Hill that NHA can rehab and sell through their affordable homeownership program. And Helen was finding homes in the Tivoli area were being snapped up before local homebuyers could even look at them. Albany realtors had been given a number to call if they had *any* listing in that area."

"Whose number?"

"Something called Livingston Properties, Inc." I told him the little I'd learned about Livingston Properties, Inc., through my brief computer search. I didn't know whether it was time to tell him about my talk with Lucas. I wasn't prepared to talk about it, and I decided to let it go for the present, but I regretted not having given more thought to the matter sooner.

"I still don't know what the hell it has to do with my murder case. It drives me crazy because we're finally starting to get somewhere – we got a set of prints, we got DNA, and now we got what your Indian friend picked up. And I'd like to just put everything we've got into finding these guys. But there's this pressure to get into all these crazy rumors, and now they're putting more people on the case, including someone who's supposed to know all about real estate and finance and all that shit, and computers. The way I see it, that's not where it's at, but it's what's happening now."

When I got off the phone with Reilly, I went downstairs, had a bowl of generic wheat flakes and a banana, then went out and took a brisk walk around the neighborhood, which brought me eventually to the NHA office, where the coffee had just finished brewing.

"Your usual perfect timing," Helen said.

"Don't know about that. Meant to be in touch with you a week ago. I'm running late on everything."

I got a cup of coffee and sat down beside her desk. I asked her if she had seen the Albany Times article. She had not, but quickly found it on the AT website and read it.

"My my," she said.

"Just so you know," I said, "my friend Lisa and I sort of planted the information about those properties with the AT."

She raised her eyebrows. "You stirring things up again, Warren?"

"You could say that. But something *is* going on around Tivoli, and it seems like the way to find out what it is... is to stir and stir and see what comes to the surface. Anyway, Lisa went to the deeds office and made a list of the recently filed deeds for that area. And we did share the list with an Albany Times reporter, the one who wrote that article. But I also wanted you to have a copy of it."

I handed her the paper copy I'd brought with me.

She studied it briefly. "I see you've got the two where I talked with the sellers. Also looks like you broke all of them down between those two buyers."

"Yes, they were all deeded to one or the other of those two – either Livingston Properties, Inc., or the lawyer you told me about, Alan Thompson. I did go and look up Alan Thompson and it's clear he's making those purchases with money from someone who wants to block what Livingston Properties is doing."

"But you don't know who it is."

"Actually I'm pretty sure I do know, and I've asked him, but he won't quite admit it. But I'm pretty sure he's not just another greedy investor but someone who cares about the preserve and the neighborhood."

"Certainly seems to treat the sellers right," she said.

"Yeah, Thompson referred to those deals as his 'Santa Clause' deals. He seems to be having a good time giving people good deals. So hang on to that list, and if we update it we'll send that to you. And who knows – if things work out the right way, maybe Thompson and his backer can play Santa Clause for NHA."

"Now wouldn't that be nice," Helen said.

After lunch I called Robert Goodwin and asked him if he'd seen the article.

"I saw it," he said. "Is that your doing? I was planning to call you and complain."

"But the deeds are public documents. Anyone can see them – and can see whose names are on them."

"Anyone can. But no one does. Unless there's someone making a public issue of it."

"I would say the one who's making a public issue of what's going on here is whoever's behind the murders. As I think we agree, the only explanation for the murders that makes any sense is that someone's trying to generate public pressure on the city to sell the preserve."

"However, I'd hoped to deal with the matter as quietly as possible."

"I know that's been your hope. Anyway I've called you now to make sure you know about the AT article, and to tell you also that the AT reporter does have information about the deeds, which of course includes the new owner's name. If they haven't already, they're likely to call Alan Thompson."

"In fact they have called him."

"Sorry, I should have warned you sooner."

"Wouldn't have made any difference of course. If the cat's already out of the bag…"

"In any case you do control those properties, and who-ever's behind Livingston Properties, Inc., knows they have a competitor. I'm curious, though – what are you going to do with those properties for the long term?"

"When this all blows over, I hope to sell them. If I can. No doubt for less than I've paid for them."

For the first time he was explicitly acknowledging that he had in fact paid for those properties – which at least made it a little easier to discuss the situation with him.

"At some point," I said, "I'd like to talk with you about the possibility of selling those homes to the Neighborhood Housing Association for their community land trust homeowner-ship program. It could be a way for you to recoup some of your investment through a single deal. And it would mean that the availability of those homes for local people would be locked in permanently."

"My understanding of that model is that the nonprofit continues to own the land but the resident owns the house, am I right?"

"Yes, with the homeowner having a 99-year lease to the land, and with the terms of that lease controlling resale of the house so it can be passed on to another lower income family."

"Intriguing," he said. "If we get to that point…"

Late in the afternoon there was an email from Lisa saying she was going to be tied up that evening, but how about tomorrow. I was disappointed – in particular because the temperature in my house had risen to about ninety degrees and I'd been hoping to spend an hour with a cold martini in Lisa's air-conditioned apart-ment. Instead, I pocketed my new cell phone, walked over to Washington Park, found a comfortable spot in the shade, and called Ronnie.

"You're actually *using* the phone I gave you!" she said.

"Yeah, You've corrupted me."

"Well I'm glad."

"I'm starting to like it. And right now it's an alternative to air conditioning. My land line is in an oven. Where I am now there's a bit of a breeze and it's quite pleasant."

"How utterly corrupt of you," she said.

Later, I walked around the neighborhood, bought a sub and a six-pack, and went home to eat supper on my front steps. When I finally checked my land line for messages before going to bed, there was a voice-mail from Reilly asking me to come to a meet-ing with "the new person on the case" at nine the next morning.

26

The new person on the case was about as different from Reilly as anyone could be. Her name was Sergeant Giselle Lopez. She was a tall, beautiful African American woman. She might have been thirty years old, but no more than that. She was elegantly dressed. Her head was cleanly shaved.

She, Reilly and I sat around a table in a small room that I assumed was normally used for interrogations, which I thought might be what I myself would be facing. I had got up early to think about how I should handle it – what I should say and what I should not say.

Lopez had a laptop open on the table in front of her and was typing rapidly, but her role wasn't going to be limited to note-taking. From the start, she assumed management of the meeting, which Reilly's body language suggested might not have been something he'd agreed to beforehand.

"Let us begin," she said, "by putting everything we know on the table – every last thing, each of us. We have asked Mr. Crow to participate in this because he has obviously been doing some research on his own, and we need to know everything he knows. But I suggest we start by asking Detective Reilly to tell us what is known as a result of his investigations."

Reilly gave a summary – emphasizing a number of times that he was summarizing "evidence, not rumors." It was a good summary and I learned things I hadn't known before. A full-scale methodical search of the preserve resulted in another site being identified similar to the one I had found. Again there was blood and duct tape. Fingerprints had been found on the tape from both sites. Semen from the bodies of both women provided DNA samples. Efforts to match both the prints and the DNA were underway. Various members of Albany gangs – some of them currently in jail for various reasons, some not – were being interrogated about the identities of Tank and Switch. Reilly was optimistic, he said, about the likelihood of a significant break-through in the near future.

Lopez then asked me to describe my own "investigations."

"I don't know as much as Detective Reilly might think I do," I said. "I haven't been conducting an organized investigation by any means."

"Never mind what Detective Reilly might think," she said. "Please just tell us what you know and how you've come to know it."

I wasn't comfortable with the breadth of her request, but I did the best I could. I described what I had learned from

Helen Hamilton and then from Lisa about the purchase of properties around the preserve. I described my interview with Alan Thompson. I mentioned that Alan Thompson was a nephew of Elwin Thompson who was a friend of Robert Goodwin, whom Reilly had interviewed, but I did not tell them I'd learned Goodwin was funding Alan Thompson's acquisitions. I thought Goodwin would deny it, and it seemed enough just to acknowledge that there was a funder who for some reason was competing with Livingston Properties, Inc. I did tell them I had made a quick trip to the city to meet a representative of Livingston Properties, Inc., named Eliot Lucas, who had refused to tell me anything useful. I did not describe my effort to scam him. I did report the little I knew about Livingston Properties, Inc., and about the apparent disbarment of Eliot Lucas.

"Contact information for Livingston Properties, Inc.?" Lopez said, her hands hovering over the laptop.

"I'll email it to you."

Her hands came to rest briefly. "Please also email contact information for Helen Hamilton and your friend Lisa. Oh, and Alan Thompson."

"Okay."

"And getting back to Livingston Properties, Inc.," she said. "Bank accounts?"

"No idea," I said. "I'm not authorized to do that sort of thing."

"Of course you're not, but did you do it anyway?"

"No, I didn't." I did not tell her I didn't know how. "But maybe you'll do it," I said.

"One way or another," she said. "We have to know where the money comes from."

"That will be very useful," I said.

"Perhaps," she said. "Perhaps not. But we have to know."

Then she typed for a time, and finally said, "Enough for today."

Reilly stood up, looked at me, screwed up his mouth and shook his head, then left quickly.

Lopez looked up from her laptop and said, "Do me a favor?"

"Sure."

"We've talked about what we know. Now I'd like to re-view any hypotheses that might make sense of what we know. Would you take a few minutes and write down and email to me what you have in mind as possible hypotheses."

"You're assigning *homework*?"

She simply nodded. "If you would. I'll get Reilly's thinking another way, but if you would email me…"

"Okay, sure."

We exchanged email addresses. I went home and wrote a summary.

My hypothesis is (1) that someone wants to acquire the 80 acres of Tivoli Park from the city; (2) that to pressure the city to sell the land, this someone is trying to persuade the public that Tivoli is a dangerous place, a threat to law and order, and a burden for city government; (3) that for this purpose this someone has hired at least two hoodlums to kill and maim a series of victims and leave them in the park – with the identity of these victims being completely ir-relevant to this someone; (4) that, free to choose their own victims, the hoodlums first did the easy thing, appropriating a victim that may already have been killed by the OGK, and that, thereafter, they seized the opportunity to attack sexually attractive young women; and (5) that the someone who wants to acquire the preserve has be-gun buying up other properties that border or face the open land so as to better control the interface between the park and the neighbor-hood. We don't know what this someone's intended use for the land is, but it is rumored that a casino is planned.

It wasn't very useful. I hadn't really got beyond the easy generalizations. I spent a few more minutes thinking of all the *ifs* and *on-the-other-hands* that could be added, but I decided not to bother with these and sent the paragraph to Lopez as it was.

I then checked the Albany Times on line and found two letters to the editor on the subject of a possible casino in Tivoli Park. One writer thought it was a great idea, the very thing that Albany needed to generate tax revenue, create jobs, and "finally give this place a little class." The other writer thought it was a horrible idea, the kind of thing that would promote all sorts of criminal activity, suck money out of the pockets of Albany's residents and "destroy the good character of this historic city."

The day was even hotter than the day before, and by five-thirty I was even readier for a cold martini in Lisa's air conditioned apartment than I had been the day before.

Greeting me at the door, Lisa said, "You forgot to bring gin."

"So gin is now required every time I come?" I hope you still have some of the last bottle left."

"There's plenty left, but the price of admission is going up nonetheless."

"Inflation?"

"Have to take my profit when I can. The rumor mill won't always do as well as it has lately. Of course if you have rumors of your own to share, I could give you a discount."

"I have amazing *facts* to share."

"Oh well then, go make us some martinis."

I made the drinks and brought them into the living room where she had settled on the sofa. I sat in my regular chair.

"So tell me some amazing facts," she said.

"First of all, our rumor mill is making life difficult for Detective Reilly. He's started to hear from the chief, who's started to hear from the mayor. There's pressure to investigate both the casino rumor and the facts of the property purchases around the park. Whereas Reilly wants to concentrate on the pieces of evidence relating directly to the specific victims and possible specific killers."

"I'm sure it's a problem for a working cop. But you're not amazing me yet."

"Okay, well, Reilly has an amazing new person working on the case with him." I proceeded to describe the meeting with Giselle Lopez.

"Is she smart or merely amazing?" Lisa said.

"At first I suspected she was all style and no substance, but now I'm not sure. She's certainly direct. She gave me a homework assignment."

"Huh?"

I described the assignment.

"Can I see what you wrote?"

"Sure. I'll forward it to you. It doesn't amount to much. When she asked me to do it, I sort of thought I would have more to say, but what I came up with was more or less the same stuff we've been going around and around with for a while now. But it's kind of nice to be dealing with a cop who is interested in finding a hypothesis that would explain the whole set of things that are going on. And who is smart with computers. She may be able to learn a lot more than either Reilly or I have about certain things – like where Livingston Properties' money comes from."

"So this person – whatever she turns out to be worth – is what we've accomplished with our rumor mill."

"We should continue to stir the pot, but, yeah, she's what the rumors have produced so far."

"I'm not so sure about more pot-stirring – at least around the casino idea. We started out to look for information from inside city government, and I stumbled on the one odd little piece of information from Jean – about the guy who asked her what she thought of the casino idea. But it hasn't led any-where. And what we've done now is just create these rumors that give the media something to speculate about but don't get us any closer to the truth."

"Yeah, we still know nothing for certain about what's go-ing on behind the scenes."

"Which leaves the rumors looking groundless and far-fetched. I mean it's going to be a couple of years, at the very least, before it will be clear whether a casino will even be le-gally possible. How credible is it that someone would be doing these horrendous things *now*, just *in case* they want to buy the preserve several years from now?"

"Not very credible," I admitted. "They would at least have to have a plan B."

"A pretty solid, profitable plan B. In fact if anyone's think-ing casino at all it would have to be as a kind of wild card alter-native or supplement to something much more predictable."

"Another brainstorm?" I suggested.

She raised her empty glass. "Can't brainstorm on just one drink."

I went to the kitchen and made two more drinks – one of them all gin, the other a conventional martini.

When I returned and gave her the martini, she said, "Remind me why we're talking about all these crazy possible uses for that land but not talking about housing."

"Housing did come up in our brainstorm," I said. "Both high-end and low-end, I believe."

"Scratch low-end. But high-end? Maybe an exclusive gated community?"

"In a future where the price of gas can only continue to rise and where living in some Saratoga County subdivision is going to be less viable, less attractive… It doesn't sound like a bad investment."

"So do housing developers and sub-dividers go around killing people in order to get the land they want to develop or subdivide?"

"I believe it could happen," I said.

"Yes, I'm afraid it's credible – though I was hoping for something more exciting."

"Well, let me tell you what happened last week. I received a note telling me to stay out of Tivoli Park and stay out of things that aren't my business, or something bad would happen to my next-door, thirteen-year-old friend Jesse."

"Shit! Not that kind of excitement." She stared at me. "But you're *not* staying out of it."

"I took Jesse to Ithaca to stay with Ronnie for a while."

"But even so… I can't believe you're still doing this."

"I'm not doing that much – and the whole thing is complicated. I'm convinced that the little I'm doing is best for Jesse in the long run."

"You *would* think that. But I'm afraid I just lost my appetite for helping you do things that aren't your business."

"Okay. I understand. I won't ask any more of you." I stood up. "It's been fun, though – doing this sort of thing with you again."

She got up and followed me to the door. "Yes it's been fun."

We found ourselves standing awkwardly at the door, facing each other, not quite knowing how to say goodbye. Finally she said, "Can I have a hug?"

We hugged. "You stubborn old mule," she said.

I went home. I hadn't finished my gin at Lisa's, so I got out the bottle of fancy whiskey Goodwin had given me. I poured a shot over a glassful of ice and took it out to my steps, leaving the door open behind me.

I was feeling bad about Lisa, and more generally bad about my own clumsy failure to think through the consequences of what I was doing. My "stirring-the-pot" metaphor, I decided, was just a way of justifying the lack of a real plan.

Or maybe I was just tired. Since returning from Ithaca, I'd been staying up late, trying to get some work done, and I hadn't been sleeping well in my overheated bedroom. It would be at least two more days before I could get back to Ithaca, but I wished I could leave right away.

27

In the morning I had emails from both Lisa and Sergeant Lopez. The one from Lisa made me feel a little better about the way our evening together had ended.

Forgot to tell you yesterday… I was in the records office again yesterday morning and checked for new Tivoli perimeter transactions. Found one more on Livingston, bought by Livingston Properties a week ago. Didn't seem right to keep it from you even though it will just help you get into trouble.

The note concluded with the address of the property.

For her part, Lopez had wasted no time in backtracking the money that funded Livingston Properties' purchases. Her email was addressed to me and Reilly.

LP Inc. has only a checking account in which they keep a minimal balance. Funds are transferred into it electronically from an entity called Excalibur Corp, and within several days most is transferred out, mostly to attorneys' escrow accounts in Albany The most recent was a week ago. There have also been some cash withdrawals, one for $10,000. Now researching Excalibur.

I sent her a reply saying Lisa had confirmed another LP Inc. purchase a week earlier.

As I was sending it, another email dropped into my inbox, a brief note from Ronnie with two more photos attached for Jesse's mother – Jesse gnawing on a barbecued rib and looking happy, Jesse holding a plastic bucket on the edge of a wide marsh and looking stoical. I printed the photos. Because I was feeling restless and wanted an excuse to get out of my office for a while, I took them next door and slid them under the door for Mina.

Then, because I was already out of my office, I took a walk up Judson and over on Livingston to look at Livingston Properties' most recent acquisition. Located on the south side of the street, facing the park to the north, it was an older, narrow wood-frame house with a more recent addition in the rear. Still more recently, the whole house had been wrapped in grey vinyl siding. Now sheets of unpainted particle board had been nailed over the windows. It was easy to believe that someone who had expensive plans for the park's 80 acres would want this not particularly attractive house – and many others like it – cleared from the area.

As I circled back toward home – down Quail and around on Clinton to Robin – I began to hear distant thunder in the west, raising some hope for a break in the hot weather.

Back in my office I found another email from Lopez, who was moving right along with things.

Excalibur has total assets of about $500 M., most of it in real estate in the US plus some in the Caribbean. Operation is very highly leveraged. See attached balance sheet. Corporation is privately held, apparently mostly if not entirely by one family. Half the board of directors are named Endicott, including CEO Henderson Endicott. Know more about them soon.
The corp was a major client of Eliot Lucas before his disbarment.

It seemed that the most practical thing for me to do now would be just to let Lopez do what she was so obviously good at doing before I tried to do anything further on my own. I was left waiting for rain and waiting for Lopez. But in the meantime she'd sent me a balance sheet to look at.

I had no idea how she'd got hold of it, whether legally or otherwise, but it was a relatively detailed account of Excalibur's financial position, itemizing major assets and liabilities as of the end of the previous year. As she had said, there was a lot of real estate. Among the real property holdings listed, there were several large leaseholds in southwestern New York State which had been booked for millions of dollars. It seemed possible, if not likely, that the leases were related to natural gas that could be extracted from that region's shale, but only through hydrofracking, which could only be done if the State of New York decided to allow it.

As Lopez had also said, the business was highly leveraged. Total mortgage liabilities amounted to more than $490 million. There was less than one million in current assets, with less than a quarter million of that in cash, which meant that more borrowing would be required if the business was going to fund many more Livingston Properties purchases, let alone fund the acquisition and development of 80 acres.

It appeared to be a very precarious operation. The major real estate investments could each result in either big profits or big losses. If the value of the western New York leaseholds depended on hydrofracking and if hydrofracking was legalized then those leaseholds might be worth many times their book value. If hydrofracking was prohibited, they would probably have little or no value. Overall, if too many investments were big losers and not enough were big winners, the company would be unable to continue servicing its debt and unable to get new loans.

It was not hard to believe that a company engaged in such speculative investments – where the future value of the assets would depend so heavily on circumstances beyond its control – might be reckless enough to try to buy Tivoli Park and might in the meantime be buying neighboring properties. Even the casino scenario was suddenly more credible.

I was excited. I found myself wanting to forward the balance sheet to Lisa, who would find it as fascinating as I did. A few days previously I would have sent it to her, but that no longer seemed appropriate. In any case, it was Lopez, not Lisa, who had come up with this information. And it was to Lopez that I needed to respond.

Sergeant Lopez, I'm impressed. Really useful stuff. I'm especially interested in those western New York leaseholds. Assuming they are about gas wells, they have value ONLY if the state allows hydro-

fracking – just as Tivoli Park might have significant value only if the state legalizes gaming and the city agrees to sell the park for that purpose.

I cc'd the message to Reilly and sent it off. I wasn't sure that Reilly made a practice of reading his email regularly, but Lopez obviously did and it felt good to be dealing with her in the way that I did most of my work, which was a matter of sending, receiving, and discussing documents through this electronic medium – not a matter of sitting at a desk with a phone in one hand while the other hand sorted through piles of paper.

A few minutes later I got a reply from Lopez.

Yeah. But the oil shale investments may be ones that will actually pay off. I'm looking now at ones that won't. For instance one of the Vegas properties appears to be a failed subdivision development. Probably no way to salvage it in that market – total loss – but looks like it's still booked at cost (millions in costs). A couple of similar ones in Florida. If an auditor insisted on marking this portfolio to market value, the balance sheet would probably look like a tsunami went through it.

I replied.

So these guys have got to be pretty desperate.

She replied.

And some Endicotts are bailing. More later.

I was awed by how much she was learning and how fast. There was no point in trying to keep up with her until the flood of information diminished. It felt like it was time to get out of the house again for a while. I also thought it might be time for another talk with Bob Goodwin. I decided to walk over to Livingston again and see if he was home.

The thunder storm I'd heard approaching earlier had passed to the north of Albany. Troy might have got a good soaking but Orange Street's brick pavement was still hot and dry. Once again there was distant thunder in the west, but I feared that this storm, too, would slide past on the north and leave me still waiting for a break in the heat.

Goodwin's apartment, however, was air conditioned. He welcomed me graciously, as usual, and offered iced tea, which I gratefully accepted. We sat at his dining table. An open book lay turned over on the table. Goodwin saw me eying it and asked, "Ever read Montaigne?"

"No. I've seen quotes from time to time that made me think I might like him, but I'm afraid most of what I actually get around to reading is project proposals and that kind of thing."

"A wonderful mind," he said. "You ought to try an essay or two."

"Probably a much more pleasant way to spend a summer afternoon than what I've been doing."

"I'm sure your work does keep you busy."

"It would keep me reasonably busy if I could concentrate on it. As it is, work's piling up as I flounder around in this Tivoli Park stuff."

"Ah," he said. "And no doubt that's what you'd like to talk about. Any new information?"

"A lot of it. The police department now has a very smart person doing on-line research relating to some of what's going on here – such as the way Livingston Properties, Inc., is being funded. She's only been on it for a day but she's already come up with a ton of information."

"Ah." He raised his eyebrows but said no more.

"Livingston Properties is controlled, and its purchases are funded by a company called Excalibur Corp. It's privately held – apparently a family-owned corporation. A number of board members are named Endicott. You may know this – or some of it – already."

He inclined his head in a way that was almost a nod. "I do know some members of the Endicott family. In general they are decent people."

"Their company is looking very shaky. They've made a number of speculative real estate investments that are likely to lose them a lot of money."

"I don't wish the company to fail," he said.

"But you are clearly trying to block their effort to gain control of properties around Tivoli Park."

"I don't want to see the preserve developed. As you've discovered, I've been trying to discourage the kind of investment in this area – by Excalibur or anyone else – that would facilitate the conversion of the preserve. Otherwise I wish Excalibur well."

"I admire what you're doing," I said. "But how well do you know the Endicotts?"

He gazed steadily at me. "I know what you're thinking," he said. "But there's no necessary link between those plans for the preserve and the murder victims who've been found there."

"No proven link as yet. But reason to suspect a link."

He continued to gaze at me in silence, until finally he said, "I suppose this is something that computer researcher can discover, so I will tell you now. It will make it easier for you and me to understand each other. My ex-wife is now married to Henderson Endicott. We were divorced some years ago – a friendly parting of our ways – and she married Henderson a year later. I thought she was making a mistake, but it was no longer any of my business. I don't want to see her hurt, and I don't particularly want her and Henderson to know that I'm the one funding Alan Thompson's acquisitions."

"I appreciate your telling me. I did sort of guess when we talked the other day that you were protecting someone, and it's good to know who that is."

"As you, too, have been protecting someone."

I thought I now owed him at least a brief explanation. "In my case the someone is a thirteen-year-old boy, a neighbor to whom I've been sort of a big brother for some time. I'm afraid he's been drawn into the margins of some gang activity and has come to know some things relating to the murders that put him at risk."

"Thank you," he said. "You don't need to tell me more."

"And you would probably rather not tell me more about Henderson Endicott. But you did say you thought it was a mistake for your ex-wife to marry him…"

"There isn't much I can say. He is of course the CEO of Excalibur and the driving force behind its investments. He is a risk-taker. He has made some brilliant investments and some very bad ones – and, I must say, some investments that made money for Excalibur but that I have disapproved of. And I

admit that I do not like the man – charming and persuasive as
he may be."

"Thank you. That says quite a lot." I stood up. "I should
get back to my desk."

"Perhaps you should take the afternoon off and read some
Montaigne – or at least take a good long walk and contemplate
the wider world."

I went home, ate a sandwich on my front steps, then went
upstairs to my hot office and checked my email. There was
nothing further from Lopez, but I sent a note to her and Reilly,
reporting what I had just learned about the marriage of Goodwin's ex-wife to Henderson Endicott and Goodwin's character-
ization of the man. I also thought I'd better report Goodwin's
role in funding Alan Thompson's acquisitions before Lopez
discovered it on her own – if she hadn't already. I said that
he had "finally tacitly acknowledged" that he was the one. It
was now more than tacit acknowledgement, but I was hoping
to avoid blame for not reporting earlier what I had already
become convinced of.

I also asked Lopez what she had meant by saying Endicotts
were bailing.

I sent the email and then forced myself to put in several
hours of work on an over-due proposal.

A five o'clock I checked my email again and found a note
from Lopez to me and Reilly.

*Re. bailing: Henderson E. is buying up stock from some other mem-
bers of the family for pennies on the dollar of original value. Can
we meet at 9:00 AM tomorrow to talk about new information. Let
me know if not possible.*

I replied that it was possible. Then I went out, loaded my
solo canoe on the pickup, and drove to Peebles Island, where I
launched into the Hudson at the foot of the island.

I paddled upstream against a moderate current and was
soaked with sweat before I reached the big island. I made my
way up along the island's east shore, then swung westward
among the smaller islands and dropped back downstream to

a sandbar on the big island's west shore, where I beached the canoe. I then waded out into the brisk current and sat down on the gravel bottom, leaned back and let the river rinse the sweat from my clothes.

On my way back down the river to Peebles Island, the thunderstorm I'd been wishing for finally caught up with me. There were a few hailstones, but mostly it was just five minutes of cold hard rain, colder than the river. By the time it was over I was looking forward to getting warm again.

28

In the morning there was an AT letter to the editor from Helen Hamilton.

To the Editor: I have just a few things I want to say about recent events in Tivoli Park as someone who has lived in the West Hill neighborhood all my life. First, the murders are tragic, and I'm sure everyone agrees those responsible must be brought to justice. But I am not writing to tell the police how to do their work, which they know how to do better than any of us letter writers. I am writing because I fear for the future of my neighborhood and the open space that our children have enjoyed for generations.

The efforts by an absentee investor to buy up all available property around Tivoli Park are disturbing. These homes, now being left empty and boarded up, are being removed from the stock of moderately priced housing available to local families who would like to buy a home for themselves. These are homes on our land, and the land is being taken away from us to serve some outsider's purpose. The homes are all around the edge of Tivoli Park. We would be stupid not to think they are being bought up because of plans someone has for the park. We would also be stupid to think those plans are for something that would be shared with us in the neighborhood. I think it is clear they want us out of the way.

Our neighborhood has some problems, but it also has some special assets, and one of those assets is Tivoli Park, which gives us a natural open space at our doorsteps. Many people in this neighborhood have happy childhood memories of racing their bikes on the trails or building their own huts and hideouts in the woods. It doesn't make a big difference to me whether development of the

park would be for a gambling casino or luxury housing or whatever.
What I care about is saving the preserve and saving the neighbor-
hood.

-- Helen Hamilton, Executive Director, Neighborhood Housing
Association

I called Helen and congratulated her on her letter before I
headed off to meet with Reilly and Lopez.

The meeting was held in the same interrogation room as
the first meeting. When I arrived, Sergeant Lopez was already
seated at the table with her laptop open in front of her. I asked
her whether she had seen Helen's letter and whether she had
contacted her yet.

"It is an excellent letter," Lopez said. "I will see her later
today and I will tell her so." For a moment her fingers moved
rapidly on the laptop's keys, as though she was making a note
to herself about something that had just occurred to her. Then
she said, "Detective Reilly will be here in a few minutes, but
tell me... Your conversation with Robert Goodwin...?" She
turned toward me and raised her elegant eyebrows.

"Yes, I took the opportunity to visit him yesterday afternoon."

"As soon as you got my emails. You wasted no time." The
eyebrows were still elevated.

"I hope you're not thinking I rushed over to warn him
about what you were finding. It was just that what you'd
learned left me wanting to do the one thing I was positioned
to do – to take the next step with the peculiar series of conversations I've been having with Bob Goodwin these last few
weeks."

"What did you tell him about my research?"

"Only that it had identified Excalibur Corp as the source
of funding for Livingston Properties, Inc., and that Excalibur
appeared to be a family-owned business – with the family being named Endicott."

"You didn't mention the balance sheet..."

"No. You had labeled it confidential."

"All right. As you could probably guess, Detective Reilly
doesn't think I should be sharing so much information with a
civilian. But you have learned certain things on your own, and
I want to know what you've learned *and* what you can tell me

about the things I've already learned. It would be ridiculous to keep your information and my information in separate silos for form's sake. That's not how I operate. I'm sharing and I expect you to share. And be discrete. So, now would you tell me about this series of conversations." Her hands hovered over the keys.

So I gave her a summary of my Goodwin conversations, from our first meeting in the park after the first body was found, up to the recent conversations when he had acknowledged funding Alan Thompson's acquisitions and admitted that his ex-wife was married to Henderson Endicott. "At first I had no idea what to make of him," I said. "No idea of whether to take anything he said seriously. But that has gradually changed as I've gotten to now him."

"You believe what he says now?"

"I'm more inclined to believe him now that he's given me a reason to understand his unwillingness to tell me certain things before. Of course if you're going to tell me your research indicates he was never married to that woman…"

"No, I'm not going to tell you that. I haven't checked that, but I have checked his financial situation. He appears to have substantial wealth – most of it apparently invested in socially screened mutual funds."

"He lives very modestly…"

"I assumed as much from his Livingston Avenue address."

"But he does buy expensive books and expensive liquor."

"I'm going to interview him this morning. Thank you for the background. And, by the way, yesterday I met your friend Raymond. An interesting guy. Also I interviewed Alan Thompson."

"A nice guy," I said. "Makes a good Santa Clause."

She gave me a brief noncommittal look and said nothing. When Reilly came in a minute later she was once again busy typing.

Reilly carried a file folder, which he opened on the table as he sat down.

"You have something for us, Detective?" Lopez asked.

"One guy's prints identified. The big guy. Ronald Worcheski, last known residence Brooklyn. Two convictions for drug possession, one for carrying a concealed weapon, one for assault. One for rape. Served seven years for the rape conviction.

Released from Great Meadows six months ago. Various aliases. One is *Tank*."

"Nothing on the other guy yet?" I asked.

"The big guy's prints were all over the duct tape in both sites. If someone else's prints were there with them, they were too smeared to do us any good."

"So the big guy does the manual labor," Lopez said. "And it's hard to say what the other guy does, except that he's said to be the one in charge."

"Also hard to say what he looks like, but the big guy should be easy. NYPD says he's not real clever and usually not real hard to find. They'll ask around, and we'll keep an eye out in Albany. See anyone six-eight, three hundred pounds, we'll check him out. And when we find him, he's going to tell us who his partner is. Whole thing may not be too hard to unwind now."

"Except the whole thing includes finding who's been paying these guys," Lopez said. "And they probably don't know where the money's coming from. They would know how it's delivered, and they might know the delivery boy, but that's probably all."

"If anyone's paying them at all," Reilly said. "For all we know they're a couple of psychos operating on their own."

"A *team* of psychos?" Lopez said. "I don't think so."

Reilly shrugged.

"We have suspects," Lopez said. "Excalibur Corp. The Endicott family. One Endicott in particular. We have large cash withdrawals from Livingston Properties' bank account. And we need to interview Eliot Lucas as soon as possible. He could be our delivery boy, or at least know where that cash was going. I'd like to go to the city today and find him." She looked at Reilly, who shrugged again.

She closed her laptop, and the meeting ended.

I went back to my house ready to do a good day's work before leaving for Ithaca at the end of the day. The storm that had caught me on the river the day before had missed Albany, but another had finally found us in the middle of the night. I'd had to get up and close my windows for the first time in more than a week. A half hour later I got up and opened them again and let the rain-washed air blow through the house. Now I was able to sit comfortably at my desk without even needing a sweat towel around my neck. It was the first solid-feeling day's work I'd been able to accomplish all week.

At six o'clock I made some sandwiches to eat on the road, gathered up the cookies and clean clothes that Mina had brought over for me to take to Jesse, and set off for Ithaca.

29

When I arrived at ten o'clock, Jesse was asleep. Ronnie got out the Jack Daniel's from the previous weekend. We sat at the kitchen table, sipped bourbon, and grinned at each other for a while.

"I feel like I've just come home," I said.

"And this place isn't even my home, let alone yours."

"Maybe home isn't a place after all."

"But sooner or later there does need to be a place to *put* it," she said.

"Yeah, I guess there does – whether it's a little cabin in the woods or a little house in the city."

"But lately I've been thinking about that a little differently. I'd like to talk about it. But not now. A long talk is not what I'm in the mood for, but first tell me how it's going in Albany."

"No, first you tell me how it's going in Ithaca for you and Jesse."

"It's going okay. Jesse's a little homesick at times, but he likes exploring the campus – alone and with me. He's full of questions about how the place works – everything from who's in charge of this whole thing, as he put it, to what do students do between classes, can they just do anything they want?" Also he's been playing basketball in the little park down the street with some local kids he seems to have hit it off with. They call him Jay-Jay. It seems there's a Cornell player named Jesse Jones who gets called Jay-Jay. He likes that."

"And for you, how is this arrangement working?"

"Well I'm not the footloose Ronnie I used to be. But then I haven't really been footloose since I came here to Cornell, and in some ways it feels good to have another person around that I'm sort of responsible for. And it gets you down here every weekend. So all in all it's a pretty good arrangement. Now tell me quick what's happening in Albany, and then we can go to bed."

"But it feels so good to just sit here looking at you and thinking about going to bed with you, and not thinking about Albany at all."

"Okay, Albany can wait."

In the morning, as the three of us ate pancakes and bacon at the kitchen table, I summarized recent Albany events, starting with Raymond's role in telling the police about Switch and Tank.

"I been worrying about that," Jesse said. "I didn't know how you going to tell them that stuff without telling 'em who told you."

"I worried about it too," I said. "I wasn't going to tell them you told me, so I asked Raymond to help me work out some story about how I heard that stuff on the street. But he pointed out that I talk too much and I'm not a very good liar and he could do it much better. So he did. And I owe him."

"Me too," Jesse said solemnly.

"And now, with the fingerprints," I said, "it looks like they could be close to catching up with the big guy, either in the city or in Albany."

"Sure hope they get the other one too," Jesse said. "The real bad one."

"He may be a lot harder to find. The police don't have fingerprints. They don't really know what he looks like. From what you said about him, it doesn't sound like he'd stand out in a crowd – unless you can think of anything else about him that would help identify him."

"I been trying to think ever since I told you, but he's just kind of regular, most ways. Not real tall, not real short. Not real fat or skinny. Ordinary kind of haircut – no cornrows or dreadlocks, no beard or anything."

"And no scars of any sort?"

"Nuh-uh. But there's his eyes."

"What about his eyes?"

"Just you can't look into 'em. Don't know what it is. Maybe you just don't *want* to see what's in there."

"Scary idea," Ronnie said.

"Yeah. Hope I never see him again."

"If they can find the big guy," I said, "they're hoping they can get him to identify the other guy, so they can go after him."

"They get both of 'em, I can go home."

"I hope so," I said. "We still have to worry about whoever's been paying those two guys to do all this horrible stuff. But at least there are some real suspects now, real people with real names." I gave them a quick summary of what Sergeant Lopez had learned. "And at the rate she's going I think we're going to know more soon."

Ronnie stood up, gathered our plates from the table and put them in the sink. "Real progress, then. Think we're going to be able to get Jesse home by Labor Day and the start of school?"

"That's the goal."

Jesse got up, ran water into the sink and began scrubbing the plates.

"Look at him," Ronnie said. "I always wanted a dishwasher. Now that I finally got one, I don't think I'll want to let him go."

"You going to have to move to Albany then," Jesse said.

"You mean if I move in with Crow, you'd come next door every day and do our dishes?"

"We could talk about it."

"You mean we'd have to negotiate? Wages, vacation time, all that?"

"Probably some union I could join, too."

"Oh," she said. "I don't know then."

"Jesse," I said, "now look what you've done. Now she'll probably make *me* wash the dishes."

"She move in with you, it's the least you could do," he said.

"Good thinking, Jesse. If I move in with him, maybe I can get you to negotiate terms for me. Maybe you could get him to agree to do all the cooking *and* wash all the dishes."

"Don't know if you want him cooking for you though. Mostly he just eats those subs from Subway. Don't think he knows how to cook most stuff."

Ronnie laughed.

"Be real nice if you did move in though."

"Thank you, Jesse. I might discuss it with him – see if he'd let me. But first we have to get you moved back into your own house with your own mom."

"Yeah."

When he'd finished the dishes, the three of us went out and walked down the street to the basketball court in the little park. There was just one kid there, but he had a ball. He was shooting long jump shots that were flying wide off the rim, so he was getting a pretty good workout chasing the ball down after each shot.

"Thinks he going to be a three point man," Jesse said. "Not showing much yet, though."

"Hey Jay-Jay," the kid said. "How 'bout a little one-on-one?"

"Sure," Jesse said. "Or how 'bout you and me take on this big guy. See if he's any good."

They ran circles around me of course. I was taller, but they were far quicker. I hadn't touched a basketball in at least ten years, and the ball seemed to have got a lot heavier in that time. It didn't feel right. My shots fell short. I was relieved when two more kids arrived and I had an excuse to take myself out of the game.

Ronnie and I then sat on a bench in the shade.

"He's pretty feisty today," she said. "Because you're here and he has a good time picking on you. When it's just me, he feels he has to be more polite."

"Well you've been pretty feisty today yourself. Between the two of you I don't stand a chance. Nonetheless, if you want to move in with me…"

"Well certainly not right away. But this gets us to what I wanted to talk about. I've been thinking more and more that I do want to live with you. Like permanently. When I finish my course work here."

"It's what I want too. The sooner the better. And I *will* wash dishes, and even cook, sometimes."

"But we've still got the problem we've talked about before. You have a life in Albany. You like living where you live. And I like it there too. I like visiting you there. But I'm afraid I'm just not a city girl at heart. I just can't picture myself living fulltime and permanently in an urban place. But I also hate the idea of hauling you up by the roots and making you live somewhere else."

"You wouldn't really be hauling me up by the roots. I'm not that rooted. In some ways I'm just a sojourner in the city."

"Okay, but as I said last night I've been thinking about a kind of alternative, and I've even done a little online research." She turned and looked at me and shook her head. "And now I'm all of a sudden feeling shy about telling you."

"But now you *have* to tell me."

"Well, okay, I've been thinking about where we took Jesse fishing on the Hoosick River. I really liked that river, that area. But I don't know how you feel about it... you grew up there... and sometimes there's that feeling you don't want to end up just where you started."

"No, in fact I've been fantasizing lately about someday having a place with you somewhere like that."

Her face lit up. "Well I've been thinking maybe *someday* doesn't have to be that far off. I've been thinking maybe we could find a piece of land, maybe with some kind of housing on it, or maybe we could just do a tent platform. You could keep the Orange Street house, and work there, and spend as much time there as you wanted, and I could spend some time there too. But we'd also have this place out in the country. And maybe someday we could build a real house on it..."

"So you've been doing some online research? Maybe looking at real estate listings?"

"As a matter of fact, yeah, I have."

"And maybe you've found something?"

"Well there is this one place... On River Road between Buskirk and Eagle Bridge. It's ten acres, mostly woods, with an old mobile home on it. I haven't seen it of course and the photos on the website aren't very good, but I can show you what I've got. And maybe you could go look at it when you're back in Albany."

We told Jesse where we were headed, and went back to the apartment.

Ronnie lifted several printouts from the top of the refrigerator and spread them on the kitchen table. One of them was a satellite photo showing the river with the road beside it. North of the road there were woods, with a small clearing, and in the middle of the clearing a tiny white patch that we presumed was the mobile home.

Another printout contained three photographs – two of them views of woods and river, one a view of what was described as a mobile home.

"It's really pretty crappy," Ronnie said. "Really more like an old travel trailer than a mobile home."

"Which might be for the best," I said. "If we wanted to use it temporarily there would be less to clean up and repair, and if we wanted to get rid of it, it would be easier to haul off."

"Anyway the location looks promising," she said. "And it's affordable."

"But maybe hard to finance. We couldn't get a home mortgage loan, or any sort of commercial loan. I'm not sure where we *would* get a loan."

"But we wouldn't need a loan. I mean I have this embarrassing but very useful trust fund. I would love to use some of it to buy us a piece of land. And if your scruples get in the way of that, well, I'll *sort of* understand, but I'll be really disappointed."

"It could be just in your name, and we could still use it together."

"No, absolutely not. If we do it, both of our names have to be on the deed. I won't do it any other way. And I hope you understand why it has to be that way."

I did understand. "Actually," I said, "I love the idea of having my name on a deed with yours – if not for this place then for some other."

We had remained standing hip-to-hip, gazing down at the printouts on the table. She turned toward me now, and I turned toward her, and we held each other for a while.

"I'll call the realtor Monday," I said. "I'll go look at it and take lots of photos. And if this isn't the right place, well, we can have a lot of fun looking at lots of other possible places this fall."

That night in bed, she said, "I can't help feeling like we've just decided to get married."

"We could do that too," I said.

"Maybe at some point, but this feels a lot more important than just some ceremony you go through just to get some kind of institutional approval for being together. This is more fundamental."

"Yes, sharing a place is fundamental. And we're not the only ones where male and female create a nest or a den together."

"But I think it's usually the female that chooses the site," she said, "at least with birds."

"But usually she does it within a territory established by the male."

"So we're doing it exactly the right way."

"Yes, although there are other ways, too."

"Such as?"

"Well the male sunfish makes a nest all by himself. I've seen one doing it, clearing a circular spot on the bottom of the pond, clearing away little stones and pieces of debris, in the hope that a female will come along and approve of his work and deposit her eggs there. If she does, then he fertilizes the eggs, and they go their separate ways and the eggs are on their own."

"So I'm glad we're not fish," she said, snuggling against me.

"I've been thinking about your friends Skinner and Pat," I said. "Did they ever get married?"

"I don't think so. It wouldn't be the kind of thing Skinner would do."

"So they just got a little piece of land and started building a log house together."

"Yeah. While living in an old trailer."

"Is it pure coincidence that we've decided to do the same thing?"

"Maybe not entirely."

On Sunday, the three of us visited Ronnie's Montezuma research site, then launched Ronnie's canoe in the Seneca River and gave Jesse a chance to do some fishing. He caught a pike, which we took back to Ithaca. We skinned and boiled the pike, then sat around the table carefully separating the y-bones from the fine white flesh, with which we made an excellent chowder.

After three large bowls of chowder, I was even less ready to leave for Albany than I would otherwise have been. I decided to spend another night and leave early in the morning.

30

I got to Orange Street at nine, opened the windows, started a pot of coffee, and went upstairs to my computer. There was an email sent Friday evening by Sergeant Lopez saying she had not gone to the city to interview Eliot Lucas. She had called the Manhattan number we had for Livingston Properties and talked to a woman – presumably the same woman I had talked to – who told her she had not seen Lucas in several days and had no idea where he might be found. She did not have a home address for him. Lopez had then contacted NYPD and asked them to try to locate him and to call her as soon as they had any information. There was no further message from her since the Friday email.

I went back downstairs and watched the coffee pot finish its work, then poured a cup and returned to my office.

I called the Hoosick Falls realtor who had listed the River Road property and arranged to meet her at the site at five that evening. Then I started a list of the past and pending work-related deadlines that I had to do something about. The list was only about half finished when the phone rang.

Reilly's voice said, "Get your ass over here."

"I beg your pardon."

"Right now. North Station."

"Why?"

"Tell you when you get here."

"I guess what you're trying to say is that something has happened and you think it is important to talk with me about it in person. Is that correct?"

"Another body in the park," he said.

"All right, I'll be over shortly."

I thought about going on with my work for a while and making him wait, but it would be hard to concentrate. I decided I might as well go talk with him now.

I found him at his desk.

"So another body was found this morning?" I asked. "Got any idea who it is?"

"No, but you might. Middle aged male. No ID on him. But a scrap of paper in his pocket had a phone number on it. I thought the number looked familiar, and I checked it out. It's your number."

"So I guess you want me to look at him."

"Start with the photos." He handed me a batch of 8x10 prints.

The photo on the top of the stack showed a man's body on its back. He was short, rather flabby, and mostly bald. There was blood on the front of his shirt. His head was turned away so I couldn't see his face. Then there were several other photos of the body and its immediate surroundings taken from different angles and distances. In some of them I could see the face, which looked familiar. There was then a close-up of the man's bloody chest. Then a close-up of the face.

"Shit," I said. "It's Eliot Lucas."

"The guy from the city Lopez is trying to find?"

"Yes, the man who might've known if those guys Switch and Tank were being paid to kill people up here. And maybe even who was paying them."

He picked up his desk phone and punched in a number. In a moment he said, "Crow's here. ID'd the body. You better come in."

In less than a minute Lopez appeared. "Who?" she said.

"Lucas" I said.

"You're certain?"

"I haven't seen the body, but yeah, this photo is definitely him."

"Shit," she said.

"Echo in here," Reilly said.

"Where'd you find him?" I asked.

"Let's go sit down and talk about this." Lopez jerked her thumb toward the door.

We went out and walked down the hall to the interrogation room and sat down at the table in what was becoming our habitual arrangement.

Reilly tossed the photos on the table and said, "Okay. So we found him on the dirt road, almost to where we found the last one – the second woman – but he could've been shot outside the park, or not. Like the first one, he was shot in the chest, big exit wound in the back, but he didn't bleed much in the place where we found him. Ears cut off. That's about it. But the big question is, what was he doing in Albany and why did he have Crow's number in his pocket?"

"Did he call you?" Lopez asked.

"No, but it's possible he tried to. I was away for the weekend."

"And no messages on your machine."

"No, not from him."

"Okay," Reilly said. "Suppose you tell us again about your meeting with him – exactly what was said."

"Every detail you can remember," Lopez said. "Whether you think it's important or not."

"Okay. We didn't talk for that long a time. We met in a place called Herm's Coffee shop."

"Not in Livingston Properties' office?" Lopez said.

"When we'd talked on the phone he described it as the place downstairs, and I assumed Livingston Properties did have an office in that building upstairs. But now I'm not sure. There's the woman who fields phone calls from somewhere in the city but I don't really know where. Maybe Herm's *is* the office."

"And how did you set up that meeting?" Lopez said. "What did you tell him you wanted to talk about?"

"I told him I knew Livingston Properties was buying everything they could get in that area around the park, and that I might be able to help them secure more properties."

"He must have wanted to know what specific properties. What did you tell him?"

"I identified the properties that Alan Thompson had purchased. But Lucas *knew* about those properties – knew Thompson had purchased them – so I told him I knew Thompson and could maybe broker their resale. I think from that point on he knew I was just on a fishing expedition, but he played along for a while. Both of us were fishing."

"Can you tell us exactly what you were fishing for?"

I was fishing for information about Livingston Properties – who was behind the corporation and why they wanted those properties. And Lucas was fishing for information about

Thompson's properties – and who was funding their purchase, and why."

"And you undertook this fishing expedition entirely on your own," Lopez said, "without bothering to tell this department what you were doing."

"That's correct. Your department hadn't shown any interest in those transactions at that time. If I'd learned anything significant from Lucas I would have reported it, but I didn't come home with much to report."

Lopez gazed steadily at me, then shook her head. I assumed she was frustrated by losing Lucas as a potentially important source of information, and was wishing she had been the one to have the conversation I was describing.

"So you're saying Lucas wanted to know why Alan Thompson – or his funder – wanted those properties. Is that correct?"

"Yes. In fact he asked why would *anyone* be investing in that kind of property in that area. I said I was puzzled in the same way by the investments in the neighborhood that Livingston Properties had made. He refused to explain Livingston Properties' investments, but he really did seem puzzled about why Thompson was buying."

"And what did you tell him?"

"I told him I thought Thompson was buying them for someone who just didn't want Livingston Properties to have them. I did try to lead him on by suggesting that Thompson might be willing to betray his funder and resell the properties if the price was right."

"You told him you could arrange that?"

"In vague terms."

"But he didn't bite?"

"He didn't really bite but he didn't really say no either."

"You think that could be why he had your phone number – because he was going to ask you to help him get those properties?"

"It's possible."

"Could that be why someone wanted him dead?"

"I don't know. But if he was skimming something for himself from the Albany purchases, and if Excalibur or the Endicotts found out about it…"

Lopez nodded. "And did the subject of the murders come up?"

"I made a point of it. I asked him what he knew, and told him I didn't want to get involved in any kind of deal that would get me killed. His response was 'So you're a cop?' When I denied it, he said, 'Yeah, you're too naïve to be a cop.'"

Reilly chuckled. Lopez kept her gaze fixed on me. "Do you think he did know something about the killings?"

"I think he did, but he certainly didn't admit it."

"So perhaps he was killed because he knew too much. If he was the go-between – between Excalibur and hired killers... or even if he wasn't the go-between but did know where that cash was going and why..."

"And especially if Endicotts assumed the police in Albany could be investigating the possible connection between Livingston Properties, Inc. and the murders, which you were, and if they thought you might talk to Lucas in the course of that investigation, which you were planning to do, and if he was the sort of guy who would talk to the police if he thought it was in his interest... and I think he was that kind of guy..."

"It fits," Lopez said. "They got to him before we did."

Reilly was sitting up straight now, fully engaged. "We know anything about family, friends, anyone who knew him? He didn't mention a wife or family of any sort, did he?"

"There's an ex-wife," Lopez said. "That's all I know, but I'll look some more, and see if NYPD can help." She stood up. Reilly gathered up the photos from the table in front of him.

I said, "Before you go, has there been any progress in locating the guy named Tank?"

Reilly shook his head. "Let you know when it's time for you to know. Right now you and I need to go to the morgue."

I persisted. "And have you had any luck finding someone who can identify the other guy?"

Reilly shook his head again, stood up and turned away. But Lopez paused at the door and looked back at me. "Couple of guys in jail awaiting sentencing who might tell us something, or not. Stay tuned."

Reilly took me to the morgue, where I confirmed the identity of the corpse. We said very little to each other in the process. Afterward he dropped me off at home, where I managed to get a few hours of work done.

At the end of the afternoon I drove to Troy, then on northward on Route 40 to Schaghticoke, and then east on Route 67 to Buskirk, where I crossed the river through the covered bridge and turned right on River Road. The property, with its little clearing and old trailer, was easy to spot. I parked just off the road, with the river down a moderate embankment on my right, and the clearing across the road on my left. The realtor arrived a few minutes later – a small, tidy woman driving a large SUV.

We walked up through the clearing to the trailer. She unlocked the door and I stepped in. She remained outside peering in. "It's in terrible shape," she said. "But I assume you're not mainly interested in this old thing. The location is lovely. The property will sell as a lovely building site."

I spent some time poking around amidst the trash that filled the place, trying to determine the condition of the trailer itself. I couldn't see any evidence that the roof had leaked, and as far as I could tell the floor was sound. The double bed in the small bedroom was a mess, but the ripped mattress could be replaced. The kitchenette had a small gas stove that would probably work if cleaned, and a small counter and sink in fair condition, though there was of course no water. All in all, the place was in better shape than I had feared it might be. It could be cleaned up and used – for however long we might want. I took a few photos for informational purposes.

As she relocked the trailer, the realtor said, "Well you're free to walk around all you want, and I'll be happy to answer any questions."

I asked about the boundaries. She was able to point out where east and west boundaries intersected the road but was unclear about how the back of the property was bounded – though she assured me that all of the clearing was within those bounds.

I asked who owned the land between the road and the river. Was it all part of the public right-of-way? Did some of it go with the property we were looking at? She said she thought some of it was right-of-way, but where the right-of-way didn't reach the river, then the space between should go with the property.

I said I would like to spend some time walking around and taking some photos, and that there was no need for her to stay. She said that she'd be happy to stay but wasn't really dressed for it, and that I should take all the time I wanted.

The clearing angled uphill into the woods. I walked up the slope through waist-high goldenrod, milkweed, joe-pie weed and blue asters. From the area furthest uphill the road was out of site, though I could see the glint of the river through the trees.

At the far uphill end of the clearing I found a spring that had been dug out and lined with stones some years earlier. Now it was partially filled with silt and the stones were beginning to tumble, but there was a modest little stream of water trickling from it and dispersing into a thick green mat of watercress. I scooped a double handful of water and tasted it. It was cold and good.

After taking a number of photos, I sat down by the spring and called Ronnie on the cell phone. I gave her a full description of the meadow and its vegetation, and the spring and watercress, and the encroaching woods.

"I can't wait to see it," she said repeatedly.

"I've got lots of photos to send you."

"If you were properly equipped for this work, you'd have an i-phone and you could be sending me photos as we talk."

"Sorry, the phone my girlfriend gave me is just a plain old cell."

"Except for one feature. But I guess she knew you're just a plain old guy who could only do one thing at a time. But never mind. I can probably wait a couple of hours for photos. But tell me more. The woods – what kind of woods?"

"Second growth hardwoods. Birch, ash, red maple." I studied the woods in front of me. "And I can see a black cherry, I think an aspen, an old apple. Most of it's a decent size for firewood. No really big trees. Except down by the river there are good-sized cottonwoods, and a couple of big sycamores."

There was silence at her end of the line. I imagined her picturing each tree I had named.

"All in all a pretty nice place," I said.

"Sounds like you like it."

"I'm really looking forward to showing it to you, and thinking about it with you. It's definitely something to think about."

"Having to wait is excruciating," she said.

"If you like the photos," I said, "we'll work out some way to get you up here by the weekend even if it means me being in Ithaca with Jesse while you're up here."

"You shouldn't have to do that. But, anyway, I'll be looking for the photos."

I walked down to the road and took more photos of the river bank and of the views up and down the river and up and down the road. Then I drove home. I downloaded all the photos to my computer and emailed them to Ronnie in several batches.

In no time at all there was a response:

Do I like the photos? I LOVE the photos. Only they don't show enough – because now I have to see all of it, absolutely everything.

PS Jesse wants to know how the fishing would be from that riverbank.

I was worried that we were both getting too excited too soon about this one place, before either of us had even considered any other place. Nonetheless, I fell asleep that night thinking about it.

31

In the morning, I awoke from a dream in which I'd been in a wooded place that at first seemed to be the place on River Road, except that something in these woods was not right. I'd then realized that I was not on River Road but in Tivoli Park, trying to figure out what it was in the woods that was not right. I knew it had something to do with two guys whose names I couldn't remember. It was the effort to remember the names that finally woke me up.

I was just pouring my first cup of coffee at six-thirty when the phone rang. I reached for the kitchen wall phone with my left hand as I took my first sip from the cup in my right hand.

"More bad news," Lopez said. "We need to talk right away. I'm at home – just leaving. Can you meet me at North Station?"

"Okay. In maybe ten minutes."

I dumped my cup of coffee into a travel mug and topped it off with more from the pot. Mug in hand, I went out, locked the door behind me, and turned to the right to walk down Orange Street to Henry Johnson Boulevard. My pickup was parked just down the street. As I passed it I realized that there was an envelope taped to the steering wheel.

I make a practice of leaving my pickup unlocked – on the theory that any skilled practitioner with a coat hanger could get a window open if they wanted to rifle my glove compartment in search of loose change or cigarettes. I opened the door, leaned in and pulled the envelope from the wheel and tore it open.

There was a sheet of paper inside that looked like the one Jesse had delivered more than a week earlier. And the clumsy writing was similar to the scrawl on the earlier note.

You were warned. We will get you and your friend Jesse unless you back off right now and stop talking to police. If you don't you will end up like the others.

I stood with one hand on the still-open door of the pick-up, trying to think as calmly as possible. I was already on my way to do more "talking to police." Was someone watching? Would they see me go into the North Station?

Did they know where Jesse was?

If talking to the police had meant talking only to Reilly, I think I might have just got into the pickup and got out of Albany. But talking to Lopez was different. I'd come to respect her intelligence, and I realized I needed to talk with her. Even if I was going to leave town I needed to be sure I'd given her every bit of information I had.

I closed the pickup door, pocketed the note, and walked, as fast as I could without running, down Orange Street toward Henry Johnson.

Lopez met me at the entrance to North Station, laptop under her arm, and led me once again to the interrogation room. It was barely seven o'clock. I was wearing the rumpled t-shirt and stained jeans I'd worn the day before, and no doubt I looked as frazzled as I felt. Lopez, however, looked as perfectly turned out and elegantly put together as ever. We sat down, she with a Starbucks cup, me with my old travel mug.

"Reilly's tied up," she said. "Dealing with another body."

"Not in the preserve!"

"In the preserve but just barely. Dumped over the gate onto the dirt road behind the school. I guess he was too big to lug further in. There probably wouldn't have been anyone big enough to do it anyway."

"How big are you talking about?"

"About six-eight, three hundred pounds, wearing a size 15 shoe. Sound familiar?"

"Tank?"

"They're checking his fingerprints now, but we're assuming it's him. Shot in the chest. Ears severed."

"Another one who knew too much, you think?"

"And who would probably be picked up sooner or later and couldn't be trusted to keep his mouth shut."

"So they've eliminated the two people who we thought could help us identify the guy named Switch and whoever was paying for the whole show."

"And their timing is good – almost as though they knew we'd started looking for those people. The question is how'd they know. Let's talk about the possibilities."

"Okay, but first…" I took the note from my pocket and slid it across the table to her. "I found that taped to the steering wheel of my pickup this morning as I was starting to walk down here."

She raised her eyebrows, unfolded the note, read it, and fixed her gaze on me. "Well, you are talking to the police."

"Yes I am."

"Who's your friend Jesse?"

I told her who Jesse was. I told her about the earlier threat, and that I'd taken Jesse to Ithaca.

"The obvious question is why didn't you report that to us at the time?"

"Okay, I'm going to tell you the whole story now. Maybe I should have reported all this earlier. I had my reasons not to, but now you need to know it all."

I started from the beginning – Jesse finding the first body and telling me he couldn't report it so I had to. I told her Jesse then didn't want to talk about anything related to what he'd found, and I said I'd started to worry about whether he and his compatriots might be involved on the fringes of gang activity, and whether that activity was somehow related to the murders.

Lopez had been listening in silence, but now said, "Jesse's black?"

I nodded.

She nodded. "Go on."

I told her about the conversation I'd had with Jesse on the way to Ithaca, including what he'd told me about Switch and Tank.

"Which, coincidentally," she said, "we learned from Raymond who, coincidentally, is your friend."

"Yes, coincidentally."

"You have an interesting set of friends – Jesse, Raymond, Lisa, Robert Goodwin. I've interviewed the last three. They were all careful not to say anything that would get you in trouble."

"Raymond and Lisa are old friends, and I sometimes use them as sounding boards when I need to sort things out."

"I believe Lisa is more than a sounding board – but no longer your girlfriend, right?"

"Right."

"You now have a girlfriend in Ithaca, with whom Jesse is staying."

"Yes."

"That was probably a good move, taking him there. You've made some other moves that weren't so good. But what we've got to deal with now is what we've got to deal with now."

She picked up the note and looked at it again. She put it back on the table and stared at the wall above my head for a time. Then she took a sip of coffee, then stared at the wall again.

Finally she said, "We were going to talk about how these people... or how at least one of them knows what he knows. And is it only one? And, if so, who? And how much does he know about what *you've* been doing?"

"The note doesn't sound like it was written by an Endicott," I said. "Maybe by the guy called Switch."

"If it's him, what he knows probably came from his own local observations or local sources, not from Endicotts. Unless Robert Goodwin is really on the Endicott's side."

"I'm absolutely certain he's not."

"Okay, we need to talk about him, but later. First let's look at what someone could know about you from the obvious sources, including the Albany Times."

"Anyone could read in the AT that I was the one who reported two of the bodies. A coincidence, but it did focus some attention on me."

"And someone *might* know about your conversation with Lucas."

"Not unless Lucas told someone – which he probably wouldn't have if he had any interest in dealing with me and taking a cut for himself."

"Okay. But if it's Switch he would know Jesse's friends, and it wouldn't be hard for him to learn from them that you're a friend of Jesse's."

"Right."

"Did any of those kids know Jesse was going to Ithaca?"

"There's no way they could know. Not unless he got in touch with one of them between 10:00 PM and 6:30 the next morning. And I'm sure he wouldn't have done that."

"But you're still worried about his safety there?" She picked up the note, then dropped it back on the table. "Of course you are."

"Yes I am."

"He'll probably be fine. The note doesn't say they know where he is. And anyway he's not a player. No one would gain anything by hurting him."

"They could kidnap him. Hold him hostage."

"That would complicate their situation unnecessarily. They don't need that, and they don't really need to put more pressure on you. You're a nuisance and an annoyance. They just want to back you off."

"But they're people who are responsible for five murders in the past few weeks. It seems their way of backing people off is to shoot them in the chest."

"However, your situation is completely different from Tank's or Lucas's. You may be helping the police – finally – but it's not like you know anything that can really hurt these guys."

"If they hurt Jesse…"

She shook her head. "Let's talk about Robert Goodwin. He is someone they might very well have reason to take out. In fact I'm not sure why they haven't already."

"It wouldn't be difficult," I said. "He still walks in the preserve most days, alone."

"If they know he's the one trying to block their property acquisitions… But they haven't gone after him…"

"Then maybe it's because Henderson Endicott would rather not kill his wife's ex-husband."

"Possibly. You said they're still on friendly terms…"

"Goodwin and his ex, yes, apparently. He admits not liking Henderson Endicott. He also said he didn't want either of them to know he was the one competing with them for property around the park."

"Do you think he already knew – before you told him – that it was Endicotts who were buying property in Albany? And if he did know does he also know *why* they are?"

"I don't know. He didn't seem surprised when I told him it was Excalibur that was funding Livingston Properties. But that may only mean he knew it was the kind of thing that Henderson Endicott *might* do."

"We need to get closer to Henderson Endicott. Goodwin's the one link we have. I need to talk with him again."

"I'd like to talk with him again myself," I said.

"He may actually be ready to tell you things he wouldn't tell me. But I'm not sure you'll press him hard enough. We could try talking with him together."

"I'm up for that."

"But not here, and not at his house."

"Maybe at Alan Thompson's office in Troy," I suggested.

"Okay. You want to call him now, set it up for today ASAP. Got a cell?"

"Not with me."

She produced her own cell phone, selected a name and made the call, then handed the phone to me. "Tell him it's urgent. You can mention the most recent killing, and the threatening note to you."

I did mention the most recent killing and the threatening message. I told him the police now believed that it was urgent to find and question Henderson Endicott and that they needed help.

He said he didn't see how he could help but of course he would be happy to meet with me and Sergeant Lopez. We arranged to meet at Thompson's office at 1:30 that afternoon.

I handed the phone back to Lopez. She then handed me a card with her phone numbers. "I want to be sure you have my cell number, and I need your cell number. And I want you to keep your cell on you and turned on at all times. We will be keeping your home under surveillance, and if there's anything suspicious, we want to know about it immediately. From now on, no freelancing. I mean absolutely none. You got that?"

"Okay. And is it possible to get the Ithaca police to keep an eye on the place where Jesse and my friend Ronnie are staying?"

"I'm going to make that call right away. I need her name and address and her cell number. As soon as I've talked with them I'll call you with a number you can give her, so if anything comes up she can call someone who'll know who she is and what she's talking about."

"I'm grateful." I gave her the information she needed, which she quickly typed into her laptop. "You could also tell them that Jesse spends quite a lot of time playing basketball in a little park just down the street from that address."

Shortly after I got home she called me with a phone number and other information for Ronnie. I called Ronnie immediately, telling her about the note left in my pickup and my conversation with Lopez before passing on the information about the Ithaca police.

After listening in silence, Ronnie said, "This is a serious downer. I've been floating in the clouds, dreaming of River Road, looking at those photos over and over. But this is a serious downer."

"I know, but I think there's very little chance that they know where Jesse is, and almost zero chance that they would make an effort to find him and do anything to him. Sergeant

Lopez agrees that they couldn't really gain anything by doing that."

"But they know exactly where *you* are," she said. "And you're the one they're trying to stop."

"But as of this past hour I've told Lopez absolutely everything I know about this whole situation, so there'd be no benefit in doing anything to me now."

"It's still scary."

"I intend to be very careful. Lopez told me in no uncertain terms that I'm not to do any more freelancing, and I agreed."

"Good. She must be quite a woman to get you to agree to that."

"It's a relief to be dealing with someone as smart and competent as she is. And I'm under orders to keep my cell phone with me and turned on at all times, and I intend to obey those orders."

"Good," she said again.

Shortly after I'd talked with Ronnie, my cell cawed.

"Making sure you've got it turned on," Lopez said. "Also let's talk about how we're going to handle our meeting with Goodwin, and what we're going to ask him to do."

32

Lopez picked me up on Orange Street and I rode with her to Alan Thompson's office in Troy. She was greeted by Thompson with a broad grin, which she returned with the first smile I'd seen her give anyone.

Thompson then showed us into a small conference room where Goodwin was already waiting. After Thompson had left, closing the door behind him, Lopez looked at me and said, "No I didn't just meet Alan this week. We're old friends." She then turned to Goodwin and said, "It's good to see you again. Thank you for taking the time to talk with us today."

"I'm happy to talk, but as I told Warren I really don't know how I can help."

"We don't either. But right now any scrap of information about Excalibur and the Endicotts could be helpful. I'd like to start by summarizing what I believe you've already told us – either me or Mr. Crow – about that subject. Then you can correct anything that's not accurate and add anything further you can think of that could possibly be relevant. And we'll have a few questions to follow up."

She proceeded to deliver a thorough summary.

"My goodness," Goodwin said. "Did I really tell you all that?"

"I think so," she said. "We have information from other sources as well, but I've tried to summarize just what we know from you – much of it of course from your conversations with Mr. Crow during recent weeks. Did I get anything wrong?"

"No, quite accurate."

"Or leave anything out that could be significant?"

"I don't think so."

"Then if we may, we'd like to ask some questions about Henderson Endicott."

"All right."

We had agreed that I would begin the questioning: "Bob, I don't think you've said whether you knew Henderson before he married your ex-wife?"

"I had not met him. I knew of him only as someone who made certain kinds of investments."

"Including some you disapproved of, you've said. Can you describe any particular investments you've disapproved of."

He rubbed his chin and shifted uncomfortably in his chair. "You must understand much of what I didn't like I knew only by hearsay."

"Of course. That's okay."

"Well, this goes way back, but one kind of thing he was involved in is what used to be called slum clearance. He'd have connections in some city government that was contemplating one or another kind of federally funded redevelopment project for some low-income neighborhood. It would be a situation where they could use eminent domain to acquire the land but it would be a slow expensive process. Slumlords would play the system to get higher prices. Federal regs would require that displaced tenants receive relocation assistance. Some older homeowners would just refuse to leave their homes until they were forced out, which of course resulted in very bad press for the city.

"So what Endicott would do – and of course others have done the same – was to begin buying up property himself, using tactics that the city couldn't use, or didn't want to be seen as using."

"What kinds of tactics?"

"This is the part that is pure hearsay. But Warren, you work in housing – you know these things do happen. Things would happen that would make people want to sell. There might be a fire, threats of other fires, other kinds of accidents happening to people who wouldn't sell or who held out for more money."

"You're talking about criminal activity."

"Almost certainly some of it criminal, but of course Endicott would keep himself several steps away from that. If there were thugs applying pressure in the neighborhood he wouldn't necessarily even know who they were. He was just an investor. But he certainly understood how the strategy he was funding works, and it was unconscionable."

"Not a very nice man."

"Oh but most people, including my ex-wife, think he is a very nice man. Charming, witty, generous with his friends..."

"Okay. So when did you begin to suspect – or did you? – that his company was buying up property in your own West Hill neighborhood?"

"I did suspect. My ex-wife quite innocently mentioned to me on the phone that he was working on a big project in Albany, and was starting to acquire property. This was several months ago. I noticed some properties in the neighborhood where for-sale signs went up but then came down again surprisingly fast. I wondered, and asked Alan to investigate. And he found it was this corporation called Livingston Properties. I didn't know if it was an Excalibur subsidiary, but I did suspect. In any case it looked to me like someone wanted to buy up the neighborhood for some purpose that would not be good for people who live here now. So I arranged with Alan to make it difficult for them. Then the bodies started turning up and I didn't know what to think."

Lopez leaned forward. "But you did think the bodies could possibly be related to the Livingston Properties acquisitions."

Goodwin shook his head slowly. He started to say something, then stopped. He raised his eyes to meet Lopez's unwavering gaze, then dropped them again. Finally he said, "Of course the possibility occurred to me."

"And the possibility that Henderson Endicott was behind the whole thing?"

He spread his hands in front of him in a who-knows gesture.

"But you have not rejected that possibility."

"No."

He studied his hands, now resting on the edge of the table. Lopez studied his face, letting a quiet moment become an extended silence – until finally he looked up and met her gaze.

"We really need your help," she said. "Five people have been killed, two of them in the past two days. It appears both of them worked for Excalibur but were expendable. They're jettisoning their baggage."

"I would very much like to help," he said. "But I think I've told you everything I know."

"You do talk to your ex-wife sometimes by phone?" Lopez said.

"Rarely, maybe once or twice a year."

"I have an address and phone number in Scarsdale. Is that where they live, she and Henderson?"

"Yes. He has an office in Manhattan of course."

"Would you be willing to call her?" I asked.

He looked at me. The idea obviously made him uncomfortable. But finally he said, "It would depend on why."

"Our problem is this," Lopez said. "We have a strong circumstantial basis for thinking Endicott is behind the murders, though keeping himself, as you put it, several steps away from the criminal activity. We do not have the kind of evidence needed to charge him, but we do think he is feeling some pressure now. Things are not going well for him. We want to increase that pressure. We want to challenge him and push him hard – force him to make a mistake. And to do that we want to get him up here in Albany, out of his sheltered Scarsdale-Manhattan world."

"So we're asking you to do something," I said, "that will go against your grain. I know you'd rather not tell your ex-wife anything you don't know to be true, but we're asking you to tell her that some people you know in Albany are interested in Endicott's project. They're interested in partnering with him and would like to discuss it with him next time he's in Albany."

"That's all?"

"That's all," Lopez said. "I'll give you a name and phone number that you can ask her to pass on to him."

"I hardly think he'll be interested in partnering with any-one."

"No, but he's likely to worry about who it is and what they know, and we hope he'll try to find out."

"So if he does call that number...?"

"He'll be talking to someone in the Albany Police Depart-ment, but he won't know that."

"All right," Goodwin said. "I'll try. But I'm not sure how convincing I'll be. She always used to know when I wasn't tell-ing the whole truth about something."

"Do your best," Lopez said. "But even if she's suspicious, she'll tell him and he'll *still* want to find out who it is and what's going on."

On the drive back to Albany I asked Lopez how she knew Alan Thompson.

"Classmates at Troy High. He's one of a little group I used to hang with."

"So you grew up in Troy, but then went to work in the big city of Albany?"

"Not exactly. I was born in South Carolina and started school there before my folks moved up here. After high school I went to NYU. After that I was with NYPD for five years."

"Why'd you come back up here?"

"Partner got a job with the state up here."

"Miss the city?"

"Who wouldn't. And the job I had there."

"How long have you been with the Albany police?"

"Almost six months."

She glanced sideways at me. "And you – where'd you grow up?"

"On a farm near Hoosick Falls."

"I don't suppose you miss *that*."

"I don't miss the farm, but I'm still half farmboy."

"Ever think of doing cop work?"

"Can't say that I have."

"A little discipline and you'd make a good detective."

"It's that *little discipline* part that would be a problem. But I do like the kind of detecting that my consulting work gets me into."

"Really? What kind is that?"

"I do technical assistance work for housing and community development organizations here and there. Which means you go into a community with a license to ask a lot of people a lot of questions, and with an opportunity to try to figure out how things really work there. So then you can sit down with the organization and try to help them make some realistic plans. Anyway it's the asking questions that's fun. It's not all fun."

"Same with police work. This is the first interesting case I've had since I came to Albany."

"So what are you thinking about next steps with Henderson Endicott?"

She glanced at me again. "We'll have to see what kind of face-to-face opportunity we can get. But what we're likely to need is someone who can do the face-to-face and play it by ear."

"Someone who's a freelancer at heart?"

"But will accept a little discipline. You up for it?"

We had just exited I-787 onto I-90 and were about to enter the ramp that would swing us up and over I-90 to the traffic light at the head of Henry Johnson Boulevard.

"If a little discipline means working with you," I said, "then I'm up for it."

"Okay. I'm going to drop down to Orange Street and let you off. Then you stay home and keep your cell on. I'll be in touch."

The temperature was working its way back up toward the 90s. Spending the rest of the day and evening in my hot little house was the last thing I wanted to do. Nonetheless, I did manage to get a couple of hours of work done before escaping with a beer to my front steps.

I had drunk only half the beer when a black and white police car cruised up Orange Street and turned right on Robin. Two minutes later my cell phone cawed.

"You're not in your house," Lopez said.

"I'm on the steps, which are part of the house. Inside the house the temperature is about a hundred degrees. Have a heart."

There was a moment's silence. Then she said, "What the hell. Just don't wander off."

I then called Ronnie on the cell, which was beginning to feel as much an essential extension of myself as cell phones seem to have become for most people.

"I feel like I'm under house arrest here," I said. "I came out here to the steps to drink a beer and cool off, and pretty soon a cop car comes by, and then immediately I get a call from Lopez telling me I'm not in my house."

"My God, Crow, she's got you on a leash. I didn't think it was possible."

"Between the two of you... You've got me thinking all these domestic thoughts about a home for the two of us. She's got me obeying orders from a cop."

"And how does it feel?"

"Thinking about a home with you feels great. Taking orders from most cops would drive me crazy. But it's actually a little different with Lopez. She's smart, and a bit of a maverick, and I kind of like working with her."

"Well, it makes me feel better to know someone in Albany is trying to keep you in one piece."

"I do prefer to be in one piece," I said. "How are things there? How's Jesse?"

"Jesse's fine. In the shower right now. Just came in from the basketball court soaked with sweat, as usual. Everything's fine. I'm even starting to think about River Road again."

"Me too. Without that place to think about, house arrest would be intolerable."

So we talked about the River Road property and the Hoosick River, and then Buskirk and Eagle Bridge and North Hoosick and White Creek and the Taconic Mountains, and then the River Road property some more.

The sun dipped below the Robin Street rooftops. A cop car went by again, and I enjoyed knowing that if Lopez tried to call me now she'd get a busy signal.

We were discussing where the trailer should be located on the River Road property, when Ronnie finally said, "I guess I'd better get off and do something about supper for the boy here. He's sitting here at the table looking hungry."

In the background I heard Jesse say, "Yeah!"

33

In the morning, the Albany Times website was overflowing with Tivoli Park stories – a front page article on the two most recent murders, a longer article summarizing the history of all five "Tivoli murders," a report on an interview with the mayor, and three letters to the editor.

The article on the recent killings identified both victims. Ronald (Tank) Worcheski was identified as "one of two men sought by the police in connection with the earlier murders." Eliot Lucas was identified as "an individual whom the police had sought to interview regarding circumstances related to the murders."

The other article offered additional information on both men. A police spokesman was quoted as confirming that "Worcheski's fingerprints were found on items associated with the deaths of the two women," and as saying that "the possibility that Worcheski raped the two women" is being "evaluated through a DNA analysis." The police spokesman also said police were investigating the possibility that both men were killed "because they knew too much about the earlier murders." The article then noted that "an unofficial source" had suggested that Lucas had been sought by the police as someone who might have information regarding a connection between the murders and the "puzzling investments being made in homes bordering the park." There was also a link to the earlier Albany Times article that mentioned the investments.

The report on the interview with the mayor quoted his very cautious responses to several questions. On the question of police progress in solving the murders, he said, "They're doing a great job in very difficult circumstances." When asked what he meant by "difficult circumstances," he said, "Well, Tivoli Preserve is a very difficult place to work." Asked what he thought of suggestions that the preserve be sold to a developer who would turn it into a safer place, he said, "The city has no such plans." When asked again what he thought of the idea – couldn't it possibly make sense for the city to explore the idea – he said, "It would be premature for me to comment on that idea at this time." His response to a question regarding possible future development of a casino in Albany was similar. "I'm on record as saying such a thing could be good for Albany's economy, but there are many hurdles to be cleared." Asked if Tivoli Preserve could be a possible site for a casino, he said, "Clearly the discussion of any site would be premature at this time."

The letters to the editor were from people who were much less reticent in saying what they thought about Tivoli Park. Two of the three writers thought it was high time the city did something about it. One said, "The city's had the darn place for a hundred years and they've never done a darn thing with it." The other was more specific: "The city ought to get off the dime and put the property on the market, or else put out a request for proposals to developers and go with the proposal that would do the most for the economy." The third letter was from Harry Cooper, President of the NHA Board of Directors. He praised and "seconded" Helen Hamilton's recent letter. He said that he himself, as a boy growing up in Arbor Hill, had "loved the freedom of having a hideout in the park." He wanted "more than anything to see the preserve go on being a preserve and be made safe once again for our children."

When I'd finished reading the AT material, I checked my email and found a note sent by Lisa that morning.

Are you okay? They're killing off guys who know too much, and I hope that doesn't include you. That guy Lucas is the guy you went to NYC to try to scam, isn't he. What does that mean?
I talked with your Sergeant Lopez. Quite a gal.
I hope you're being careful, but I don't suppose you are.

I sent her a quick reply, saying she'd be amazed by how careful I was being, and promising to tell her more later.

Then my desk phone rang.

Robert Goodwin said, "Warren, I wanted you to know I did call her, and told her what you asked me to tell her."

"Good. Thank you. Do you think she'll get the message to Henderson?"

"She said she would. And she said, 'Well he's in Albany now, so it should be easy enough for those people to meet with him.'"

"That's very helpful. Have you told Sergeant Lopez this, or should I tell her?"

"I'd appreciate it if you'd tell her."

I thanked him again and told him I hoped we could get together soon under pleasanter circumstances.

I then called Lopez's cell from my cell and told her what Goodwin had reported.

"Okay, I'll check the hotels and get back to you quick."

In almost no time she called back. "Okay, he's at the Marriott. Registered for two more nights. Pick you up in ten minutes. We'll take a drive and talk about this."

We were headed north on I-787, the morning sun glinting off the river on our right.

"First question," she said. "Do we wait for him to contact us, or do we call him at the Marriott, or maybe even just walk in on him?"

"I think we should follow through with the story Goodwin introduced for us – at least give the guy a chance to call the number you gave Goodwin. If he doesn't call we can always do it the other way. And by the way, whose number is that – who will he be talking to?"

"Me. It's a different phone but I'll be answering it – as someone who handles someone else's schedule."

"And who's the someone else you'll arrange a meeting for?"

"You still up for this?"

"Yes."

"Okay then it's you. We'll wire you up. I'll be nearby with an audio receiver and recorder, and we'll see where we get to."

"And this will happen when – at the earliest?"

"If he calls before, say, mid-afternoon, I might try for the end of the business day or evening. Otherwise tomorrow."

"And how I handle it will depend partly on what you pick up in your phone conversation, but we should talk about possible approaches now."

"Right. And the possible questions you may get from him. I might get a hint of what he'll ask, but probably not much of one. I'll just be your secretary or administrative assistant."

"I find that part hard to imagine."

"Well, work on it. I see you as a spare-no-expense wheeler-dealer type who lives large, or wants to look like he does. He has to have a secretary."

"All right, I'll work on that. But I'm just wondering if it wouldn't be even better if *you* were the self-assured wheeler-dealer and I was your administrative assistant."

She chuckled. "You think that's what I look like? A black female bald-headed wheeler-dealer?"

"A beautiful black female bald-headed dealer-of-some-sort. He'd be awed by you and wouldn't know what to make of you. He wouldn't be able to pigeon-hole you. He certainly wouldn't see you as just some guy pretending to be a wheeler-dealer type."

"Interesting idea. But I think we'd better stick with the more obvious way of casting this thing. We don't want to confuse him."

"In that case I'll probably need to borrow some clothes, so I won't confuse him by appearing as a wheeler-dealer in a t-shirt and old jeans."

"You're not saying that's all the clothes you have, are you?"

"Well, in addition to jeans I have a couple of pairs of khakis, a sports coat that came from the Salvation Army, a suit that I bought for my high school graduation…"

"All right, I'll see what I can do about that. But let's talk about what kind of deal you've going to propose to him. One approach would be to suggest there's something you can do for him that would make his deal work. Presumably something under the table – in return for some kind of under-the-table compensation."

"And what I could do for him might be a matter of *not* telling other people certain things."

"Like the fact that his company is ready to crash."

"Or that the late Eliot Lucas was employed by a subsidiary of his company that was buying up property."

"Or take a chance and say you know he's been negotiating with the city to acquire the park, and the media would love to know about it."

"Some kind of threat then…"

"A serious enough threat so he has to react."

We had come all the way up 787 to Cohoes, then continued on Route 32 to Waterford. We were now crossing the bridge to North Troy. To our left was the stretch of the river where I often paddle my solo boat. On the far side of the river she pulled into the parking lot of the Hannaford supermarket. She parked on the edge of the lot closest to the river and shut off the motor. She leaned back in her seat and for a time stared straight ahead through the windshield.

Finally she said, "All right. We don't know enough to offer him a credible deal. We do know enough to present a credible threat, which would mean provoking a reaction that puts you at risk."

She gave me a questioning sideways look.

"There could be some protection," I said, "in leaving him afraid that I know too much but not letting him know exactly what I know or how I learned it or who I've talked to about it. He couldn't just take me down without learning those things."

"It would have to be extremely well managed," she said. "But all right, let's let it stew for a while." She turned in her seat and looked at me as though sizing me up for the first time. "How tall are you?"

"Er, about six-one."

"Waist and inseam?"

"Okay, thirty-three, thirty-two."

She pulled her cell from a jacket pocket and made a call. "Hello Alan," she said. "I'm working on this guy Crow – trying to get him into some decent clothes for one day in his life. Tell me, what's your waist size and inseam?"

She listened to his answer, then said, "The size might work. And yeah I know it's unusual, but it's only for a day, and I'll get everything back to you professionally washed and ironed."

She listened for another moment, then snapped the phone shut. "He says he's got a whole hamper of clothes you can try on as long as they all come back washed and ironed."

"Yeah, right. But I'm not sure I want to spend the rest of the day trying on clothes."

"Don't worry," she said. "I'll take care of it. We're going to put you in a suit."

As we made our way down Second Avenue – crossing, one after another, the many short streets between 126th Street and Hoosick Street – I asked her what Reilly was doing. "Is he still on the case?"

"Oh, yeah. Doing his piece of it. He's now got DNA evidence that it was Tank who raped the two women."

"Just him? Not the other guy as well?"

"His semen. Doesn't mean the other guy wasn't a nasty part of it. Maybe holding the women down. Maybe just standing there getting off on the whole scene."

"Or maybe just not giving a damn. Any progress in finding him, that other guy?"

"Reilly's still working his way through a long list of prisoners, parolees, and various other losers he knows who might sell him information that might or might not be accurate and might or might not be useful. He'll keep at it. He's good at it – and I'm glad it isn't me who has to do it. But I don't know how much he'll ever find in Albany. This is not a guy who spends a lot of time in Albany."

"So you and Reilly have got the work pretty well divided up."

"Sure. The work splits out that way. Reilly's after Switch. I'm after Henderson Endicott."

"Of course one could wind up being the way to get the other."

"We'll see."

We had turned onto Hoosick Street and crossed the river on the Collar City Bridge and were now back on I-787. It was only nine o'clock. I was thinking about the long day ahead of me. "What I think I'm going to do when I get home," I said, "is take a very long walk. I've got to get my mind around this thing we're doing. I've got to think, and I've got to walk to think."

She was silent for a time. Then she said, "I'm not going to cuff you to your desk. Don't forget your cell."

I was walking across Lincoln Park, headed for Morton Avenue, when the cell cawed in my pocket.

"He called," Lopez said. "You've got an appointment at nine tomorrow morning."

"Okay. What'd he sound like?"

"Like the mister-nice-guy Goodwin said everyone thinks he is. Didn't ask any questions but he's looking forward to meeting Mister Crandall in the morning."

"Crandall. What's Crandall's first name?"

"James."

"Okay. Known to his friends as Jim."

"Could even be Jimmy. Possibly Jamie. Take your pick."

"Where are Jimmy and Henderson meeting?"

"An office on North Pearl, in a building that it turns out Excalibur owns."

"And do you have a suit for Jimmy?"

"One of Alan's suits. It's at a tailor's now, on Clinton Avenue, where you've got an appointment this afternoon for a fitting. They'll do the alterations while you wait."

"You're amazing."

"And I've got a gadget for Jimmy. A modified smart phone, which Jimmy's going to take with him in the morning, and which he'll manage to leave behind in that office. It has Jimmy's schedule in it. And Jimmy's contacts. We have to leave too much to chance here, but we'll hope Endicott finds it and is as snoopy as he should be. What he finds should help to persuade him that you are who you say you are. The thing will also pick up and transmit anything said within fifteen or twenty feet of it. I'm going to swing by for you again the end of the afternoon. We'll go over the gadget and some other stuff."

Once again we were headed up I-787 – this time in the midst of a hoard of commuters driving north out of the city.

"So let's talk about who Jimmy is," Lopez said.

"Besides being a wheeler-dealer."

"Right. He's got to be some kind of wheeler-dealer. But that's not how his resume describes him."

"I've been working on his resume," I said. "As it stands I've got him with a mix of banking, public relations and security experience. I've got him working for Norstar Bank when he first came to Albany. The resume claims that he helped shape a public relations strategy around Norstar's merger with Fleet Bank, and suggests that the strategy involved both keeping the public from learning about it too soon and, when it was finally announced, making it sound like a good thing for Albany, which of course it wasn't."

"I've never heard of Norstar Bank. How long ago was that? How easy would it be for him to check your story?"

"Something like twenty years ago, so I guess you wouldn't have heard of it, and I don't think it would be easy for him to check the story. Norstar was an Albany-based bank that was getting pretty big, buying up other banks in other states. Then it was merged with Fleet, which was based in Providence, and for a little while they were Fleet-Norstar. Then the Norstar name disappeared, and not long after that Fleet was acquired by Bank of America."

"Okay. Nice angle, and buried deep enough. But what's he doing now?"

"His own consulting business – dealing with corporate PR, with some emphasis on managing the message so the public won't hear what you don't want them to hear. I thought I'd do up a little brochure for him tonight."

"I like it – Crandall Consultants: Message Management for All Occasions."

"Yeah, something like that. Maybe *Discrete Message Management*. Maybe so discreet that it would be a matter of policy for him to never identify his clients to anyone. Keep it hard for Endicott to check Jimmy's stories."

"Okay, He's sounding less and less like a wheeler-dealer, but I like where you're going with this. Still, if we use the rigged smart phone we'll need to enter some names that he can really call."

She was now exiting 787 onto Route 378 westbound.

"That will be the hard part," I said. "Real names he can call."

"We'll work on it," she said. "We've got all night."

"I was kind of hoping to get some sleep."

"Yes, you have to sleep. But I don't."

"Maybe Jimmy's so discreet he doesn't even *have* a smart phone."

"If we don't like what we've got in the morning we can drop the idea, but let's see what we can come up with first."

At the intersection with Route 32 she turned right and drove north into Watervliet, where she eventually turned left onto a quiet residential street and parked.

"I love these things," she said, lifting the smart phone from the pocket of her blazer.

She gave me a quick tour of the device's features and showed me how to enter Jimmy's contacts.

"When you get home, send me your draft resume and I'll work up a few fictional contacts and send those to you. If you're okay with who they're supposed to be, then I'll match them up with some people in the department so there'll be certain people he can call who'll play along with the story."

"But only a few – you mean he's only got a few contacts? How convincing is that?"

"We'll give him more, a longer list, but we'll only try to put real people behind a few that are going to look like the most relevant people for him to check with."

"Seems kind of elaborate and artificial."

"The whole gig is artificial."

"Well, yeah."

"Obviously it can't work for more than a little while, but we're just trying to gain as much time as we can. The longer we can play him, the more likely he'll give us something we can nail him with."

"Okay, but I'm going to be a real guy sitting in Endicott's office, and I will really know certain things that have got to worry him. I'd rather just *be* that guy without having to worry about this damn gadget."

She looked at me, then turned back and stared straight ahead through the windshield, until finally she said, "All right, you *are* the one who's going to be sitting in his office. We'd better do it your way."

"Good. Thanks."

"So your angle is going to be you could help him with PR around development of Tivoli Park...."

"Or at least that might be my foot in the door. My opportunity to show him I know some things he would rather no one knew. You can put a wire on me and we'll see what we learn. And if I can arrange a follow-up meeting, he won't have any easy way to check me out before that meeting."

She nodded, dropped the phone back in her pocket, and put her car in gear. "Okay, Warren. I'll take you home and you can do your brochure and then email that and your resume to me."

"I will, and look forward to your suggestions. And may I call you Giselle?"

"She smiled. "Not quite. My friends call me GL." She raised her right palm toward me. Clumsily I completed a high five.

"Okay, GL."

Back at home I ordered a pizza, went upstairs and got to work on the brochure. By eight o'clock my desk was covered with pizza crumbs and I had a draft brochure, which I sent to GL along with the draft resume. Then I poured myself a jigger of Goodwin's rye whiskey and went out to the steps, where the day was fading and cooling.

I sat for a while, looking at the quiet street and sipping strong liquor and letting my mind empty out. I was savoring the prospect of calling Ronnie, but, as I was savoring, a crow cawed in my pocket.

"So I bet you're sitting on your steps drinking beer," Ronnie said.

"Sitting on my steps drinking a little of Goodwin's whiskey and looking forward to talking with you."

"But making me wait."

"Yeah, I guess so. Sorry."

"I'm teasing. A few minutes doesn't matter. It's just that sometimes it feels like Jesse and I are having to wait way too long. Or really, it's not so much the waiting as it is not knowing what's going on and worrying about what's going to happen. I'm starting to have nightmares about it. Last night I had a really awful one."

"I really am sorry. We've got you in a really uncomfortable position."

"Wait a minute," she said. "It was my idea to bring Jesse here."

"I know. By *we* I don't mean we in Albany. I mean you and I."

"Okay, so stop apologizing. Just get this damn thing done. Somehow. Whatever it takes. Jesse and I'll be fine."

"How's he doing?"

"A little more homesick but hanging in. The basketball helps – along with frequent orders of barbecued ribs."

"Tell me about your nightmare." I said. "Unless you'd rather talk about something else."

"It was too murky and confusing to describe. We were in the middle of this huge place – Jesse and I – and we didn't know how to get out, and we were supposed to meet you but you weren't there and we had no idea how to find you, and it was just this overwhelming no-exit-forever feeling. When I woke up and saw daylight in my window I was so relieved I wanted to cry."

"Jesus, Ronnie…"

"And now I'd like to talk about River Road."

So we did.

"I just hope it wouldn't mean you'd wind up commuting to Albany every day," she said. "I don't want to turn you into a commuter."

"No way. It's the last thing I'd want to do. Probably I'd go to town only for meetings – the meetings that couldn't be done with conference calls or Skype. Or I'd go and stay for a few days, from time to time, when I needed to be there. Anyway, a lot of my work isn't *in* Albany."

"Okay then – if it feels okay to you."

"It does. And I hope *you* don't wind up commuting to some distant wetland every day."

"Of course it will be at least a year before we can really talk about anything more than weekends…"

For a while we continued to ramble around in the fields of our future – even reaching that field where the question was how could we both do the things we do and have a family too.

When we finally said good night, I went indoors, poured another jigger of rye, and went up to my office and checked my email. GL had marked up my Word files, using Track Changes. She was a good copy editor. She hadn't tried to change too much, but did have some useful ideas. I made the changes, sent the revised files back to her, and printed out copies for myself.

Then I took my drink back out to the steps and sat for a while longer, again letting my mind empty out and the whiskey seep in.

When I eventually went to bed, I fell asleep almost immediately and slept until dawn.

34

The office where I sat with Henderson Endicott appeared to have been recently and expensively remodeled, though the building as a whole looked somewhat the worse for wear. Endicott was behind a large desk, tilted back in a leather-covered desk chair. I was seated in an armchair in front of the desk. A very attractive young woman was serving us coffee.

"I hadn't realized you had an office here in town," I said.

"Oh I don't really. We bought this building out of foreclosure. I'm just making temporary use of this one office." He turned to the young woman. "Edie love, thanks for the coffee, and now there's really no need for you to hang around. Why don't you go on back to the hotel, or whatever you like. I'll call your cell if I need you."

She smiled, nodded, gathered up a large shoulder bag from a desk chair, and left.

"Edie travels with me often," he said. "Good secretary and good company, in a lovely package. Can't ask for more than that."

"I suppose not," I said, still trying to find my balance.

He was in his shirtsleeves, without a tie. His suit coat hung on a hanger by the door. He was tall, blond, handsome, and seemingly completely at ease.

I was wearing my assigned suit and tie, feeling overdressed and ill at ease. I busied myself taking a file folder from my briefcase and then taking the resume and brochure from the file folder.

I slid the papers across the desk toward Endicott. "In case you have questions about my firm or my personal qualifications."

He picked them up, glanced at them and set them aside. "Thank you. But of course I'm primarily interested in why you've proposed this meeting. I believe you got the impression from Robert Goodwin that Excalibur is planning a major project here in Albany. However, that is hardly the case."

"All right. I don't know how far your planning has advanced, but what I do know I learned not from Robert Goodwin but from my own observations and other local sources. Bob Goodwin is simply a friend through whom I was able to contact you."

"Ah, so you've heard rumors, and you want to know if Excalibur really does have plans in this town. Well your curiosity is understandable. But what makes you think there could be a role for you or your firm in connection with this *rumored* project?"

"It's more than rumored. A subsidiary of your firm has been purchasing real estate around the boundary of Tivoli Park. An investment in those properties makes sense only if something of significance is going to happen on the land that is now Tivoli Park."

"Well that's true in a sense, but these are very long-term investments. The world is changing fast. It's absolutely inevitable that Tivoli Park will be developed sooner or later. But the land belongs to the city and at present it's not for sale."

"So you're buying and boarding up a bunch of old wood-frame homes, and you're going to hold them empty, paying taxes and insurance year-in-year-out, because you think, someday, something – you don't know what – is going to be developed in Tivoli Park that could possibly increase the value of those properties. With all due respect…"

He laughed – an easy laugh. "All right, I won't ask you to believe that. You can assume we have some plans – some very preliminary plans."

"And that you're discussing those plans with people in city government."

He shrugged and waved a hand in front of him, as though waving aside something of no importance. "You still haven't answered my question – what role can you possibly see for yourself?"

"Okay. Possibly a role in brokering some investments. Possibly a role in handling local PR."

"I'm not looking for investors. Excalibur has assets of almost half a billion dollars."

"So you could finance acquisition, pre-development, and development costs by borrowing against those existing assets as well as the Tivoli land."

"Sorry, but I'm not about to discuss financing strategies with you."

"Which is understandable, given the precariousness of your company's finances."

He raised his eyebrows. "I beg your pardon."

"It's no secret that your assets include large, heavily mortgaged subdivision projects in Las Vegas and Florida that are dead in the water. As well as other highly leveraged projects with futures that are questionable at best. It doesn't take a genius to calculate that Excalibur has got to be close to bankruptcy."

"I have backers lined up," he said, "whom I'm not at liberty to identify." He pulled the resume and brochure back in front of him on the desk and looked at them. "You mentioned local PR as something you could offer. Why would I need local PR?"

"Have you been reading the Albany Times?"

"From time to time."

"They're already publishing complaints about someone developing a casino in Tivoli Park."

"Surely the paper hasn't reported any such thing. It would be stupid and irresponsible, and no publisher would risk it."

"The Albany Times has simply reported that there are such rumors. They've published letters to the editor commenting on those rumors – most of them negative comments. They've reported an interview with the mayor in which he was asked whether the city is in fact planning to sell the preserve for such a purpose."

"Which he of course denied."

"Of course – but without closing the door on the possibility. My point is just that the Albany public has already taken an interest in the possibility, and voices are being raised against the idea. If you do want to do something with that land – and it's pretty obvious that you do – then you have a PR problem. And you need help from an experienced PR professional who's familiar with the local scene."

He made a tent of his hands on his desktop and studied me calmly, almost smiling. "And this PR professional would be you."

"It could be. Of course if you didn't want me on your side…"

He continued to study me. "What you seem to think you know about Excalibur's assets… what do you base that on?"

I knew it would sound glib, but I had to say something. "I'm a skilled researcher," I said.

He shrugged, then rotated his desk chair and gazed off toward the windows on his right. After a time he said, "I'm curious. Suppose you give me an idea of what you see such a PR campaign entailing."

"Planning that kind of campaign would have to start with a discussion of what you want it to accomplish – with what part of the public, and on what timetable."

"No it would not start that way." He swung back to face me directly. "It would not start with me giving information to you. It would have to start with you telling me something useful."

"I could do that. I have an on-the-ground knowledge of the park and of the neighborhood around it. I know who your opposition will be, and what their specific concerns are. I know a lot that would be useful to you. But I'm no more interested in being the first one to ante up useful information than you are."

He nodded, smiling. "I guess we're at a dead end."

"Not necessarily," I said.

"Then how do you suggest we proceed?"

"I'm wondering if you've ever been on the land – been inside the preserve. Most people in Albany have actually never been there, even if they drive up and down Livingston Avenue every day. I expect the same is true of you."

I had only a vague idea of where I was going with this, but at least I thought the actual preserve was a subject I knew more about than he did.

"I know everything about the place I need to know," he said.

"I'm sure you've had people studying its possibilities for certain development agendas – mostly based on topographic and geological maps and satellite photos. Maybe one or two of them have explored the place on foot, but I'm sure you've never set foot there."

He shook his head. "What are you getting at? I still don't know what the hell to make of you."

"I'm just suggesting we go take an actual walk in the park together."

He laughed, still seemingly at ease. "A walk in the park? Fellah, give me a break."

"If you have an hour to spare, why don't we just go have a look at the pig in this poke you're trying to buy. I think I could show you a few things you ought to know."

He studied me in silence. Eventually he said, "I should probably tell you to get out of here and stay the hell out of my way if you know what's good for you. But I'm still curious. What the hell – an hour?"

"No more than an hour. Probably less."

"And what is it you want to show me that I ought to know about? Should I bring an engineer? A landscape architect?"

"No, these are things you yourself need to know."

"Then why not just tell me about them now?"

"You have to see them or it would mean nothing to you."

He shrugged. "Okay, why not? I wouldn't mind looking at the place. Not right now but maybe this afternoon."

"Name the time then."

"Say three o'clock?"

"Okay."

"And where will I meet you?"

"You know the trailhead by the Green Charter School off Northern Boulevard?"

"I'm sure I can find it."

"Okay, I'll see you there at three."

"That was really dumb," GL said. "Of all the places for a follow-up meeting, that is the worst place imaginable."

I was at home, in my office, on my cell phone. "But for him too," I said. "It's not his kind of place – not in its present condition. And as long as he's behind a desk in some office somewhere, he's just too smooth. I'll never get him to give away anything important in those surroundings."

"So you're taking him into the woods."

"Into the preserve a little way. I want to get him standing on the ground where the people were dumped whose murders he's responsible for."

"Where it's just you and him. It was not my intention to set up some kind of high noon confrontation between the two of you."

"I don't see it that way, but it was the only way I could think of to push him."

"In a place where it's just you and him and whoever else he arranges to have there. I can't *cover* you there."

"I think you can put more people out there than he can."

"Well that's true," she said. Then, after a period of silence, "Anyway it's what we've got to do. Give me a little time to think about it. And in the meantime I'll send someone to your house with a Kevlar vest, and they can make sure the wire's set up right on whatever you're going to be wearing. We don't want you leaving it in your suit coat."

35

It was Reilly who brought the vest. Tossing it onto a chair in my front room, he said, "These things aren't worth shit. In this hot weather I wouldn't even think about wearing it if I was you."

Out of curiosity, I looked at it anyway. My ultra-light solo canoe is made of layers of Kevlar fabric bonded and stiffened with resin, and I was curious about what a Kevlar vest would be like. It seemed to be composed of many layers of woven material – not rigid, and maybe wearable enough in cool weather, but I had to agree with Reilly. I had no desire to walk around in such a thing on a hot August afternoon. Besides, I thought that if anyone was going to try to shoot me in Tivoli Park, they would have plenty of time to put a bullet in my head if a shot in the chest didn't do the job.

"You want to just take it back with you?" I asked Reilly.

"Naw, just leave it here till later. Don't want to have to explain to Lopez why I didn't make you put it on. But you'll need a little more than that t-shirt to hang this wire on. Not the suit you wore this morning, but not just a t-shirt either. We could just give you a cell phone with an open mike to put in your pocket, but this thing here will give us better reception of what's going on around you."

I went upstairs and put on an old worn-thin work shirt. When I came down, Reilly bugged the shirt.

"I'm going out to the car," he said. "When I get there, say a few words quiet-like, and maybe..." He looked around. "Maybe go in the kitchen and get a spoon or something. Stand back by the door there and toss it into the sink. If I can hear that, you're all set."

He left, and through the window I watched him go to his car and get in.

I muttered, "Oh my God, there's a cop out front."

He gave me a thumbs-up.

I went into the kitchen, picked up a fork from the table and lobbed it into the sink.

In a minute Reilly was back at the door. "Working good," he said. "Now just, whatever you do, stay with the route. No last-minute bright ideas of your own."

"Right. I absolutely intend to stay where my friends know where I am."

I walked over to the charter school, arriving at the trailhead a few minutes before three. Henderson Endicott arrived in a white Mercedes almost exactly at three o'clock.

"Let's make this quick," he said, stepping out of his vehicle. "I'm due in the city at six."

He was still dressed as he had been in the morning. I could see the suit coat hanging inside the Mercedes.

"It won't take long," I said. "Follow me." I headed up the narrow trail between thickets. "Nice day for a walk, isn't it."

"Um, I suppose," he said from behind me. "But I don't see how you're going to show me anything in this place except a lot of bushes."

"It opens up in places," I said.

Halfway up the trail, he said, "This is beginning to feel rather ridiculous."

"Don't worry, it's going to make sense."

At the intersection with the trail coming down from the head of Judson, I stopped and let him catch up.

"This is the first place," I said, pointing.

"What? What about this place?"

"Right there in front of you. That's where one of the bodies was found. The second one actually. A nice young woman. If you look carefully you can probably still see her blood on the ground there. She was very bloody. She'd been badly beaten. And raped. And of course her ears were cut off."

"Did you bring me here just to try to shock me?"

"No. But that young woman, whose name was Beth Ellsworth, was killed just because someone needed another body in order to shock and frighten local residents. Very pretty young woman. Lovely smile. I used to see her sometimes when we both happened to be jogging down here. It's her smile that I remember. Wonderful smile. But never mind. Let's take a look at Tivoli Lake. It's one of the features your landscape architect will be focusing on, so you should see it."

I led the way down the main trail past the pond.

"I'd be interested in knowing what you do plan to do with this body of water," I said. "I suppose you may have to drain it. If it's a casino you're planning, you're going to need a lot of parking space. Even so, I bet your landscape architect wants to keep the pond – but replace that boring stretch of reeds with more exotic plants. Maybe redo the whole area to make it look like some wild Adirondack Pond."

"I'm not amused," Endicott said.

"Okay, we'll walk on down to the dirt road, so you can see what you've got for vehicle access and how close it is to the railroad tracks."

Where the trail joined the dirt road, I stopped again. "And this is where the third body was found. The other young woman. She too was quite pretty. She too was beat up. Raped and beaten to death. Because someone needed still another bloody body to scare the public and force the city to sell the preserve."

He was studying me calmly now. I'd been afraid he would just turn around and leave, but it looked like he'd decided to ride out our excursion and learn as much as he could about what I knew.

"Okay, let's walk on up the dirt road here – give you a sense of the whole area."

At the place where I had gone into the woods and found where a body had been worked over, I stopped again. "This is interesting," I said. "In there a little way is the place where the police found where someone's body'd been on the ground. There was blood and a piece of duct tape there, which it turned out had fingerprints on it. Prints of the big guy, called Tank, who raped both those women. They found an ear in there too. Only one they ever found."

Endicott's eyes remained fixed on me, but he said nothing.

I led the way on along the dirt road, then turned left up the trail toward Park View Apartments.

"Show you the back side of the apartment complex," I said. "It's right up against the preserve, so you'll need to do something about it. But maybe you're already trying to buy it."

He was coming along silently behind me.

"And while we're up that way, I can show you where they found the first body. The guy named Ben Higgins. They don't even know if he was actually killed by Tank and Switch. Could've been shot by some gangbangers who didn't like him. Anyway Tank and Switch made use of the body to serve their employer's purposes. Probably drove it to the parking area behind the apartments, carried it down the trail a ways, cut its ears off, and left it there. So people would find it and be frightened."

"And after that, we'll go back down to the dirt road and back out toward the gate. We'll pass where the fourth body was dumped. That would be your man Eliot Lucas, who knew too much about the whole deal, and so had to be killed by Tank and Switch. Then at the gate we'll see where Switch dumped Tank, who of course knew too much about the other killings, and sooner or later the police were going to catch him and question him and he would talk to save his neck. So Switch had to kill him."

From just behind me came a piercing whistle.

I turned to see Endicott with his two thumbs together at his mouth, producing a second all-but-ear-splitting whistle.

"Calling your dog?" A smart-ass remark wasn't going to change things. I was on the edge of panic.

"In a manner of speaking," he said coolly.

I continued up the trail, but I'd lost my grip on things. I was now thinking defensively – or trying to. If he'd called in his support, what were my options? Where were my own supporters in relation to where I was now?

GL had done a diagram of the whole preserve, with Xs at the points where police personnel were to be stationed. One X was back where this trail left the dirt road. Another was up where the trail came down from the apartments. And one was in between. But I didn't know whether the in-between one was still ahead of me or if I'd already passed it.

I wasn't even sure how far behind me Endicott was now.

I started to turnaround to look, but was caught up abruptly. Someone had grabbed my wrist and pinned my left arm behind me. At the same time something hard and sharp pressed into my throat just beneath the right corner of my jaw. A very sharp knife point against a very vulnerable part of me.

Twisting to the left as far as possible to lessen the pressure of the knife, I was able to see the brown-skinned man who gripped my wrist with his left hand while his right arm wrapped over my shoulder to press the knife into my throat.

The man's dark eyes looked through me. Looked beyond me – focused somewhere on up the trail, as though he didn't see me at all, or saw me only incidentally, as an object that was in his way and had to be disposed of.

I remembered Jesse's description of Switch's eyes: "You can't look into 'em."

The man could kill me without ever seeing me. I could die trying to look into eyes that couldn't see me.

Now he spoke in a quick, thin voice: "Where you want this one?"

From just beyond him, Endicott's voice said, "Not like the others. Take him into the woods – the thickest part you can. Kill him with the knife, not the gun, and leave him out of sight. I don't want anyone finding this one anytime soon."

The pressure of the knife tip increased, pressing me leftward, turning me toward the woods. I felt blood begin to run down my neck.

A sudden wave of sound erupted around us. Something – many things together – thrashing upward through branches.

The man jerked backwards, stumbled, lost his grip on my wrist, and the pressure of the knife point was gone.

I pivoted and found myself bringing my right fist around and up into his jaw as he tried to catch his balance. It knocked him backward onto the ground, but he managed to sit up and began fumbling for what I realized was a gun in a shoulder holster.

From nearby a voice said, "Drop it or I'll shoot." It was GL's voice.

But he was getting the gun free of the holster.

There was a gunshot, overpoweringly loud. The man's body jerked and rolled. The gun flipped to one side.

As I picked it up, I saw Endicott heading off at a fast run around the bend in the trail toward the apartments.

GL stood over the man, who I was sure was Switch. "It's his shoulder," she said. He'll live. But what the hell *was* that? All that... all those..."

"Turkeys."

"Come on. Seriously..."

"Seriously, it was turkeys. A brood of wild turkeys. I've been watching them growing up through the summer, but I hadn't seen them fly until now."

"It was like the whole woods exploded," she said.

Then Henderson Endicott reappeared coming back around the bend in the trail, with Reilly walking behind, a gun pointed at the man's back.

Waiting for an ambulance, the three of us sat in Reilly's car in the parking area behind the apartments. We had just listened to the recording of the recent action, in which Endicott's voice was clearly audible saying, "Not like the others... Kill him with the knife."

"I think we got him," GL said.

"For one attempted," Reilly said. "The five actual murders could be harder – and Endicott's role in those harder still."

"You think a guy like Switch isn't going to talk?" GL asked. "You think he's going to protect a guy like Endicott from five counts of conspiracy to commit murder?"

"I don't know," Reilly said. "Just don't count your convictions before they're in the bag."

After that, both Reilly and GL were sternly silent. I was feeling shaky and needed to talk.

"So you were the one posted at this trailhead," I said to Reilly. "Endicott must have run right into you."

"Yeah, I'm coming around the bend – gun in my hand after Lopez's shot – and here he comes, running like a son-of-a-bitch. Should've seen his face when he saw me."

"And you," I said to GL. "How'd you wind up right there where I was?"

"I was back at the other end – back near where that first trail connects with the other one. After you and Endicott went by, Switch came along, trailing behind, just out of your sight. So after he'd gone on by, I trailed along after *him*."

"So all my friends were there when I needed them. The two of you, and the turkeys."

"Amazing," GL said.

"Yes."

"Friggin lucky," Reilly said.

"Yes, that too."

36

"How does it feel to be home?" Ronnie asked Jesse.

We were eating breakfast at Mina Johnson's kitchen table. I had called Ithaca when I got home the evening before. Jesse had then called his mom, and by sunup he and Ronnie were on the road. Mina arranged to stay home from work, and now had produced a huge celebratory breakfast that included scrambled eggs, ham, home fries, biscuits and sausage gravy, pancakes, syrup, sweet rolls, and coffee.

"Feels pretty good," Jesse said. "And they got real good food here."

Ronnie pointed a finger at him. "Come on Jesse – you saying *I* didn't feed you good?"

"Not too bad – specially when you take me out for those barbeque ribs."

"I think you been spoiling him," Mina said.

"Naw, it was *good* for me. Like this big breakfast's good for me. Going to make me big and tall so I can get a basketball scholarship to Cornell."

"Or big and tall and *smart*," Ronnie said. "So you can go to college one way or another, basketball or not."

"I like what I'm hearing here," Mina said.

"Warren says I'm already smart. But my jump shot – I got to work on that."

"You're already smart like you're already athletic," Ronnie said. "Still have to work on your jump shot *and* your math and science."

"Yeah, okay, but school doesn't start for a week. Got to get in all the basketball I can while I got a chance. Gonna call CJ and see if he wants to play." He had a cell phone in his hand.

"And where did you get *that*?" Mina wanted to know.

"Bought it."

"With what? I gave you money to take with you in case you really needed something. Not so you could go and buy yourself a phone, which we already got one of right over there."

"But I do need a cell. And I earned the money for it myself."

Ronnie nodded. "He did. I hired him to enter my research findings in my database. He did a good careful job, and I paid him for real value received. So he went off to Radio Shack and bought himself a phone."

"My goodness," Mina said. "But is there going to be a big bill every month?"

"Didn't pay for no monthly plan. Just bought a bunch of minutes. Enough to keep in touch with my buddies."

"I hope they're not the kind of buddies that will get you in trouble. You don't need any more of that kind."

"I know, Mom. Going to be careful about that."

Mina pursed her lips. "You know what – I think I'm going to get *me* one of those things. So I can check on you every little while. Make *sure* you staying out of trouble."

Jesse looked at Ronnie. "Shouldn't have showed it to her," he said.

Mina smiled. Ronnie laughed.

"So, does CJ like basketball?" I asked.

"Yeah, and he's real good."

"Excellent. Play basketball with CJ and keep him out of trouble."

"Keep us both out of trouble."

"There you go," Ronnie said.

"No one's eating any biscuits," Mina said. "And that sausage gravy's just sitting there."

Jesse and I both reached for the biscuits. "I'll fix that," Jesse said.

"I'll help," I said.

After breakfast Jesse went off, with a basketball under his arm, to meet CJ in the little park on Quail Street. His mom went to work happy. Ronnie and I went to look at the River Road place after picking up the key to the trailer from the realtor in Hoosick Falls.

"What do you want to look at first?" I asked. "The riverbank? The woods? The spring? The trailer?"

"Oh, the trailer. Definitely the trailer."

"It's not the prettiest part."

"Doesn't need to be. I think you said something awhile back about how it's the female that picks the nesting place."

"Yes, and it *was* the female who found this place."

"But ten acres is not a nest. A nest has to be little and cozy."

"The trailer is little all right. I don't know about cozy."

"We'll see. Come on."

We walked up through the meadow, opened up the trailer and went in. I watched her inspecting the trash-littered interior.

"As I said, it's not the prettiest part."

"It needs a good cleaning, and, no, it's not pretty, but it *could* be cozy. And it doesn't need to be out here in the middle of the meadow. It could be moved over there by the woods. Maybe by the spring. And we could get some of that metal and asbestos chimney material and have a woodstove in here. We'd have plenty of firewood."

"It's starting to sound sort of cozy."

"Okay, now let's go look at the spring."

We found a place near the spring where, with a little pick and shovel work, the trailer could be set up and leveled. Then we sat down by the spring and for a while just soaked up the feeling of the place, not saying much, nibbling watercress.

Eventually Ronnie said, "I vote yes."

"Then it's unanimous." I said.

When we returned the key to the realtor in Hoosick Falls, we gave her an offer for a dollar amount twenty percent below the asking price.

"I'll call the sellers right away," she said. "You're likely to get a counter-offer, but it's been on the market more than a year, and I think you'll find them eager to deal. And – may I say – I'm delighted that you want it. I think it's a sweet opportunity for a young couple like you."

Back in the car, Ronnie said, "Yeah, sweet. At least she didn't call us a sweet young couple like I was afraid she was going to."

We headed back to the Capital District by way of Route 7, and along the way we stopped at the Man of Kent pub to celebrate with some English beer.

The next morning we walked over to Livingston Avenue to have coffee with Bob Goodwin. I wanted Ronnie to meet him. I also wanted to see how he was feeling about what had happened with Henderson Endicott. I was afraid he might be feeling bad about having used his ex-wife – or having allowed GL and me to use her – to get to Henderson, whose arrest had been reported the day before by local media.

But he was his usual gracious self. He responded to Ronnie with the kind of smile that her grin elicits from most people. He poured coffee for us, and tea for himself. He asked questions about Ronnie's research. We talked about the Montezuma marshes, and he recounted stories he'd read about the difficulty of developing the Erie Canal through those expanses of wetland.

Finally he turned to me and said, "All right, I *am* curious about what's going on with Henderson. The news reports yesterday said he was arrested in *connection* with the Tivoli Park murders – along with someone named Juan Gutierrez who was arrested as a suspect and is in the hospital with a gunshot wound. The AT treated it as a major story but most of it was just a rehash of what was already known about the murders. It said very little about what Henderson's connection to the murders might be – and nothing about who Juan Gutierrez is, or what either of them is being charged with. I'm guessing that you know quite a lot more."

"I didn't catch up with the AT article yesterday, and I don't know what charges have been or will be brought, but I can tell you what happened in the preserve."

I gave him a very general account of what GL and I had planned and of my experience in the preserve with Endicott, including the confrontation with Switch, who apparently had now been identified as Juan Gutierrez. "So," I concluded, "Sergeant Lopez did witness Gutierrez holding a knife to my throat, and did hear Endicott telling him to kill me – and there's also an audio recording of that. But beyond that, a lot now depends on what Gutierrez and Endicott will say about each other – what each says the other had to do with the actual murders."

"My God!" Goodwin said. "You must have been terrified!"

"I was about to be – but I didn't really have time."

"Because of the turkeys!" Ronnie said. "He hasn't told you the good part. He was saved by turkeys. And I'm never going to eat a turkey dinner again."

"I don't understand," Goodwin said.

Ronnie told him about the turkeys. "And if that turkey habitat hadn't been protected," she said, "they could not have saved Crow."

Goodwin got up and went to one of the windows, where he turned away from us to stare out across Livingston Avenue toward the preserve.

"And no matter what happens to Endicott now," I said, "that place has been saved."

He remained standing with his back to us, saying nothing.

"And you played a critical role in making that happen," I said.

"No."

"But you did."

"Well, but only in the sense that I also played a role in wrecking my ex-wife's future. In the sense that I played a role in getting you almost killed. In the sense that the flapping of a butterfly wing can play a role in creating a hurricane somewhere else some days later."

"The so-called butterfly effect," Ronnie said. "Except in this case there was a turkey effect."

Goodwin turned around and looked at her, then shook his head and laughed. "Humbling, isn't it?"

"Yes," she said. "There are billions of butterflies out there. Along with zillions of other bugs. And birds – all sorts of birds. In this case there was a major crow effect."

"And a major Goodwin effect," I said.

"Enough," Goodwin said, sitting down at the table with us again. "Let's talk about real estate. What am I going to do with all these damn houses I've bought?"

Epilogue

Labor Day Weekend was just days away. On Friday Ronnie and I would drive to Fisher Lake. On Saturday we would make our way to Wilder Ponds – and would stay in the campsite on Little Wilder where we had spent Labor Day the year before.

But before leaving town – on Thursday evening – we had a small party in the little house on Orange Street to celebrate the purchase agreement Ronnie and I had signed, which, as Ronnie said, was like getting engaged, only better.

Raymond brought a bottle of Wild Turkey, "an offering to the turkey gods," he said, "for saving Crow's sorry ass."

Bob Goodwin brought various other expensive bottles. Lisa brought Martini makings. Reilly brought a six-pack of Coors. Helen Hamilton brought a jug of iced tea and a cake. Jesse and Mina brought two liters of Coke and another cake. Zera and GL and GL's partner Laura had got together and cooked up something like a bushel of Buffalo wings. Ronnie and I, with strong encouragement from Jesse, had purchased barbecued ribs for the occasion.

Together we more or less filled my front room and kitchen. The house was hot but we had the door and all the windows open, and it was a cloudy day, so the place was almost comfortable.

I was sitting next to Raymond in the front room by the door. In the corner to my right, Bob Goodwin and Helen Hamilton were talking earnestly. Helen's eyes were very big. Bob had just told her he wanted to donate the Santa Clause properties to NHA's CLT homeownership program.

Across the room, close together on the sofa, GL and Zera were deep in what appeared to be an intense conservation, though I couldn't hear what they were saying above the laughter coming from the kitchen.

"They look like old friends just getting back together," I said to Raymond.

"They just met this week," he said, "but they found something they have in common."

"And what is that?"

"Where they came from."

"Really? But GL's from South Carolina, and Zera's from…"

"No, I mean they came from the same kind of roots. Like I've told you, Zera's family is from a Garifuna community in Honduras, where her people have been living on the beaches for about three centuries, hanging on to their own culture, and their own language with its mix of Indian and West African sources…"

"You're not saying GL has Garifuna roots too…"

"No, but similar. GL's family's from the South Carolina low country. Gullah people."

"Okay… people who came there originally as slaves from the coast of West Africa and are still there."

"Yeah, they knew how to grow rice, so the plantation owners, who didn't want to live in the low country, put them to work on the rice plantations and more or less stayed away themselves."

"So the two really are similar," I said. "Like the Garifuna, the Gullah were able to hang on to a culture of their own. Both of them stayed out on the very edge of the continent, at least partly free from the oppressive societies at their backs. And at least partly connected to where they came from."

"Exactly. They didn't get sucked in. Staying on the edge that way was never an option for most of us – most African Americans and Native Americans, except maybe the Inuit up on the arctic edge. But then there are other ways of staying on the edge, too."

"Like your way," I said.

"Yeah, I have my way, but I think everyone in this house manages to stay on the edge in one way or another."

"I suppose so, in one way or another. And you think that's a good thing?"

"Not entirely. Living on the edge has its downside." He drained the last of his Wild Turkey. "But I sure as hell wouldn't want to get sucked into the *middle* of this out-of-control society of ours."

I clicked my empty glass against his. "Me neither. Here's to the edges."